LOVE & DECEPTION

THE LOVE & RUIN SERIES BOOK TWO

J.A. OWENBY

1

Reality was like a black-and-white TV with bad reception —flickering in and out. Clear one moment and fuzzy the next.

The cold November night air should have sent my teeth chattering into overdrive, but I felt nothing as I stared, speechless, at Andrea Wallace. She'd stopped me outside my dorm building and began blabbing something so inconceivable my conscious mind refused to register the information.

"Gemma, did you hear what I said?" Andrea spoke softly while taking a cautious step closer.

I narrowed my eyes at this girl, whom I'd met only once before, and tried to wrap my head around the shocking news she'd just hit me with.

This was not the way my night was supposed to play out. Right now, Mac and I should be moving our stuff out of the dorm and into Hendrix's house.

I was still moving in with Hendrix. But not tonight.

Tonight, fate had once again thrown me a massive curveball.

Tonight, my mother had died in a car accident, and I was on my way to the airport and back to Louisiana.

"I heard you, Andrea," I said, void of emotion.

Apparently she didn't believe me because she repeated her news with more force.

"I'm pressing charges against Hendrix Harrington for raping me."

My conscious mind may have been struggling to process her statement, but my subconscious understood her just fine.

I dropped my overstuffed duffel and punched my fist into her face, sending her reeling backward. She yelped, her eyes popping open wide with shock as she landed ass first on the sidewalk. My hand smarted from the contact, but other than that...I felt no remorse for what I'd done. Bending down, my stare never left her while I picked up my bag again.

"And, as I said, my mother just died, and I have a plane to catch," I informed her.

Logically, I knew the grief and anger were waiting to erupt, stirring just beneath the surface. The problem was I had no idea when it would happen. Right now, as far as I was concerned, numbness could continue to claim me.

Andrea covered her jaw and whimpered. Sadness flickered in her stunned expression. I spun on my heel and walked away.

"I'm going to let that go, Gemma. I'd probably have done the same if my mom had just died. But a word of advice...if I were you, I wouldn't come back. For your own safety, stay away from Spokane," she called after me.

I refused to turn around or acknowledge her warning. Everything inside me had officially checked out. I calmly walked toward the Uber waiting at the curb. The driver would most likely charge me for the additional time it had taken me to hit someone for the first time in my life.

"Thank you for waiting."

The middle-aged woman behind the wheel merely nodded and drove away from campus.

Leaning my head back against the passenger seat, I stared blankly out the window as Spokane lit up the evening sky with all her twinkling lights. As we drove over the Monroe Street Bridge, I focused my attention on the Spokane River snaking its way through the heart of the city, twisting and turning.

My thoughts floated to Hendrix and memories of eating breakfast on his back patio while the river rushed past us, the clean, fresh smell of the water tickling my nose.

Dammit, Hendrix should be with me. He should be next to me in the car, holding my hand.

Maybe it was a good thing he was at rehearsal tonight and not answering his phone. Because after the bomb Andrea dropped on me, I wasn't sure what to think of him right now.

Was Andrea telling the truth? What could she possibly have to gain by lying about something as serious as rape? My stomach lurched. How well did I really know Hendrix? I'd been fooled before.

Regardless, Andrea had planted a seed that would linger in the back of my mind like a pesky fly, constantly buzzing in the background.

All I knew for certain was that Mom was dead, and I was on my way back to Louisiana.

The only comfort in this mess was Ada Lynn.

My feelings roared to life as the Uber driver slowed to take the airport exit. Anger and fear ripped through me. I squeezed my eyes shut and fisted my hands in an attempt to contain it all in front of this total stranger. I couldn't let it loose yet. Not until I reached the safety of my house in Louisiana. I could fall apart then.

"What airline?" The driver's abrupt question shook me out of my thoughts. She hadn't uttered a word the entire twenty-five-minute drive, for which I was thankful. I wasn't in any mood for small talk.

"Alaska," I replied after glancing at my email from Ada Lynn.

"Got it," she said, expertly maneuvering across lanes in the direction indicated for Departures, then pulled up to the curb adjacent to an Alaska Airlines sign. I stepped out of the car, grabbed my bag and thanked her. Then I turned and stared at the automatic doors, watching them whoosh open and closed, my body frozen in place. As soon as I walked through them, my life would never be the same. I was going home, but instead of feeling excited to see Dad and Ada Lynn, I only felt dread. Because a huge part of me was now gone.

People hurried past me, their luggage rolling behind them, and conversations taking place on their phones. I watched dumbly as they passed by. All of this ordinary life was taking place while my world fell apart right in front of them. No one even knew the difference. I wondered how many times I'd walked by others and had no idea if they were okay or if they were living hell on earth like I was.

"Gemma!"

My head snapped in the direction of the familiar, deep voice. Hendrix. Shit, with the Andrea drama I'd forgotten I'd texted him to meet me at the airport.

"I got your message," he said, breathlessly catching up to me. "What's going on? Why are you leaving?" His focus bounced between my duffel and back to me. Worry and confusion clouded his handsome features. Briefly, my heart came to life and then the light flickered out again.

"Ada Lynn called. Mom was killed in a car accident tonight," I said, my own voice sounding foreign to me.

"What?" Hendrix gasped and stepped forward, preparing to hug me.

I walked backward and dodged him.

"Don't touch me." My tone was hushed while people passed us. This wasn't anyone's business. I'd been taught to keep the dirty laundry behind closed doors, and now wasn't the time to break that rule.

"What? Gemma, I don't understand. Let me come with you. Please...don't shut me out."

My breath hitched, and my pulse raced in panicked bursts. I wanted him with me, but if there were any truth to Andrea's words... I couldn't ignore the situation.

"You can't."

His eyebrow rose in question. He ran his hand across his jawline and waited for me to say more.

"You need to stay away from me," I stammered.

"What? Gemma, what's going on? Why are you acting like this?" He reached toward me, and I stepped back again. I placed my duffel bag between us as a barrier.

"Andrea Wallace said she was going to press charges against you for rape."

I watched as his mouth dropped open and his eyes widened in slow motion.

"You don't believe her, do you?" His voice cracked, thick with shock and anger.

"Look at me and tell me you've never been with her," I dared, my chin jutting up with defiance.

He swallowed visibly. "I—I," he stammered. "It's not like that." His hand cupped the back of his neck, and he paused.

An ache spread through my chest. He'd been with her?

"Hendrix?" I asked, afraid to hear his answer.

"It was before you and I ever met. I told you'd I'd dated other girls, but I'd never been in love. Not until you. We went out a few times and kissed, but that was all. I swear to you. Nothing else. I never slept with her. I'm telling you the truth. Please, you have to believe me." His striking blue eyes pleaded with me.

"I don't know what to think right now. My mother is dead, and the one guy I've trusted is being accused of the worst thing I could think of. I've only known you for three months, and I can't ignore what Andrea said. Especially not after my own experience..." I paused, my pulse pounding in my ears. "This is all too much to handle. I need some time apart, Hendrix. Please, don't contact me. I'll reach out to you if I want to talk."

Hendrix shook his head in disbelief. "You can't mean that, Gemma. You're in shock about your mom, which is totally understandable, but you're not giving me a chance here. Let me prove to you this isn't true."

Pain filled his face as he reached out to touch me again and quickly pulled his hand back.

Grief and disbelief reared up inside me, and I white-knuckled my bag. I wasn't sure which was ripping me apart more, losing Mom or losing Hendrix. But the moment the realization hit me, my emotions faded to black again.

"What do I need to do? I can't lose you," he said, his jaw tightening with desperation.

"Ada Lynn told me if I didn't hurry, I would miss my flight. I have to go. Goodbye, Hendrix."

"Wait, please," he said, grabbing my arm.

My attention dropped to his hand and traveled up again to his haunted expression.

"Hendrix, my mother is dead. Ada Lynn and Dad need me. You need to let me go."

He dropped my arm. "I know you're in shock and not yourself right now. But deep inside, you know I would never hurt you, Gem. Never. Catch your plane, and while you're in Louisiana, I'm going to prove that this girl is lying. You have my word. I didn't rape her or anyone else."

At this point, I had nothing else to say, and I walked away from him.

The airport doors whooshed open, and I stepped inside and located the baggage check-in. With a quick glance over my shoulder, my attention landed for the last time on Hendrix. His hands were shoved in his front jean pockets, his face etched with pain and sadness as he watched me. With each step, I moved farther and farther away from the one person who breathed life into me, earned my trust, my love, and then ultimately crushed me.

Half an hour later, I watched the lights of the city fade away and said a silent goodbye to Spokane as my plane made its way to Louisiana. Even though it had only been a few months since I'd stepped off the Greyhound and onto campus, it felt like a lifetime. I was no longer the same girl who'd snuck away in the middle of the night. I would walk into my parents' house a changed person.

2

_E_ven in November, the temperatures in Louisiana drifted between the upper sixties and lower seventies. After several months in Washington, I'd forgotten the humidity here was stifling. Although it was cooler, since it was three in the morning, I quickly shed my coat upon arrival.

An eerie feeling washed over me as I stood on the sidewalk outside my house and stared blankly. Mom's missing white Suzuki left a gaping hole in the driveway next to Dad's Jeep. The streetlights filled the neighborhood with a soft glow. A dog barked in the distance, but the rest of the street was quiet. I debated whether to call Dad or just use my key to let myself in. He knew I was coming, and I doubted he'd be asleep anyway.

Somehow, I managed to place one foot in front of the other. As I approached the house, I noticed the peeling yellow paint had been replaced with a new soft beige. Mom's favorite color. In her mind, if you had a nice neutral background, you would have no problem matching furniture and pictures. You had the freedom to work with any color you wanted.

Dread filled me as I made my way up the porch steps and pulled open the screen door, the familiar creak breaking the stillness of the early morning.

I fumbled for my key in the front pocket of my boyfriend jeans, but before I could fit it in the keyhole, the door swung open.

"Gemma," Dad whispered hoarsely.

His brown and gray hair was plastered against the side of his head, his eyes puffy and rimmed with red. I hadn't even cried yet.

"Dad," I said with a gentleness that I didn't feel, "I'm here." He stood back while I walked inside. The familiar smell of Mom's floral perfume tickled my nose. She always said a well-dressed woman never forgot to put on fragrance before going out.

I put my bag down and hugged Dad. His arms wrapped around me tightly.

"I'm so glad you're here," he said, smoothing my hair. I rested my forehead on his shoulder, the shock of Mom's death hitting me hard as I scanned the living room. One of her crossword puzzles was tucked between the pages of a Colleen Hoover book resting on the coffee table. Her knitting bag sat next to the couch, overflowing with pink, blue, and purple yarn. Her presence filled every corner of the house. But she would never walk through the front door, work in her garden, or cook dinner for us again. She was gone.

In one split second, grief overtook me. I fell to my knees, a guttural cry slipping from deep inside me. Dad sank to the floor and pulled me onto his lap. As I sobbed, he rocked me like he did when I was little and had been upset about something. Dad's shoulders shook, and our tears fell together. Memories of her laughing, crying, and baking all bombarded me. Everything she'd done for me after the rape and pregnancy, everything she'd done for Dad during his treatment...this was what she got in return? How could God be so cruel?

Eventually, my cries fell silent. Dad and I remained sitting, holding tightly onto each other. It had been years since I'd sat in the middle of the floor like this. Finally we let go, and I stretched my cramped legs out in front of me. The flight home had been agonizingly long.

"What happened with Mom?" My voice was raw from crying, and my head began to throb.

"She—she was on the way to the pharmacy to pick up my prescriptions." He choked on his words, breaking down and sobbing again.

"Oh, Dad," I said. "It wasn't your fault. Mom always took care of the errands for us. It was just something she enjoyed."

He wiped his eyes and continued. "A car was speeding and ran the red light. Your mother never had a chance. The impact was so intense, she—she never felt a thing."

I gasped, covering my mouth with my hands and shutting my eyes against the scene his words evoked in my mind.

"She didn't suffer?"

He nodded, his jaw tightening. "It was instant," he murmured.

We sat in silence as I attempted to wrap my head around everything. It didn't make sense. But accidents like this never did. Anger flickered to life inside me, and I stood, no longer able to sit still. I extended my hand to Dad and helped him off the floor.

"Have you eaten?" he asked, leading us into the kitchen. He flipped the light on, and I squinted at the sudden brightness.

"No," I said. "Not sure I could keep much down right now, anyway."

"I understand. Your mom just went grocery shopping yesterday, so the fridge and pantry are full if you're hungry."

"Thanks."

"You look different," he said softly. "In a good way. Just different than when you lived at home."

"I guess a lot has changed since I left for college in Washington." My heart jumped into my throat as I mentally flipped through the last few months with Mac and Hendrix. I missed them already. A hollow ache tugged at me when I reminded myself I was no longer allowed to miss Hendrix. My future with him was unknown right now.

Forcing Hendrix to the back of my mind, it dawned on me I

needed to apologize to Dad and make things right while I had the opportunity. Losing Mom had reminded me how short life was.

"Yeah, about that. I'm so sorry I left like I did. It was such a shitty thing to do, go behind your back. I just...You would have stopped me. Once I got to Spokane, it was like I'd been in a trance the last several years and suddenly woke up."

Dad pulled out a chair at the kitchen table and sat down.

"I realize it's after three in the morning, but I'd really like some coffee if that's okay?" I asked, leaning against the kitchen island.

His brow rose slightly. "It actually sounds good. When did you start drinking coffee?"

"During all of the long hours of studying in a noisy dorm. Mac would often make a run to Starbucks for us in the morning, and sometimes in the evening, too. The classes were more challenging than my online courses, so I had to work harder. It was a nice change, honestly."

"No more baggy clothes, either."

I scooped the coffee grounds into the filter, filled the maker with water, and flipped the switch to brew.

My shoulders sagged with exhaustion. "I made a really good friend who helped me make some positive changes. I've mentioned her to you before, Mackenzie. Mac for short. She...well, she's different." A small smile pulled at the corner of my mouth as I recalled the first day we met. "Mac has a very bubbly personality." My eyebrow rose with my words. "Actually, that's an understatement, but I'll tell you more about her another day."

"I would love to hear about Washington. I've always wanted to see the Northwest but just never made it. Life took some dark turns before I had a chance to go."

I nodded and grabbed two cups as the brown liquid finished dripping into the pot.

"Still like milk in yours?"

"Yeah," he said, stifling a yawn.

Placing the steaming mugs on the table, I pulled out the chair next to him and sat down.

"We have to plan the funeral," I muttered, staring at nothing in particular and sipping my drink.

He nodded, his dark lashes glistening with moisture.

"What—" My eyes fluttered closed with the mere idea of asking. "What did Mom want? Did she want to be cremated or—?" My sobs choked off my last words.

Dad reached over and rubbed my back as hot tears fell down my cheeks. "Yeah. She left detailed instructions."

"She did?" I shouldn't have been surprised. Mom was a planner. She never left things to chance. "Shit," I muttered.

"Language, please," Dad said in a stern voice.

I frowned and shook my head. I was nineteen, and he was still pulling the parent thing, even during his grief.

"I'll try, but I'm not making any promises." I caught myself and scrambled to explain why I'd just talked back to my dad. "What I mean is it's not on the forefront of my mind right now, so if I slip, please cut me some slack."

He grimaced. "I know it was hard on you, Gemma. What you went through broke us all. I guess you really didn't know what to say or how to express what was going on inside you during those years. When you were so depressed, and no one could get you out of bed, we were worried we might lose you. We were afraid you might—commit suicide."

I leaned back in my chair, seeing his perspective for the first time. He'd never said anything like that to me before, acknowledging I'd not only lost my body and child...but my voice.

"Why didn't you ever say anything? We just stopped talking, Dad. After you told me I had to carry Jordan—" I gawked at my mistake. Dammit, my mind was so fucked up over Mom, and Hendrix, that shit was just flying out of my mouth.

"What?" Dad glared at me as he leaned forward. "How do you know his name?" Fury coursed over his face.

I answered him with my silence. There was no way I was having this conversation now, mere hours after losing Mom. I couldn't take it.

"Goddammit, Gemma! How do you know?" He slammed his fist

on the table, our coffee spilling over the mugs and across the surface. Dad had never acted like this before. Terror shot through me with his response. Reeling from his anger, I shot out of my chair, sending it toppling backward.

My breathing came in short bursts, and I wrestled with my feelings. How could I have messed up like this?

"Do. Not. Ever. Talk to me like that again," I said, steel weaving through every word. My body tensed as I turned away from him, grabbed my duffel from the living room, and made my way to my old bedroom. Shutting the door, I leaned against it, my hands trembling with his outburst and my response. Had I made a mistake coming back to him even under the circumstances? I crumpled to the floor, my quiet sobs shaking my shoulders.

3

I finally crawled into my bed at 5 am, physically and emotionally exhausted, but I couldn't sleep. Images of Mom's Suzuki, broken and smashed, played on a loop in my mind. Dad assured me she didn't suffer, however that was little comfort when I imagined what the impact had done to her body. I cried off and on until a pounding headache took over, and I thankfully slipped into numbness.

My phone vibrated on my nightstand.

The same secondhand nightstand Mom and I had painted white and decorated with colorful flower stickers a few months before I was raped. Rolling over, I picked up the phone. Mac's message flashed across the screen.

Yo, bestie. Did you make it to Louisiana alright?

I squeezed my eyes closed and debated if I wanted to text her right now. My mood was in the shitter, and I didn't want to bring her down with me. However, I owed it to her to let her know I'd arrived safe and sound.

Yeah. Been home for a few hours. Why are you awake? It's after three in the morning there.

Black dots flickered across the screen while I waited for her reply.

We've been up all night worried sick about you.

We? I replied.

Yeah, as in your bestie and your boyfriend.

Shit. Had Hendrix not told her what happened?

I don't want to get into it now, but Hendrix isn't my boyfriend anymore. You can ask him for details. It's no longer my business what you two discuss.

There was no immediate response, and I imagined her zeroing in on him, asking a million questions all at once.

He told me, but I don't believe Andrea for one second and deep in your heart, neither do you, Gemma. But for now, just take care of yourself. When is the service?

She wasn't going to argue with me? I chewed my lip, my chest aching with the events that had transpired in less than twenty-four hours.

We talk to the funeral home Friday. It's closed today for Thanksgiving.

I wish you were here with us instead of planning a service for your mom. This sucks in a million ways.

She didn't have to tell *me* that.

I should try and get some sleep. You should too.

I doubt we will, but I'll try. Miss you already, Gemma. Big hug.

You too.

The phone went silent, and I placed it on my nightstand, tears brimming in my eyes again. If things hadn't gone to shit, I'd be next to Hendrix right now with a smile on my face.

I kicked the thought to the curb, rolled over, and stared at the wall. I hated this fucking room. I hated this fucking house. And I seriously hated fucking Louisiana. It had stolen my life from me. Twice.

As hard as I tried, sleep evaded me. It was Thanksgiving Day, but I had nothing to be thankful for. The house felt deserted, too quiet. The usual holiday sounds and aromas I loved—Mom bustling around in the kitchen, basting the turkey, kneading her homemade dough, sautéing celery and onions for stuffing—were gone forever. No one would be celebrating this year.

Since we couldn't plan the funeral until tomorrow, and I had nothing to say to Dad after his explosive reaction about Jordan, I planned on spending the day next door with Ada Lynn.

I showered and dressed in a fresh pair of jeans and a baby blue V-neck shirt. No way would I show up at Ada Lynn's a complete wreck. She'd taken charge after my pregnancy and gotten me through the depression that almost ruined me. This time, it would be up to me to help my family through. I grimaced. Truthfully, I should be with Dad, picking up the pieces, but I couldn't. Not yet.

Ada Lynn usually woke at the crack of dawn, so a little after seven, I rang her doorbell.

The door creaked open, the chain pulling tight as one eye peered at me.

"My blue-eyed girl," she cried as she undid the chain and flung open the door.

I rushed in, my heart overflowing with grief and happiness, swirling together to make a complicated, sticky mess of my emotions. Nothing in the world made me happier than seeing her, but I wouldn't be here if Mom hadn't died.

We stood in the doorway, holding each other, crying. No words were necessary.

"I'm so sorry," Ada Lynn whispered, her warm breath tickling my ear. The familiar scent of cinnamon and apple filled her home from her favorite air fresheners. She planted a kiss on my cheek and pulled back. Then took my hand and gave a gentle squeeze, her eyes traveling up and down my body. A flush crept up my neck at her scrutiny.

"You're beautiful," she said, her expression filled with wonder. "Absolutely stunning."

My lips pursed. It was one thing for Ada Lynn to notice, but I knew the changes I'd made would bring attention and I wasn't interested in any of it. For a fleeting moment, I considered shopping for bland, baggy clothes again, but I didn't have the energy. My mind was in such a fog, I wasn't even sure how I'd ended up on her porch. All I wanted to do was stay in bed and cry. This time, I couldn't. I had to find something to hold onto that would propel me forward. Mom wouldn't want me to waste any more years of my life.

"How about something to drink?" Ada Lynn asked, ushering me inside.

"Coffee sounds good." I followed her into the kitchen. It was as neat and tidy as when I'd left. The only difference? She'd changed her everyday tablecloth out for the fancy lace one she reserved for Thanksgiving. "You're the only good thing about this trip," I muttered. "Sit, I'll get the coffee going for us," I said, pulling her chair out for her.

Ada Lynn sat down at the table, and I grabbed the mugs and milk. I joined her with fresh drinks and sipped at my steaming cup.

"College will do that to ya." She smiled sadly, pointing at my coffee.

"Dad asked me when I started drinking it, too. Guess I never thought about it. Mac would make a Starbucks run on long study nights or early mornings before tests. Right now it's more of a comfort. Plus I'm not sleeping, but I highly doubt anyone else is either."

"No, it will be a while before any of us has a full night's rest again." Her hand trembled slightly as she lifted her mug. She had brushed her hair straight back, flattening some of the gray curls down. Typically, she had it styled at Betty Blue's salon before a holiday, but not this one. Nothing about Thanksgiving would be normal again. Ever.

"Washington has been good to you," Ada Lynn said and smiled gently.

I nodded. "A lot changed after I left." I leaned back in my chair, staring at my cup, my mind flipping through the memories.

"How's Mac?"

I couldn't stop the sad grin. "Love her." I rubbed my hands over my face, attempting to wipe away the deep sadness building inside me. For Mom. For Hendrix. "Other than you, she's my best friend.

She's chatty as hell and pushy at times, but her heart is so good. She's like you in that way."

Ada Lynn's eyebrow arched in anticipation of a full comparison and took a sip of her drink.

"She knows when to push me and when not to. Like you did after the baby."

I bit my thumbnail and thanked the heavens I'd not slipped up and said his name again. If I were honest with myself, there was no way I could hide it from Ada Lynn even if I wanted to. I would have to tell her, but I wasn't sure now was the right time.

"It takes a special kind of friend to know when to push and when to back off. Timing is essential. The person has to be ready to hear what you have to say. If they're not ready, it just bounces off them like a ball off a brick building. Nothing soaks in."

I remembered the day Ada Lynn showed up at my house and stormed into my bedroom. I'd been so consumed by depression after Jordan's birth, I'd given up on life and refused to get out of bed for weeks. Finally, she'd had enough. She came over and hauled me to the shower, scrubbed me clean, and told me to show up at her house the next day. It had been precisely what I'd needed.

"And you, Gemma, process things. You take your time and think things through. When you finally make up your mind about something, there's no changing it. I had to study you a bit to understand when the time was right to drop some wisdom into you. Once I got the hang of it, I would say what I needed to, then back off and let it seep inside you. It worked every time." She smiled widely while she revealed her secret to motivating me. "And look at you now."

"Have you seen my life lately?" I twirled a lock of my hair around my finger, wondering if anything ever knocked Ada Lynn down. The coffee pot gurgled in the background.

"Now before you start to argue with me, I know things are dark right now. No doubt about that. You've been through hell and back before and conquered it. You will again."

She nodded as if her words made it so. Then she pinned me with her all-knowing eyes.

"So full of secrets," she said. "You know I'm here when you're ready."

I stared at her, speechless. Did she realize other things were going on or was she referring to Mom?

I responded to her comment by redirecting the conversation. "Did you know Mom and Dad had their wills prepared after my pregnancy?"

"I did."

I swallowed hard, struggling to maintain my composure while I crumbled inside.

"Dad told me yesterday. He also explained why they chose that time to do it."

"We were all scared we were going to lose you. Your poor mother agonized over it so much there were nights she would sneak into your room while you were sleeping and sit on the floor, watching over you."

"What?" My hand flew to my mouth in astonishment. "No one ever said anything."

"That's the funny thing about parents, they don't often tell you about the sacrifices they make, because to them it's not a sacrifice at all."

Unable to control it any longer, tears streamed down my cheeks.

"She was so proud of you," Ada Lynn said fiercely. "When you made it to Washington, she came over and thanked me for helping you."

I turned away in the chair, tugged my legs into my chest, buried my face against my knees, and full on ugly cried. Mom had been my biggest supporter, and I'd never known. Now she was gone.

I heard Ada Lynn's chair scrape across the linoleum as she stood up, then moved around in the small kitchen. She returned and set a box of tissues in front of me on her pretty Thanksgiving tablecloth.

"Thanks." I grabbed one and blew my nose. "Why didn't anyone tell me this stuff?" I asked, confused. Placing my arm on the back of my chair, I laid my head down and peered at her through swollen eyes.

"We couldn't. You would have worried about her, and it would have done more harm than good. Now everything has changed. You've changed."

"I have." I wiped my face with the Kleenex and took a deep breath. "I need to take care of Dad, but I don't know what to do. We got into a big fight last night about—" My focus dropped to the floor and back to her.

"Jordan," I blurted.

The color drained from her cheeks as I stared at her.

"Good God." She covered her mouth, her hand trembling.

"Dad got super pissed when I accidentally let the name slip."

"How did you even know, Gemma?"

I updated her on the letter I'd found the night I left for Washington. It was too painful to tell her about Hendrix going with me, so I kept it simple and told her a friend had driven me to Seattle. She didn't pry, but I suspected she knew she wasn't getting the entire story yet, either.

"I'm stunned you went to see him, but I understand. I would have done the same." Her brown-eyed gaze filled with sadness.

I shrugged nonchalantly. My emotions were on overload, and I couldn't handle talking about it anymore.

"Anyway, Dad found it necessary to swear at me and slammed his fist into the kitchen table."

Surprise flickered to life in Ada Lynn's expression. "I imagine it was a big shock, Gemma. I don't support him losing his temper, but under the circumstances...You may not realize this, but your mom worked hard to be a buffer between you and your father. She kept a lot of disagreements at bay and tried to protect you the best she could. He finally started to soften when he was diagnosed with lymphoma after you left. Your dad has always had a temper. I think it might be wise for you to tread lightly for now."

"Is he a ticking time bomb or something?" I was astonished Ada Lynn felt it was necessary for me to be careful around my dad.

Her focus dropped to the table before she looked at me again. "He might be," she whispered. "There's only so much a person can handle, and I think he's reached his limit. When you two need some space you come over here, you understand?" Her voice grew stern with her instruction.

I nodded, mulling over what she'd just told me. Had my dad abused my mom? He shoved religious stuff down our throats, but I'd never seen him raise a hand to her. He hardly ever yelled. But I had been so full of grief and lost in depression that maybe I'd been blind to it.

"Gemma," she said, reaching across the table for my hand. Her skin was cool to the touch. I squeezed her thin fingers, "it is not your responsibility to become your father's caregiver."

"That doesn't make any sense. Why would you say that? I have to take care of him. I'm the only one left to do it."

"No, ma'am. I realize you have to stay for a bit, but not long. You get your butt back to Washington. Your dad has made his choices, and you've lost years of your life. It's not your responsibility to take care of him when he can get back up and do it himself."

I scooted to the edge of my seat, my intense stare never leaving her. "What are you keeping from me?" My fingers thrummed anxiously against the table.

Ada Lynn leaned forward in her chair, holding my gaze until I backed down.

"Not today. Today is about your mom and our love for her. We're going to remember how selfless she was, all the good she did, and be grateful we had those years with her."

Defeated, my shoulders slumped. This wasn't what I'd expected to come home to. Dad was drinking, and Ada Lynn wanted me to return to Washington.

4

After my enlightening day with Ada Lynn, I slipped back into my house around eight that night. Dad snored loudly from his recliner, beer bottles littering the coffee table. I frowned. Dad wasn't a drinker. We never had beer or anything stronger in the house, at least that I was aware of.

I quietly gathered the bottles and discarded them in the garbage can located in the garage. I didn't want the house to stink. Everyone would expect us to have a gathering for mom as soon as possible. The last thing we needed was for the town to gossip about the house reeking of alcohol when they stopped by to pay their respects.

The kitchen didn't look like it had gotten any use today. I didn't blame Dad for not cooking. Not only was he most likely not hungry, but he and Mom spent a lot of time in here.

My attention traveled across the room, recalling Mom wearing her red and white checkered apron. She owned every inch of this kitchen. We were allowed to make a mess everywhere else, but not in here. If we forgot to load our dishes or wipe the counters, she'd threaten to not cook for us. A giggle escaped me as I imagined the stern expression, her hands on her hips, scolding us like we were toddlers. Dad and I would grin at each other and then clean up the offense.

A chirp sounded, and I reached in my back pocket for my phone. I frowned as I stared at the message.

I love you.

I fought the overwhelming urge to reply to Hendrix and ask him, if he loved me so much, then where in the hell was he right now when I needed him? Sadness stirred to life inside me when I reminded myself he would be here if I hadn't shoved him away. Fucking Andrea. For all I knew, she was a crazy person just wanting to stir up trouble by tossing around false accusations. Still...rape was nothing I would ever take lightly, and now she had me questioning who Hendrix really was.

I placed my phone on the kitchen counter, choosing not to respond. What would I even say?

Another chirp sounded, and I reluctantly picked up my phone again.

There was no message this time, just a song forwarded to me from his Spotify. When I tapped on the link, "I Can't Breathe" by Bea Miller began to play. The haunting lyrics of the very first song Hendrix and I sang together floated out of my phone speaker.

Chills ran down my body, and a million emotions stirred deep inside me as I recalled that evening.

Mac had dragged me to an outdoor concert on campus. I was still new to the school and was so out of my comfort zone, nervous and afraid. Until I saw Hendrix appear on stage. I'd had no idea the guy who sat at my table in the library every day, despite how rude I was to him, could sing!

When things went sideways after the concert, Hendrix and Mac came to my rescue. Hendrix walked us back to our dorm, and Mac insisted he sing a song. When I quietly joined in, my world opened up. It was the first time I'd sung in five years. It was also the first time I'd looked at Hendrix and really seen him.

I hiccupped as the tears started, swearing at him under my breath for sending me the stupid song. Was this how he was feeling, too?

Broken, unable to breathe, and wanting to go back in time? I wanted to be with him, but if Andrea's words were true, he was a monster. There was a full-on war inside of me. I didn't know what to believe right now. Not only was Mom gone forever, there was the possibility that my relationship with Hendrix would be ripped away. My heart couldn't take anymore.

Dad's snoring grew louder and snapped me out of my dark thoughts. If he caught me crying this hard, he'd ask questions. Turning off Spotify, I grabbed my phone and went to my room. I shut the door softly behind me and picked up my duffel bag, flinging it onto my bare mattress. Ada Lynn's words ran through my mind as I began to unpack my belongings. What wasn't she telling me? Why did she want me to leave so quickly?

An unbearable silence filled my room while I put away my clothes in the white dresser drawers and hung them in my closet. I'd always been a neat freak, but it helped me feel as if I had some kind of order in my life. At this point, I was struggling to find rhyme or reason, so a clean room was essential.

I shook out my wrinkled sheets and made my bed, tucking each corner underneath the mattress. Smoothing the material out, a pang of guilt gnawed at me with Ada Lynn's earlier words. I had no idea Mom watched me sleep during the nights I was so depressed. Opening the closet, I stood on my tiptoes and pulled down my comforter. I'd needed it in Washington, but my duffel had only had so much room.

After my bed was made, I returned to unpacking my bag. I chewed my lip as I pulled out a navy-blue T-shirt and held it up. A cry lodged itself in my throat while I brought it to my nose and inhaled deeply. Hendrix. His woodsy aftershave still lingered in the fabric. How had I gotten his shirt mixed in with my things? It didn't matter. I was relieved I had a part of him with me. I brought it to my nose again, my eyes fluttering closed. How was I going to make it without him? Pulling off my shirt, I then pulled his on and allowed myself to feel his arms around me, his lips on mine, his gentle touch on my body. Every fiber of my being screamed for him. I reveled in the scent and softness of his shirt on my skin, and then I tugged it off, folded it, and tucked it into the back corner of my dresser drawer.

Even though it wasn't nine yet, I changed into my Winnie the Pooh pajamas and climbed into bed. I sat crossed legged in the middle of it and did the only thing that felt right. I clicked the favorites on my phone. One tap later, the phone was ringing in my ear.

"Bestie?" Mac said, surprise filling her voice.

"Hey," I mumbled. "I...I didn't know who else to call."

"Gemma, talk to me," she said gently.

"It's all such a huge mess. Mom, Dad, Hendrix. What am I going to do?" I asked, sobbing into the phone.

"I know it is, and your relationship with Hendrix will work itself out. Before you realize it, you'll be back on the plane and home with us."

"I wish."

"You're not coming back?" Mac asked wistfully.

"I don't know. I don't know anything right now."

"Makes sense, but I don't like it. I don't know how to help. Hendrix is the one that's good at consoling people. I just ramble about shit. Like, I don't even know if I help or not. What should I say? What should I not say? Maybe I shouldn't say anything at all." She paused for a second.

I couldn't stop my smile. This is what I needed. Mac, rambling on and on. She was the best distraction ever.

"I miss you," I said.

"I miss you, too. What can I do? What do you need from me?"

"This. I just need my best friend." I glanced around my stark white room. It never bothered me before, but if I stayed, I'd need to hang some pictures or something. A splash of color would make it look less like a hospital room.

"Makes two of us. I know it was Thanksgiving and we spent it with our families, but there was a huge hole in my heart today. You should have been with Hendrix and me."

"I know." I tucked a stray piece of hair behind my ear and pulled out a tissue from the box on my nightstand.

"Tell me what you ate," I muttered.

"Really? You want to know about the food?"

"Yeah, just tell me about your day. It's all I need."

As Mac went on for ten minutes about helping her mom cook, burning the rolls, and playing Monopoly with her cousins, I felt like I was next to her again. Sharing a dorm room.

Her chatter slowed, and I yawned.

"So, my talking puts you to sleep?" She giggled.

"I haven't slept since I left."

"I wouldn't have either."

"I screwed up, Mac. I don't know what to do," I gushed.

"About Hendrix? No, he understands, and he's here the minute you want to get back together. He just wants to prove he's innocent, so regardless if you're together or not, he's going after the truth. He won't bother you with it yet. At least not until he has some answers, and you're not so messed up about your mom."

"Stop, Mac! No, it has nothing to do with Hendrix." My heart fluttered a little bit with her words. A part of me calmed knowing he would take me back, all I had to do was say yes.

"Oh."

"I slipped up to my Dad about Jordan."

"Oh shit."

I could only imagine the look on her face.

"Yeah. It didn't go well at all." I filled her in on how I'd let Jordan's name slip, how Dad had flipped out, and how it was a good thing he didn't know I'd gone to Seattle and seen Jordan. I also told her about my strange conversation with Ada Lynn and that she'd insisted I get my butt back to Washington as soon as possible.

"Nothing sounds good about this," Mac mumbled.

"I know, but I can't leave. Not now. He saw me through my worst days, and no matter how much we argue, I need to take care of him right now."

"But Gemma, Ada Lynn told you not to stay. I thought you

listened to her." Mac's voice was filled with concern.

"I do, but she said don't stay for long. I don't know what that looks like yet."

"I'd be super torn if I were you. I'd want to stay and take care of my dad, but at the same time, I'd want to go back to Washington."

"Yeah, sums it up pretty well. Unfortunately, I no longer have a place in Washington to live. So even if I were here for only a week or two, where would I go?"

"What? Shit, fuck, damn."

"Well said." I fiddled with the hem of my shirt, my mind too overloaded to figure out much beyond arrangements for Mom.

"It's alright. The only thing you need to deal with right now is the funeral. Get through the next few days, and I'm here for you every minute you need me. I'm only a call or text away. The rest of the shit...let me work on it. We can apply for housing together or something. If you want to come back, we'll make it happen. Got it?"

"Yeah," I said softly. Whether she realized it or not, I needed her to help me fix things. Not only did I need someone in my corner for moral support, but she had connections and could help us find a new place to live. There was no way I could make it back by myself without her help. Not after the drama with Hendrix. I yawned, feeling emotionally and physically depleted.

"You get some sleep if you can and call or text me tomorrow."

"Thanks, Mac. Love ya."

"You too, bestie. You, too."

I ended the call and massaged my aching temples. Twenty-four hours ago, I was kissing Hendrix goodbye before he left for band practice. I'd run up to my dorm room and waited for Mac so we could move into his house. Now, I sat alone in the wake of my mom's death.

I snuggled under the blankets of my freshly made bed and stared at the ceiling. If I listened to music tonight, I'd only think about Hendrix. So I let my thoughts drift back to Mom. Fresh tears spilled down my cheeks as I realized I would be planning her funeral tomorrow. There were only so many times my heart could break before I would no longer be able to piece it back together again.

5

The next several days passed in a complete blur. It was as if someone else had taken over my body, and I was watching from the sidelines. Relatives flew in from all across the country, and a ton of people showed up from our community for Mom's funeral. The house was packed after the service, the majority of mourners staying all afternoon and part of the evening. Our freezer was so full of food, I almost couldn't close the door. Well-meaning folks always felt the need to stock the kitchen with food after the funeral of a friend or family member, but here in the South, they went overboard —funeral potatoes, mac & cheese, fried chicken, pasta salads, chess pie...you name it, they brought it. It wasn't like Dad or I had an appetite.

A perma-smile had fixed itself on my lips as I played hostess and assured everyone we would be okay without Mom. I was lying. Dad and I had claimed our parts of the house and stayed away from each other. Eventually, we would have to have a real conversation about Jordan and how long I planned to stay, but it wasn't time yet.

Relieved when the last person finally left, I got started cleaning up the mess. I'd declined offers of help, preferring to be left alone with my thoughts. After gathering bottles and cans in one bag, food garbage in another, I went out to the garage to dump the trash and was startled at the number of empty beers that were quickly stacking up. Dad had passed out drunk every night since I'd been back. The only time he ever left the house was when he was out of alcohol. Granted, I was giving him his space, but an uneasy feeling tugged at me. It was disconcerting watching him fall apart like this. Maybe his drinking wasn't anything new, and Mom had kept it hidden from me.

When I returned from the garage to continue picking up, Dad was in his recliner, beer in hand. I'd lost track of how many he'd had over the last several hours. My gaze traveled across the room and it dawned on me he wasn't going to lift a finger to help me. I stomped toward the kitchen and grabbed another trash bag, tossing everyone's silver Solo cups in it along with paper plates, napkins, and plastic flatware. Why in the hell people didn't take care of their mess themselves was beyond me. It wasn't like I didn't already have a big enough of a shitshow to clean up: my life.

I dropped my half-full bag to the kitchen floor and frowned when I heard the sound of the doorbell. The clock on the microwave showed it was after nine at night. It was pretty late, but I hurried to answer the door anyway. Someone might have forgotten a phone or handbag from earlier in the day and only just realized it was missing.

I opened the door and my mouth fell open. I shot a look in Dad's direction, but he was focused on the TV, utterly oblivious to anything else around him.

"What are you doing here?" I hissed while I stepped out on the front porch.

"Gem," Hendrix whispered, "I know you don't want me here, but I had to see you."

I shook my head in disbelief. How in the hell was Hendrix Harrington standing on my porch in Louisiana?

"It took me a few days, but I finally wore Mac down until she told me what was going on with you. I'm worried about you and your dad." He shoved his hands in his jeans pockets and glanced around cautiously.

His burgundy sweater sleeves were pushed up his forearms. It was too warm for a sweater in this part of Louisiana. Apprehension flickered across his face, and he appeared tired after the day of travel. And although in my mind I didn't want him here, I did, and my heart sang for the first time since I'd kissed him goodbye—the night everything fell apart. Now, he'd flown across the country for me, risking the rejection. This couldn't happen, though. Dad would flip his shit.

"We're fine," I muttered. "Mac has a big mouth."

"It's not her fault this time. She wasn't going to break. In fact, she refused to talk about you at all. I uh...I had to bribe her, actually."

My eyebrows knitted together. "You bribed her?"

"Yeah," he said sheepishly.

"Well, I'm sorry you came all this way for nothing." I folded my arms over my chest for emphasis, pain twisting my heart into knots. "You're not welcome here."

"Gem, please. Can't we talk?" His voice cracked in barely a whisper.

"No. Go. Home." With that, I stepped back inside my house and shut the door in his face.

"Who was that?" Dad asked, not even bothering to look away from the TV.

"It was nothing. Just someone I used to know."

Anger burned inside me, and I made a beeline for my bedroom. I grabbed my phone and shot off a text to Mac.

WTF?

OMG! I'm so sorry! He's brutal when he wants info.

Mac! My dad is drunk again. Do you know how much shit would have hit the fan if he had seen H?

Shit. Are you ok? Did you at least talk to him?

I smacked the palm of my hand against my forehead. What was she not understanding? There was nothing to discuss.

No, Mac! I don't want to see him or talk to him right now. I need space, and you both need to get it through your damned noggins.

Tapping my foot, I waited for Mac's response, but none came. Shit. She was mad, but so was I. Like, what the hell? How in God's name did they think Hendrix showing up at my door would be a good idea? No meant no. Isn't that what he used to tell me?

As quickly as the anger took over, exhaustion was riding on its coattails, settling in right behind it. This ongoing rollercoaster was insane. My emotions were bouncing everywhere. I hated Hendrix one moment, and the next I was still deeply in love with him. It was eating me alive. There was only one thing to do. Cut him out completely. No more thinking about him, no more texting, or listening to songs he sent me. At least while I was here in Louisiana. Besides, my hands were already full, and there was a good possibility I would have to find a way to move on without him if what Andrea said was true.

My phone chirped with Mac's reply.

I'm sorry. I am. Please don't hate me.

I sank onto the edge of my bed. There was no way I could hate Mac. Hell, I couldn't even be mad at her for very long.

I know you're worried, but you have to respect my wishes concerning your brother. I'm fucked up right now. Nothing makes sense, and I don't even know how to make it through all of this.

Dots flickered across my screen.

Not another word about him.

Thanks.

In my mind, the conversation was over. I numbly flipped through Spotify, turned on a playlist, and shoved the phone in my back pocket. Adjusting my earphones, I proceeded to clean up the house.

The bright sunshine woke me the next morning. I wondered why the sun was in such a good fucking mood. Groaning, I forced myself out of bed. With all the people over yesterday, I'd not had a chance to talk to Ada Lynn. She was grieving just as much as we were, and I needed to check on her.

After making some coffee, I slipped quietly out the front door, not wanting to wake Dad. The moment my feet hit the porch, I gasped and stumbled, splashing coffee over the rim of my mug. Thank God I had caught myself and didn't face plant, though.

"What the hell?" I whisper-yelled. Then stared, speechless, as Hendrix sat up slowly from the porch swing. His hair stuck up on one side of his head, and he rubbed the sleep from his eyes. He glanced down in surprise at the bright orange and yellow blanket now crumpled up in his lap, and then looked at me.

"Morning." He cleared his throat and waited for me to respond.

"You slept out here? On my porch swing?" I asked astonished. "You can't be here." My attention dropped to my black and white Converse tennis shoes and slowly back to him.

"My plane doesn't leave until this afternoon, so I had to give it one more try." His shoulders slumped forward, and sadness flickered across his face.

"Does that mean you're giving up?" I asked.

"It means I'm leaving to go back to Washington."

My heart sank. I wanted him here with me, but every time the idea formed inside me, Andrea's words wrenched me back to reality.

"What do you want, Hendrix?" I asked, leaning my left shoulder against the front of the house. He looked beautiful on my swing, with his messy hair and burgundy sweater accentuating those piercing blue eyes. His normally close-cropped beard had grown out a bit, making him appear sexy as hell. I wanted to sneak him inside and make love to him, but I couldn't. I'd made my decision last night.

"You," he whispered, his gaze sweeping over me. "I miss you so bad it's fucking killing me," he said, his jaw tensing.

"You know why. It's not like I didn't tell you." My fingers wrapped tightly around my coffee mug, attempting not to shake in front of him. There was no way I'd let him know how much he affected me.

He stood and tried to smooth his hair down.

"It's not true, Gem. Somewhere inside you—you have to know she's lying."

"My life has changed, Hendrix." My eyes held his, my heart almost gashing a hole inside my chest. "Mom is gone, and I need to look after Dad." Tears welled in my eyes, and I blinked them away.

"Let me help. I should be next to you at night, holding you while you fall apart. Please," he said so softly I almost didn't hear him.

I stared out at our front yard, attempting to articulate my next words. I paused and looked at him. "I wish I could, Hendrix. You were my reason. You gave me something to believe in. But Andrea's words ripped me apart and shook me to my core. Right now, when I look at you, I'm right back in that alley five years ago."

"So, this is it?" he asked, standing and stepping toward me. He took my coffee mug from me and set it on the porch swing.

"I've been trying to tell you that I need time, Hendrix. And even with time, I can't guarantee I'll come back to you." Frustration welled up inside me. It was almost as though we were battling over the library table again.

His eyes filled with compassion, searching my face and then fixating on my mouth. An unwanted tingle traveled through my body.

"Then let me kiss you one last time, Gem." He moved toward me and slipped his arm around my waist, but he didn't pull me into him.

His fingers trailed down my cheek, sending shivers down my back. I straightened, my body rigid, trying to fight the effect he had on me.

"One more," he said while he brought me flush against him. His other hand tilted my mouth up to his, and my breath hitched as he kissed me tenderly, slowly, savoring every second. I'd missed this. I'd missed him.

My fingers automatically skimmed the back of his neck, threading through his long dark hair. Our lips parted, his tongue gently caressing mine. Warmth and longing spread through me, and I moaned softly against him.

His hands cupped each side of my head as we lost ourselves in each other. I leaned my hips into his, feeling his erection through his jeans. Hendrix's response to our kiss was just as strong as mine.

Andrea's image flickered across my mind, the desperation in her expression that night clinging to my memory. My eyes flew open and I gasped, stepping away from him.

A flush spread up my neck and cheeks. I wiped my mouth and

stared at him. "There you go. Your final kiss." I crossed my arms over my chest and huffed. He'd found a weak moment and taken advantage of it.

He grew serious and leaned forward. "Gem, you don't kiss someone goodbye like that if you don't have feelings for them," he whispered in my ear. "Know that I love you." He kissed my cheek and then walked away, leaving me breathless and flustered on the front porch.

I bit my lip as I watched him, working hard to maintain what little dignity and composure he'd left me with after the kiss. But no matter what I felt in the moment, I had to let him go.

He glanced over his shoulder and gave me a small wave before he got into a rental car and drove off down the road.

Once he was gone, I sank to my knees and let the sob that had been choking me free. After seeing him, there was no way I could do it again. When he had first found me, I was broken. But now—I was shattered.

Standing up, I smoothed my hair and cleared my throat. I picked up my coffee and the blanket off the swing. Clutching it to me, I walked to Ada Lynn's and rang her doorbell.

"Morning," she said, eyeing me.

"I noticed you didn't say *good* morning," I muttered.

"By the looks of it, it's not a good morning for you. Come on, shut the door behind you."

I did as she said and followed her into the kitchen.

"Well? Talk to me." She placed a fresh cup full of steaming comfort in front of me.

"Is this your blanket?" I held it up for her to see. Not that she could miss the bright orange and yellow colors in it.

"It is," she nodded.

"What was it doing on my porch swing this morning?"

A soft chuckle escaped her as she sipped her drink.

"What's so funny? I just wanted to know how it ended up at my house?"

"I sure have missed you, my blue-eyed girl."

"Ada Lynn," I sighed, exasperated.

"Mr. Hendrix Harrington, huh?"

My eyes popped open.

"You knew who he was?" I leaned forward in the kitchen chair, anxious.

"Well, not before last night. I heard the commotion next door and kept an eye on him after you'd gone inside. Although I wasn't positive it was him, I did suspect. He's the only young man you've ever talked about. So I went on over and brought him a blanket after it grew dark."

"Why in the world would you give a stranger a blanket and permission to stay on my porch swing?"

"He wasn't a stranger after I introduced myself. In fact, he shouldn't have been a stranger at all, Gemma."

I didn't miss the stern tone in her voice. My face flushed crimson.

"I—I. You can't tell Dad," I pleaded.

She chuckled again. "I won't say a word to him, I'm not stupid. However, Hendrix sure did take a risk coming down here for you. I don't just mean with you telling him to go away, either. There would have been hell to pay if your dad knew."

"I know. It's why I told him to leave."

"So you told him to leave because of your dad?"

"It's complicated," I stammered.

"That's what Hendrix said, too." She took another sip of her coffee.

"What did he tell you?" My fingers nervously drummed on the kitchen table, afraid to hear about the conversation.

"He told me how he met you."

"Behind the library?" I yelped.

"Yeah. I wish you'd told me how much you'd struggled," her expression clouded with emotion.

"I was so determined to make it. For you. I'd made you a promise," I said.

"And you did. But I didn't know how much Mac and Hendrix had a part in helping you through it all. That boy sure does love you."

I blanched with her words. "How do you know? You talked to him for one evening."

"I'm eighty-three. I've seen a thing or two. No boy flies two thousand miles to see someone, risking rejection, if they don't care. They sure as hell don't sleep on an old porch swing, hoping for one more opportunity to fix things. I know he offered to stay, and you told him no."

"Sounds like he told you a lot." I chewed on my thumbnail, trying to settle my nerves. Had Hendrix told her why I'd broken things off with him?

"I'll tell you something else. You changed. I don't mean just your clothes and hair, I mean here." She patted her hand over her heart. "Only one thing I know can change someone like that."

"What?" I asked, holding her gaze.

"Love. You love Hendrix, and he loves you. I haven't seen that kind of love very often. And no, I didn't miss that kiss this morning."

My ears flamed red. "That was a private moment, Ada Lynn," I muttered.

"Then you shouldn't have had it on the front porch in front of the entire neighborhood." She laughed. "I've been in love before, too." Her face grew grim, and I wondered if she was remembering the love of her life. He'd passed away before I'd met her, so I'd only heard stories.

"I'm not sure if it can be fixed." I blew out a breath.

"Says who?"

"There's more to it. Plus we just buried Mom. I don't have time for a relationship right now."

"Mm-hmm." She shot me a look that told me she knew better than the bullshit I was spewing. I had nothing but time on my hands.

"Well, you don't have to figure out the rest of your life all in one day. If you're staying for a spell, then we need to hammer out some details. You need to enroll in college somewhere. You're going to have to look after your dad for a bit, too. Maybe a little part-time job would be good for you. I'll let you use my car whenever you need it. However, if it were up to me? I'd prefer you pick up your phone, make things right with that boy of yours, and jump on the first plane to Washington." She tapped her pointer finger on the table while she emphasized the word Washington.

"Are you trying to get rid of me?" I whined.

"No, honey, I'm trying to protect you," she scolded. "You're a smart girl. Go live your life and let your dad live his."

"I can't leave yet. I can't walk away from my family again. Regardless of Dad's reaction with my slip up about Jordan—I can't leave him alone yet. Plus, I have nowhere to live in Spokane. I'll need some time to work out details with Mac before I go back."

Ada Lynn nodded. "Okay then. You chew on what I said and decide if you're staying for a while. I suspect a few months won't hurt anything as long as you're enrolled in school and stay out of your dad's way."

6

No matter how hard I fought, I slipped into a deep depression over the next few weeks. Funny how I created a new routine, friends, and a small social life in Washington, but the moment something awful happened, the old me stepped right back in. After a million calls and texts from Mac, I turned my phone off. I even skipped spending time with Ada Lynn. That hadn't happened since right after I'd had Jordan.

Dad and I didn't speak much, either. We'd grunt at each other in passing, but that was the extent of it. It worked for me since he stayed drunk. At one time I would have thought he was pathetic, but now I couldn't even manage to judge him for it. Hell, I barely got out of bed myself.

For whatever reason, today I got up and showered. After dressing in clean clothes and brushing the tangled mess called my hair, I walked into the kitchen, grabbed a can of orange juice from the freezer, and made some. My taste buds puckered with the first drink, the acid burning my throat as it went down. Coughing, I looked over at the calendar. Somehow December had arrived, and we were in the second week. Shit. A moment of clarity washed over me, and I wondered if Dad had checked the mail or if the bills had been paid.

I'd always checked it before I left for Spokane, but Mom managed the bills.

Sliding my feet into my flip-flops, I walked onto the front porch. Blinded by the sunshine, I raised my arms in a lame attempt to protect my eyes. I glanced over at the porch swing, remembering the last time I'd seen Hendrix. Kissed him. The pain of losing him speared me. Pushing the memory away, I hopped down the porch steps.

Approaching the mailbox, I saw that it was stuffed to capacity and overflowing onto the open lid. What the hell? Guess it answered my question. Dad hadn't bothered to bring in the mail, which meant the bills hadn't been paid. This wasn't good. Regardless if I used it often or not lately, I liked my electricity and hot shower.

I tugged on an envelope that jutted out between the others. The familiar handwriting scrawled out my name and address. I pulled another letter out, the same thing. Frantic, I pulled them out one by one, checking the return address. All the same. Twenty-one letters were in my hand. Hendrix had written me twenty-one times. I swallowed the ball of emotions that threatened to erupt while I continued to unload the overstuffed box. Bills and junk mail were all that was left.

I hurried back into the house and dumped it all on the kitchen table, separating the items by importance. My anxiety hummed beneath my skin, and I rubbed my temples. I'd never paid for electricity, gas, or phones. I knew Mom used her laptop, which was in a little nook/office in the kitchen, to pay the bills online. But I'd purposely avoided that whole area, hoping Dad would take the initiative to handle things.

I grabbed the stack of papers, sank into her chair at the makeshift desk, and willed myself to not cry. I missed her so much. Every time I finished one of the chores she used to do so easily, my heart ached with memories.

Ripping the power bill open first, I snooped around her computer. Guilt chewed at me for poking around where I shouldn't be, but someone had to keep the power on. Eventually I found Mom's Excel spreadsheet and monthly budget along with her account numbers and passwords. She and Dad shared a joint account, and I cringed as I logged in. Dad would be pissed, but if he wasn't going to take care of the monthly shit, I had to.

Exhausted after several phone calls and taking care of the essential items, I laid my head on the table. A dull throb had turned into a full roar when my eyes landed on the stack of letters from Hendrix. Chewing my lip, I debated on whether to open them. I was curious, but it was more than I could manage right now. I grabbed the stack of letters, went to my bedroom, and stuffed them in the back of my dresser drawer along with his shirt. A pang of sadness broke through my numbness. He must have tried to call or text me. Eventually I'd turn my phone back on, but not today.

"What the hell is all of this?" Dad roared.

My entire body tensed, and I hurried back into the kitchen.

"It was me," I said gently from the doorway. "We were late on the power and water bill, so I had to dig for Mom's information to get things taken care of." I folded my arms over my chest and leaned against the door frame, searching his face for any kind of appreciation.

"You left it all a mess," he said, peering at me with bloodshot eyes. His hair had matted itself against the side of his head, and I could smell the alcohol from across the room. I resisted the urge to open the kitchen window in front of him. All it would do is piss him off.

"We're okay now, they won't turn anything off."

He nodded and turned away from me. His shoulders hunched forward as he shuffled toward the fridge and removed another bottle of beer.

"Do you want something to eat for dinner? I'll cook if you do." Seeing him in this state pierced my heart. He hadn't even gone down this road after my rape, but maybe Mom was the reason for that. Guess it was more evidence of how much she had been the glue that held us together. But even more than that, I worried if he didn't take care of himself, the cancer might come back.

"Like what?"

"Whatever you want. I can grab some takeout, too if that sounds better. We do have a full freezer of casseroles to choose from."

The goal was to get some food in him and help him sober up. If I had to, I'd borrow Ada Lynn's car to pick up a pizza.

"Casserole works." He moved past me and into the living room where he then plopped down into his recliner, the TV roaring to life.

My shoulders sagged with relief. At least he wanted to eat some food. Neither of our appetites had been good recently. It would probably help me as well.

An hour later we sat in the living room together and ate our lasagna. It was the first time in years I'd watched TV with him. Loneliness squeezed my chest. I could almost hear Mom's voice and laugh if I listened hard enough.

To my surprise, the doorbell rang. No one had called or stopped by since Mom's service, so maybe a friend of hers was stopping by to check on us. It was weird how everyone crowded us the first few days then disappeared when we needed them the most.

I placed my plate of half-eaten dinner on the now cluttered coffee table and glanced at Dad. He'd cleaned his plate.

"I got it," I muttered and stood. It wasn't like he'd made a move to get up himself. Slow-burning anger twisted inside me toward him. I wasn't his slave. I was his daughter who was just as fucked up as he was right now.

I swung the door open.

"Hi, bestie!" Mac waved and bounced on her toes.

"Mac?" I gasped.

"The one and only. Since you turned your phone off, I'm here to check on my bestie. I just had to finish finals first. My mom would have totally kicked my ass if I flunked out this term. But here I am, live and in person."

Tears welled in my eyes, and I threw my arms around her, knocking her off balance.

"I'm so glad you're here."

"Me too! I hate not seeing you," she whined and returned my embrace.

I peered around the door at Dad who was still immersed in his TV show.

"Oh, uh, well. Shit—I," she said, fumbling for her words.

"Shh," I hushed her. "My dad is here, so no swearing."

Mac nodded vigorously.

"I need a place to stay," she whispered sheepishly.

"Shit." My hand flew to my mouth. "Well, come on in. It's not much, but neither was our dorm room."

She waltzed in, her suitcase rolling behind her across the wood floor.

"Shew." She fanned her nose, her eyes growing wide. "You start a brewery you didn't bother to tell me about?"

My face fell. Not only was I embarrassed, but how was I going to find the energy to manage Mac around my dad? I was used to shit flying out of her mouth, but he wouldn't like it.

"Dad?" I approached cautiously, unsure of his response.

"Huh?"

"Dad, I have a friend here."

"Hi, Mr. Thompson! It's so nice to meet you. Gemma has told me wonderful things about you and Mrs.—" She stalled, hand extended in front of her realizing she'd just brought up my mom. "I'm here from Washington." The color drained from her cheeks while he stared at her.

"She's dead," he said, his tone cold.

Mac dropped her hand. "I know sir, and I'm so sorry. I'm here to help in any way I can. Like first, we've got to get this house smelling better." She scrunched up her lightly freckled nose.

I gasped and gave her a smack on the back of her noggin. Dad looked at me and then back at Mac. His face a mix of anger, grief, and hopelessness.

"Maybe it wouldn't hurt to have someone else around for a bit." He settled back into his recliner and turned his attention back to his TV show.

Before my bestie could say anything else, I tugged her by the hand and back to my room.

"Shit!" She yelped, releasing her suitcase and slapping her palm against her forehead.

"Shh! These walls are paper thin, Mac. You'll have to keep it down. Surely you have an indoor voice, right?" My eyes pleaded with her. If this was what it was going to be like, it would be more stressful with her here than not, and I really needed her.

"Yes," she whisper-yelled.

"Better." I grinned at her. "I can't believe your here."

"Well, what the hell?" she asked, waving her hands in the air. "You totally shut me down." She shrugged out of her coat and tossed it on my bed. "Good, your bed is big enough for both of us. It also looks like you have managed to lose weight which means you're not eating. So now you're not talking to anyone, and you're not eating? Just a wild and crazy guess, but I don't think this is what your mom would have wanted for you, but what do I know? It's not like she's talking to me from the other side."

"I can't even go there right now." I held up my finger to warn her not to push me.

"Fine. I know how hard it was for Hendrix after Kendra died, so I'm a little prepared to help. I'll give it my best try at least."

"Let's hang up your coat and put your clothes away."

She nodded and lugged her suitcase up on my bed.

"Good grief, Mac. How much shit did you stuff in there?" I asked, eyeing the bulging zipper.

"Long enough to stay until school starts again."

"Three weeks?" Turmoil mixed with relief inside me.

"Well, at least I hope so. Hendrix only booked my ticket here. He hasn't booked my flight home yet."

"He flew you down here?" I chewed on my thumbnail while I waited for her to hang up her coat.

"Yeah. When you wouldn't respond to our texts or calls, he got super worried something awful had happened with your dad. Ya know, since he's drinking so much. Hendrix has a bit of a hot spot with it after Franklin. He has been out of his mind with worry. Like, he's not eating, writing music, nothing. Anyway, he shipped my ass down here to make sure you were functioning and to cheer you up." She flashed me her adorable toothy grin, and everything inside me crumbled. Even though I was trying to be strong for Dad, I'd done a lousy job at it. With Mac here, it dawned on me that I couldn't carry all of this on my own.

I embraced her again, unable to hold back the emotions any longer.

"Thank you," I said softly.

"Hey, it's what besties do," she said, hugging me in return and gently patting my back.

"Now we just have to figure out how to keep you out of trouble with my dad, so you can stay."

"Shit. I'm so sorry, Gemma. You know I don't mean anything when I blurt crap out. But seriously, girlfriend, we have to do something about the smell. He needs a shower, and it's warm enough to open the windows and let some fresh air and sunshine in."

"I know. I need to wash clothes and clean. Tonight was the first time we even ate dinner, not to mention we sat in the same room together for any real length of time. He's drinking instead of eating, and I can barely stomach the idea of food."

Mac unzipped her suitcase, and I opened the dresser drawers and scooted my stuff over, allowing her half of each drawer. My focus landed on the stack of letters and Hendrix's shirt. I discreetly tucked them underneath my socks and panties. She would want me to open them if she knew.

"How's Spokane?"

"Cold. We had a bunch of snow right before I left. I wasn't sure I was going to be able to make it to you or not."

"I'm glad you did. It's been so quiet here, I don't think I've realized how much I've missed human contact. Even classes and the library..." My voice trailed off.

"One way or the other, Gemma, we will get you back there."

I nodded and focused on the floor. "It's not the trip there, it's a place to live," I explained.

Mac shoved her unfolded clothes in her side of the dresser and closed the drawer. I winced. I'd forgotten how messy she was.

"I've been working on it. Most of the time they don't allow off-campus housing unless you're a junior or senior. But there are exceptions, and sometimes it's just about who you know."

"Yeah?" Hope filled me for the first time since I'd been home.

"Mmhm. Even if those didn't work, who says I can't stay here for a while and attend the university? I looked it up, and it's only twenty minutes away."

"What? You'd stay in Louisiana and attend here? Why?"

"Hello! You're my bestie!"

"Mac, there's no way you'd want to go to college here."

"Don't you think that's *my* decision?" She removed her now empty suitcase and tucked it into my closet. I sat on the edge of my bed, and she joined me.

"Like old times, huh? Us sitting on your bed talking." She bounced a little, then settled down.

"Yeah, but Mom was alive, and I was happy with Hend—."

"I know. But back to the school thing."

A frown creased my forehead. She never let anything drop that easily when it concerned her brother. She was up to something.

"Mac?"

"Yes?" she asked, grinning at me.

"What did you do?"

She swallowed visibly. "It's like this." She clapped her hands together and bounced on the bed again.

I reached over to still her. "What. Did. You. Do?"

"I transferred to the university already. I start in January. Tada! Surprise!"

"Shit! Are you screwing with me right now?"

"Nope. The old stepdad made some calls, and I've got a dorm room, and all of the logistics are taken care of. I'll stay as long as you do and when you're ready, we'll transfer back up together. I'll even have a car in a few more days. It should be delivered in front of your house soon."

"I don't understand. You're uprooting your life? What about Asher? Did he finally decide he wasn't leaving his fiancée for you?" My eyes widened as it continued to sink in.

Tension eased from Mac's body, her expression growing serious. "First, because that's what family does for each other. And fuck Asher. He's playing with my heart, anyway. I figured it's good for me to get away for a while, too. Plus I get to experience a new culture, food, and friends. It will be a great learning experience. When you're ready, we'll go back. For now, I have three weeks, and I'll only be a few minutes away versus states and states away. Good God, that was a long day of travel."

I stared at her, stunned. Never in a million years did I think she'd be telling me she was here to stay as long as I needed her to.

"I'll take it." I nodded, tears spilling down my cheeks.

"Gemma, don't cry. It's going to be alright. Losing a family member sucks ass, but you're not alone. Ever."

I dried my cheeks with the palm of my hand and looked at her, attempting a smile.

"I cry all the time, Mac. I'm a fucking mess. Just try to give me some space when I need it."

"Nope. Can't do it. You've had your space for almost a month. You've shut Hendrix and me out, and we're the people that can help you the most. So no, I won't give you any more space. We're getting out of this house, you're going to enroll in at least a class or two, and I'm going to help you put your life back together again. And in case you haven't met me yet, I don't take no for an answer."

I giggled. She definitely wasn't the best with boundaries.

Her stomach growled, and her nose scrunched up. "I'm starving, please tell me you have some food. If not, we can go out and grab dinner if you have access to a car."

"I just made some lasagna."

A lopsided grin spread across her face. "My favorite."

7

*H*aving Mac at the house was an adjustment, but so far things had gone well. In the first few days, we'd cleaned the house, aired it out, pulled food from the freezer, and cooked it. It was the first time in over a month that Dad and I ate on a regular basis. When I wanted to give up and crawl into a corner, she got me out of the house. Typically it was for a walk, but just taking a few minutes to step outside and get some fresh air seemed to help.

For whatever reason, Dad was also on good behavior. He eased off the beer and stopped being so snappy toward me. Mac even made him smile a few times.

One of the best parts about Mac being here was I could finally introduce her to Ada Lynn.

I'd been avoiding her for the last two weeks, wallowing in my own misery, and I felt like total shit for not being there for Ada Lynn. She was hurting, too. So as Mac and I stood on her porch waiting for her to answer the door, I held my breath.

She opened the door, her eye peering through the crack. It shut again, and then I heard the sound of the chain being removed.

"About time," she chided and motioned us inside.

"Hi," I said, my face heating with embarrassment.

Ada Lynn wrapped me in a hug and patted me on the back. "Good to see you," she whispered.

"Hi!" Mac bounced on her tiptoes while she beamed at Ada Lynn.

Ada Lynn chuckled and reached for Mac's hand. "From what Gemma has previously shared with me, I'm going to take a wild guess that you're Mac."

"That's me. I'm so excited to finally meet you! When Hendrix told me he'd bought my tickets the first—no, that was Gemma—the second thing I thought of was that I finally get to meet you!" Mac let out a miniature squeal and moved in for a hug.

An excited smile graced her features as Ada Lynn grinned and returned her embrace.

"You're right, she's a chatty one," she said to me. "I just made a pecan pie fresh out of the oven, you two come on back to the kitchen."

Mac's enthusiasm for the pie was hilarious. Then it dawned on me.

"One small piece for you and that's it." I raised an eyebrow at her and grabbed the plates and forks for us.

Mac's face fell with disappointment. "Medium piece?" she asked, her eyes pleading with me.

"What are you two going on about?" Ada Lynn asked while she brought the pie over to the table.

"Sugar makes Mac hyper. So, I'm cutting her off at a small piece."

"Oh lord, you get more hyper?" Ada Lynn asked, her eyes popping open wide.

Mac sank in her chair. "I don't mean too, and I rarely eat any desserts or sugar. Your pie, though," she straightened her back and took a big whiff, "smells so amazing!"

Ada Lynn shot me a look. "Well, you won't be at *my* house all night, so you take as big of a piece as you want."

"Ada Lynn!" I playfully nudged her with my elbow. It was the first time I'd joked around with anyone in weeks. Maybe Mac being here was a good thing.

Mac took a plate, and Ada Lynn cut the pie and dished it up.

"Oh my God! This is amazing," Mac said around a mouthful of food. "Wait until I tell Hendrix about your cooking, Miss Ada."

My brow arched at the Hendrix and Miss Ada comment.

Ada Lynn chewed and swallowed her food while my cheeks flamed red. I hadn't forbidden Mac to talk about Hendrix, so she hadn't known any better. But I was sure Ada Lynn would take full advantage to ply her with the million questions I'd refused to answer. It wasn't like I was jumping at the opportunity to ask her about the evening she talked to Hendrix, either. I was still unsure of the full extent of their conversation that night on the porch swing, and I was too scared to ask.

"I'd almost forgotten. Hendrix is your brother, right?" Ada Lynn dabbed at her mouth with a napkin and placed it next to her plate.

I groaned and placed my fork down. Here she went, digging into my business.

"Step," Mac muttered around her mouthful of pie. "Sooo good," she said, her eyes rolling upward in sheer pleasure.

"How is Hendrix?" Ada Lynn pried.

I shot Mac a look, my expression pleading with her to not talk about him, but she ignored me.

"Heartbroken," Mac said, shoving another bite into her mouth.

"He's not the only one," Ada Lynn replied, her head tilting toward me.

"Right? Like they just need to get their shit fixed and get back together again."

I cringed at Mac's words.

"Oh, sorry, I said shit. Sorry, Gemma. Sorry, Miss Ada."

"Just a wild guess, but I figure you know why these two broke up?"

Ada Lynn wasn't going to give up. She had tapped into a fountain of information, and she was going to milk it for everything it was worth.

"Oh my God. You don't know? I figured Gemma would have told you by now." Mac winced when I kicked her under the table, but kept her eyes on her pie. I assumed the sugar had kicked in because she suddenly had diarrhea of the mouth. Way worse than normal.

"You won't believe this! Andrea Wallace stopped Gemma on her way out of the dorm the night she was flying back here. And wow did she stir up a shit storm. Let me back up a little, so it all makes sense. There's a rapist on campus named Brandon, and all the girls know about him. It's how Hendrix and Gemma met, actually. He was harassing Gemma, and Hendrix stepped in. Man, I wish I could have seen that! One of these days Hendrix is going to beat his ass into the ground, and I do *not* want to miss it."

I watched as Ada Lynn's mouth gaped open in horror.

"Mac!" I yelled. "Enough! You have no right to share my personal life without my permission." I smacked my palm against the table while the anger roared to life inside me. "Ada Lynn, there is a reason I've not shared this with you. Mac, shut the hell up right now or get back on the plane and go home," I fumed at her.

Mac sank in her chair, tears welling in her eyes. "I'm so sorry. I'm so sorry. I don't know what's wrong with me. Maybe Mom's right and I'll never be able to keep friends unless I get back on the medication." She covered her mouth, pain etching across her features. Her leg began to bounce as her eyes focused on her now empty plate.

I sighed. Ada Lynn silently stared at her partially eaten pie.

I rubbed my hands over my face, wishing none of this had ever happened. Mac knew all my issues and that I didn't want anyone to know about the Brandon incidents. What the fuck?

"Ada Lynn," I whispered, taking her frail hand in mine. "Are you alright?"

She gazed up at me, her brown eyes clouding with turmoil.

"Is this why you came home? This is why you aren't in a hurry to go back? The rapist?"

"Part of it. Since it's all out in the open, most of it anyway, I guess we should just put it all out on the table. I'll answer whatever questions you have." Tension crept up my neck with the idea of sharing.

I glanced over at Mac as her hand moved toward another bite of pie. My chair flew backward, and I hopped up, snatching the plate away from her. "No more. Ever," I said, staring holes in her as I sat back down again.

She nodded. "Sugar messes me up pretty bad. I just forget until I have it again, but then I want more."

"Well I won't ever forget," I snapped.

I inhaled sharply. "Alright, let's see if I can possibly get through this in one piece." I turned toward Ada Lynn. "I'm going to just blurt everything out, and it will most likely include several swear words, so I'm sorry. But so much is going on, and I can't try to explain it and watch every word that comes out of my mouth, too. I'm already on eggshells with Dad so please just let me say what I need to."

Ada Lynn nodded, and Mac remained quiet for a change.

"I'm not sure where to begin. Life was such a whirlwind. And yeah, what Mac said is true. Brandon is a bad guy and he, for whatever reason, targeted me."

"I know why," Mac squeaked, raising her hand slightly.

My brow shot up. I motioned for her to provide the information.

"Unfortunately, it was the way Gemma dressed when she first arrived. Brandon could smell an easy target ten miles away. After Hendrix stood up to him on Gemma's behalf, it became revenge. Those two have a nasty history."

I drummed my fingers on the table anxiously. "I figured. I'll never forget it, either. Hendrix and Brandon literally stood toe to toe. Brandon backed down, but he spit on Hendrix first."

"What? And Hendrix didn't beat the shit out of him right there?" Mac's hands fisted with her words.

"Anyway," I interrupted Mac before she could continue, "Hendrix and I became friends, and I got closer to Mac. Oddly enough, I didn't know they were step-siblings for a while. Then, there was a concert and..." My voice trailed off, my mind rehashing the details of the night. "There was a fight, and Brandon pointed the cops toward me saying I'd started it. He put a restraining order on me, too."

"And the cops believed him! Rat bastards," Mac piped in.

"I've got this, thank you, Mac." I took a deep breath, trying to control the ebb and flow of my frustration with her. "I don't know if the cops believed Brandon or not, but that night I learned that

Brandon is the dean's son. It sounds like he gets away with a lot, including hurting girls on campus."

Ada Lynn reached for my hand, her bony fingers tightening around mine.

"Unfortunately, I did have a run in with Brandon one evening, and Mac was the one who helped me after the assault."

Ada Lynn's shoulders shook as she broke down and cried.

"Shit. I'm so sorry. Ada Lynn, I'm okay. Mac and Hendrix both helped me."

I kneeled on the floor and wrapped my arms around her.

"If anything worse had happened—" She sobbed.

"It didn't. I'm fine. Mac was there, and then Hendrix got involved." I peered at Mac, my heart softening again for all the times she'd saved my ass.

Ada Lynn peeked over at Mac.

"You helped keep my Gemma safe?"

Wide-eyed, Mac glanced at me then back to Ada Lynn.

"Yes, ma'am. We helped each other."

"Thank you. I know we had a hiccup tonight with the sugar but thank you for helping her when I couldn't."

"And I'll do it again, Miss Ada. As long as she lets me stay around, anyway." Mac's head hung in shame, and Ada Lynn reached over and patted her hand.

I slid back into my chair as Ada Lynn pulled a tissue out of the Kleenex box and dabbed her red, swollen eyes.

"I'm so sorry, Gemma. I didn't mean to bring the whole mess up and hurt you. Unfortunately, I didn't understand your reasons for keeping it to yourself, and now it's too late to undo the damage. You've already lost your mom and so many precious years. Your mom's death had a huge impact on me, too. I've noticed I'm not quite myself lately."

"It's okay, Ada Lynn. I do think we need to stop for tonight, though. It's awfully hard on all of us."

She nodded, and I peered over at Mac. "How are you miss blabbermouth?" How the hell did I end up taking care of everyone when I was barely holding onto the edge of a cliff myself?

"Okay," she responded, embarrassed.

I nodded and let it go for now.

"Ada Lynn, it's getting late so let's at least get comfortable in the living room."

I led Ada Lynn to her chair, Mac following silently behind us. She tilted her head toward the matching recliner to the one Ada Lynn had sat in, and I nodded. I settled into a corner of the couch next to Ada Lynn's chair. Her body shuddered with a deep breath, and I took her hand.

"I'm sorry," I mumbled.

"My girl," she looked at me wistfully. "What I would give to keep you protected from the world."

"You have. You were the only person who saved me the last time. Even though things aren't settled yet, Brandon will get what's coming to him."

A soft snore interrupted our conversation. I turned toward Mac and muffled a giggle against my arm. I'd never known anyone who could piss me off as much as she did, and I still loved her like crazy. My heart melted a little.

"Ada Lynn," I said, gaining her attention and nodding in Mac's direction.

"Good Lord. How in the world can she sleep like that?" Mac's head was hanging nearly upside down off the arm of the chair, one leg draped across the opposite arm.

I barked out a laugh, my hands immediately covering my mouth, not wanting to wake Mac. A fit of giggles shot through me while I peeked at her again. Ada Lynn's chuckle wasn't far behind. I propped my arm up on the sofa and stared at my best friend. A soft sigh escaped me.

"Although she messed up tonight, Gemma, you've got a really good friend there. We're all affected by the loss of your mom. And Mac seems like she's been holding a lot of stuff in."

"How in the hell can she hold anything in? You heard her full-on

gush without taking a breath or even thinking about the consequences. I had a good reason for not sharing all of the details with
you. You're on heart and blood pressure medication. I'd never forgive
myself if—" I was unable to finish. Silence filled the room, and I
struggled to regain my composure.

"I'll have to go sometime, but it's not today, so stop worrying."

A tear snuck down my cheek. My attention drifted from Mac to
Ada Lynn.

"Do you love him?" Ada Lynn asked out of the blue.

Leaning back into the couch, I sank into it, clutching at the collar
of my shirt. My emotions were flying everywhere tonight from anger
at Mac to fear of losing Ada Lynn.

An agonizing ache spread through my chest, and for a brief
moment, I allowed myself to think about Hendrix. How he'd flown
two thousand miles to see me. How he had sent Mac when I refused
his calls. His kiss goodbye, his gentleness the first time we made
love.

My heart split in two as a gut-wrenching moan escaped me
followed by a wailing cry. I'd not taken any time to really digest everything that had happened over the last few months. I'd stepped foot in
Spokane and kept everything shut in so tightly. I'd been afraid if I
looked at my new reality, I'd run right back to Louisiana. But Hendrix
had been my reason to stay. His love had brought me out on the other
side of my past but then left me broken. Somehow, I was whole with
him. Until...

"Let it out, Gemma. We all need a good cry." Ada Lynn leaned
over and rubbed my shoulder soothingly.

I curled up on the couch and sobbed. I cried over Mom, I cried
about Hendrix, and I cried over everything that had come to light
tonight, forcing me to no longer hide from it. How had life flipped
over and become such an insane nightmare?

My shoulders shook as the tears continued to flow.

The chair creaked while Ada Lynn stood and reached over for the
blanket, covering me up.

"Let it all out. You've got to face things head on before you can come out stronger on the other side." She paused and sat back down. I peered at her through swollen eyes.

"What if I can't? What if I can't make it through this time?" I hiccupped.

"Gemma, the first love is the hardest to get over. But let me assure you, only two things can happen. You and Hendrix will realize how much you mean to each other and figure out a way to get back together, or you won't. Time will pass, and the days will get a little easier, but you'll never completely get over your first. I've not met a woman yet who doesn't go all doe-eyed when she talks about the first man she fell in love with."

"Really? I don't know if that's good or bad." I wiped my stuffy nose and propped myself up on the arm of the couch.

"Do you want to tell me the rest?" Ada Lynn asked gently. This time she wasn't charging in like a bull for information.

"I don't know if I can." The thought of repeating Andrea's accusation made me nauseated. "Are you sure you can deal with it?"

"You have my word that if I can't, I'll tell you," she assured me.

Mac let out a snort, and we laughed softly for a moment. A part of me felt terrible for jumping all over her earlier.

"Brandon..." My voice trailed off, as I gathered the strength to continue. "He hurt one of Mac's friends." I pursed my lips in disgust. "I was luckier than she was, though. The night he assaulted me I escaped. I sprayed him in the face with pepper spray, but I caught some of it, too. Mac was there in a split second and helped me wash as much of it off as we could. I knew that night she was a real friend. Plus she's a huge Hendrix fan." I smiled, reflecting on the adoration in Mac's tone when she spoke about him. "She really loves her brother, and he's so good to her. He knows how to work with her when she's stressed and a massive ball of activity. He—he lived with Mac and her mom after his little sister was killed in a hit-and-run accident. She was four, Ada Lynn. Hendrix watched the entire thing happen."

Ada Lynn gasped. "How horrible. I suspect he still carries the weight on his shoulders."

I nodded and recalled our first kiss right after he'd told me about Kendra, the sensation of his lips still lingering on mine.

"He and Mac grew super close afterward. So when Mac kept telling me what a great guy he was, and he expressed some interest in me. I...I figured he was safe. Not once did he ever push me, either. Even with the ugly hat and horrid clothes, he treated me as though I wore a crown on my head. Eventually I—I fell in love with him," I said so softly I wasn't sure if she had heard me.

"Help an old lady out here. What in the world is the problem then, Gemma?"

My body shuddered as a chill traveled through me. This was the most challenging part to tell her. She would probably tell me to run, never look back, and stay in Louisiana. I twirled a strand of hair around my finger while I gathered my next words.

"The night I left...Andrea Wallace stopped me right before I got into the Uber to leave for the airport. I'd only met her briefly once before. She said she was pressing charges against Hendrix for rape." My heart thundered in my chest as I waited for her reaction.

Thick tension filled the space between us and then Ada Lynn's laughter split it wide open. When she slapped her thigh, I flinched. Shit, I'd pushed her over the edge.

"Are you alright? I've said too much. I'm sorry. No more. I'm done." I positioned my hands in a T calling for a timeout. She had finally cracked under all the stress.

Ada Lynn chuckled a bit longer then sighed. "I needed that laugh."

"It's not funny!" I snapped. "You know what I've been through. Even the tiny flicker of the idea he would harm someone—" I stammered.

"No, it's not, but the idea of the young man I met on your porch swing being a rapist is hilarious."

I'd not seen this one coming at all. Honestly, my feathers were ruffled. How could she take this lightly?

"Gemma, I know you, and you've scrutinized this from every angle possible on the days you could stand to think about it at all."

A sheepish smile spread across my face. Sometimes it was an invasion of privacy with how well she knew me.

"Tell me about Brandon."

"What? No, no." I shook my head adamantly.

"I need to talk you through this, just work with me. What did you see when he looked at you?" she asked, surveying me keenly.

Fear traveled down my spine, goosebumps rising on my arms. "His eyes were cold, hard. He loved attention. His friends looked up to him, but it was almost as though they were afraid of him, too." I peeked at her to see if she was doing okay. "He hurt me," I whispered. "I couldn't scream against his hand when he forced me against the building. He was so rough. Vicious." My voice cracked with emotion. Misery twisted my insides into knots.

Hints of anger flickered across her face, but she continued. "Now tell me about Hendrix. When did you meet him?"

My body relaxed as I recalled Hendrix in the library after the first incident with Brandon. "It was my first day there. Brandon had made some rude comments about my clothes, and he was sexually suggestive. Ignoring him, I somehow made it past him and his groupies, but I had a horrible panic attack. I slipped behind the library and dropped to the ground, my legs trembling so hard I couldn't stand. After I recovered, I went into the library, grabbed a book, put my headphones in, and sat down. I don't remember how long I sat there when a hand tapped the table in front of me, gaining my attention. His eyes were gentle, filled with concern. He wanted to know if I was okay. I had no idea what he was referring to at first, but then he said he'd seen me behind the library."

"Did he make fun of you for your panic attack?" Ada Lynn asked.

My brows knitted together. "No, the opposite," I said quietly.

"Gemma, he's no more a rapist than I'm Wonder Woman."

I grinned at her, imagining her wearing a skimpy outfit with cool bracelets. She might not ever know it, but she was my Wonder Woman.

"I know what you've been through, but when you can, try to take a step back and think of all the ways Hendrix is different than Brandon. And how he's different than the man who hurt you so badly. Don't give up on him yet."

"I don't know. Andrea...she...people are different behind closed doors."

"Yes, they certainly can be, but if you're willing to see the truth that's in front of you, there are always signs and hints of their real nature."

I had a feeling Ada Lynn wasn't just referring to Hendrix.

"I know Hendrix has a battle in front of him, but he knows it, too. He also realizes you're worth fighting for. No rapist sits all night in an uncomfortable porch swing to see the girl he loves, even if it's for a goodbye."

"You don't think so?"

"I don't think, I know. But this isn't my journey my blue-eyed girl. You'll have to figure out what's right for you. And knowing you, Gemma, you'll need some kind of proof that is so solid you can't fire a million holes through it. Just think about it. Chew on it for a bit."

"I will." She was right. Hendrix would have to prove beyond a doubt he was innocent, or my mind would have a continual fuck fest with me. At the same time, I knew Ada Lynn was speaking the truth. The night of Mom's death, I'd been overwhelmed with shock and confusion. Instead of confronting Hendrix and hearing what he had to say, I stepped back into my old habits and retreated inside myself again.

Mac finally shifted in the chair, snorting as she curled up into what I hoped was a more comfortable position.

Even though the evening had sucked overall, I was glad I no longer had to hide anything from Ada Lynn. I hated keeping secrets from her.

"You get some sleep, now."

Ada Lynn stood, handed me the pillow from the other end of the couch, and I slid it underneath my head. She brushed the hair from my face and then walked away, leaving me with my own thoughts.

8

$\mathcal{I}$ woke up, stiff and aching from sleeping on the couch. Mac was still splayed out over the recliner, totally snoring. When I stumbled into the kitchen in search of coffee, Ada Lynn peered up at me over her newspaper.

"Quite a night last night, huh?" she asked, sipping her coffee.

"I feel like I have a hangover. But honestly, I don't even know what one feels like."

"Good. At least you didn't go crazy partying while away at school."

Stifling a yawn, I filled my cup with coffee and leaned against the counter. "Do you want to go outside this morning?"

"I do, it's beautiful out."

Ada Lynn led the way, and we settled into our assigned rocking chairs.

"I've missed this. When I was in Spokane, and the days were really tough, I thought about our time together on your porch. It always seemed to help me not feel so alone."

"I missed it, too. It was lonely after you left, but you were really good about keeping in touch."

"Not as good as I should have been. Guess I got wrapped up in singing and all the crap with Brandon."

"Understandable."

We sat in silence for a while. I suspected Ada Lynn was processing the events from the evening before. Hell, I was. I was still pissed at Mac, but I was sure we'd talk about it.

The screen door creaked open, and Mac stepped onto the porch.

"Grab the chair there and join us," Ada Lynn said.

"You sure?" Mac asked, shyly.

"Yes," I said. "But we're waking up and enjoying the silence." I raised my eyebrow and gave her a stern look of warning. Sometimes it helped to set expectations for Mac.

"Yeah. I feel like shit. Miss Ada, your pie was amazing, but I don't think I can ever indulge again."

"In no way would I be offended if you declined. I'll try not to tempt you again, either. Gemma needs some meat on her, though, so I'll slip her some when you're not around." Ada Lynn winked at me.

We enjoyed the stillness of the morning as we drank coffee together. It was nice sitting in my favorite rocking chair with my two best friends.

We all perked up when a silver Kia Optima pulled up in front of my house. A medium height, muscular guy, wearing a maroon Kia polo shirt got out and began walking up the sidewalk to my porch.

"Who are you looking for?" I called over to him.

"Mackenzie Worthington."

Mac stepped forward, nudging me with her elbow.

"He's hot for an older dude," she whispered.

"Mac, stay focused." I quietly laughed at her and looked back toward him. "And you are?" If someone were looking for Mac, he'd have to go through me first.

He adjusted his glasses, running a hand over his tan, shaved head.

"I'm Josh Swensen from the dealership. Mackenzie bought a car from us, and I'm just delivering it to her, ma'am."

"I'm Mackenzie." Mac bounded down the porch steps and over to the car. I watched as Josh handed her the keys as another Kia pulled in behind Mac's new car, collected him, and drove away.

I hurried down the steps toward her.

"Wow! Ex-stepdad bought you a new car, huh?"

"Right? I can't fucking believe this. Look, leather!" She lit up like a Christmas tree. "Come on, let's go for a ride and test it out."

"We'll be back in a few minutes!" I called to Ada Lynn, giving her a little wave as I settled into the passenger side.

"What happened to your other car?" I asked, fastening my seat belt.

"Sold it. Plus now that I have this one, we can drive back to Spokane together. At least I hope so."

She pulled out onto the road and glanced at me quickly.

"Mac, we need to talk." I didn't want to have this conversation, but her outburst last night had gutted me. "I'm used to you blurting stuff out, but last night was rough. It was like you were on drugs and couldn't stop."

She inhaled sharply. "I'd understand if you want me to go back to Spokane and never speak to me again."

Staring out the window, I pondered the idea seriously. Last night had been a breach of trust. What if I couldn't confide in her anymore? I didn't want to hide things, but if I wanted her in my life, I might not have a choice. On the other hand, she was my best friend, ADHD or not.

"Turn here." I motioned for her to take the next left. "I'll take you on the tour of downtown while we talk. Don't blink because you'll miss it." I forced a laugh. "It's not much compared to Spokane."

"I understand if you need to think about having me around. I have to visit campus today, anyway. There's a meetup I joined for newbies. Figured it would help me get settled in and hopefully make friends before school started. I'll be gone for most of the day which will give you some space."

"Alright." I paused briefly. "What did you mean last night, Mac? About your mom and the medication." I realized I was prying, but I wanted to see if I could help.

Mac's body went rigid.

"Is the medication that bad?" My eyebrows arched in surprise at her reaction.

"Yeah, it is. It caused depression and I couldn't sleep. So the doctors put me on meds for those issues, too. I was so groggy in the morning I couldn't make it to school on time. I felt like a zombie."

"That sucks," I muttered. I had no idea she'd dealt with all of that. Other than her outbursts and high energy, she didn't talk about the challenges.

"It did. Mom said there are some new medications on the market now."

"Do you think you might try one?"

Mac shrugged. "I don't like being like this, Gemma. You should be inside my head. It's way worse than what you see. Like, right now while we're talking, I'm thinking about school: How am I going to adjust here? If you'll still want to be my friend? Did I blow it so bad last night we can't fix it? How pissed Hendrix is going to be with me, how pissed I am at myself, how much I like this car, that I miss Spokane, and I failed my best friend horribly."

"Wow, that's a lot."

"Not even the tip of the iceberg. Mom banned me from sugar years ago. So when the pecan pie hit me—it really hit me hard. Sugar is not my friend."

"That's an understatement. Three bites of pie and you were like a different person."

She tossed me a frown and gave me a quick half shrug.

"I mean, you do blurt shit out, but never like that." I leaned back against the headrest and stared out the window. "Turn right at the light." I paused. "I'm sorry I yelled at you last night."

"I had it coming. I'm surprised Ada Lynn is still speaking to me."

"She's not like that. Patience is her ninja skill." I shifted in my seat and looked at Mac. "If you want to see a doctor I'll go with you. Maybe a medical doctor isn't what you want, but what about some counseling to help you cope?"

Mac glanced at me. "You'd go with me? To either?"

"Yeah. I want you to be happy. You *deserve* to be happy."

"It would be nice to have some relief. I'll think about it."

I didn't want to push anymore. As her bestie, I'd support her with it. If this idea didn't pan out, we'd think of something else.

Over the next twenty minutes, we took a break from our deep discussion, and I pointed out the YMCA, library, my favorite ice cream shop, and some of the other highlights in our little town. It had been years since I'd been downtown. I'd practically been a shut-in after the rape. Even though the layout and buildings looked the same, I noted a lot of new stores, too.

"It's cozy and pretty laid back, unlike Spokane."

"Very laid back." I rubbed the back of my neck, attempting to release some of the tension that had built up. We needed to finish our conversation. "I want you to stay, but only if you can work harder on controlling your mouth, Mac. I love you like a sister, but you fucking slayed me last night. Ada Lynn is on heart medication and if it had been too much for her..."

"Oh my God. I didn't know, Gemma. You know I think the world of her. I'd never in a million years want to hurt Ada Lynn. I know what she means to you."

"I know, and that's part of the problem, your heart and your mouth don't always line up very well."

My stomach clenched as she wiped away a tear that had slipped down her cheek. This was tearing me up, but I had to give her some boundaries.

"First rule, *no more sugar*," I said firmly.

"Agreed."

"Second, you have to stop swearing around my dad at least. You're doing better, but he's super religious, and he doesn't like it. He thinks it's inappropriate for a young lady."

Mac nodded.

"If we can dial those two things down, I think we'll be fine. You only have a few weeks before school starts, anyway."

"Yeah. I'll be out of your hair by then."

"Mac, I don't want you out of my hair. You're my best friend. But I do think it's important to find some effective coping techniques for you. Alright?"

"Yeah. And what about when I start school?"

"What do you mean?" I asked, my brow raising in question.

"Will we still hang out?"

"Of course we will. We can meet at the library, and I'll work on my online class while you study. You can come over on the weekends as long as Dad is doing okay. I know the change is tough and you've given up a lot to be here with me. I remember what it was like the first day I stepped off the bus and onto campus. You were there for me from day one."

Mac's grin briefly lit up her pretty features. "Yup, scared the shit out of you, didn't I?"

"I wouldn't go that far, but I was definitely concerned at first."

Silence settled in the car as she drove back to my house. Ada Lynn was no longer on the porch, so we quietly entered my house. It was almost ten, and Dad must have still been asleep because I didn't see him anywhere.

"I need to shower and get ready," Mac said, collecting her clean clothes.

"You know where everything is."

She attempted a smile and then disappeared down the hall. I flopped backward on my bed, staring at the ceiling. Suddenly I wished Mom was here, so she could give me advice about how to help Mac. Tears slid from my eyes, dropping silently on my bedspread.

I waved as Mac pulled away from the house and toward the university. She seemed really down after our conversation about her ADHD, but I didn't blame her. We both had challenging conditions that affected us and, at times, controlled our lives. I couldn't imagine living with ADHD like Mac. My depression was hard enough to handle.

Just as I turned to go back into the house, a white pickup truck pulled up to the abandoned house across the street. What the hell?

Ada Lynn must have seen it, too because she shuffled onto her porch. I shielded my face from the sun with my hand and watched while another truck pulled up.

"What's going on?" I called to Ada Lynn from my porch.

She cupped her ear, and I realized she couldn't hear me over all the commotion.

I hurried next door and joined her, flopping down in my rocker.

"I wonder what's going on? How long has that house been abandoned, anyway?"

"A few years at least," she replied, eyeing all the activity. Curiosity was evident in her expression.

"This is the most excitement we've had in this neighborhood for a while," I commented.

"Maybe a family will move in with some kids your age."

I chuckled. "Most kids my age are away at college, not at home taking care of their drunk dad."

Ada Lynn gave me a concerned look. "You keep me posted. If he gets out of hand, don't care what time of the night it is, you come on in and sleep on my couch or in the guest bedroom."

"I wouldn't want to scare you."

"You won't. First thing in the morning I'll check to see if you're around. You have an extra key, so use it."

"Yes, ma'am."

We sat in silence and watched as a crew of six men carried lumber and other construction materials inside. Shortly afterward, the usually quiet neighborhood was filled with the sounds of hammering and sawing.

9

*C*hristmas came and went. I felt terrible for Mac since we were in no mood to celebrate. But she was a good sport, and we played cards and board games while Dad drank and watched TV. We split our day between my house and Ada Lynn's. She'd cooked us her traditional Christmas ham and sweet potatoes, but she had been thoughtful and not made dessert.

For the next two weeks, Mac did her best to keep her mouth in check, and we hadn't run into any more hurdles. Needless to say, when it was time for her to start college, a hollow ache seeped inside me. The house was empty without her, and even Dad missed her nonstop talking.

I was excited about my English Lit class. It wasn't a full load, but it was enough for now, and Mac and I had set days to meet up in the library.

I'd been consistent with checking the mail, and every day I received a new letter from Hendrix. Mac still had no idea he was writing to me. The stack of unopened letters in my dresser drawer was growing, and at times I wanted to read them, but I couldn't open that door. It was too painful.

Ada Lynn and I continued our daily routine of sitting on the porch and chatting. Our main topics of conversation were the renovations going on at the house across the street, Mac, and my dad. There wasn't much to discuss yet about my class since it had just started.

"Hm, I just realized the crews haven't been across the street today."

"I suspect they're finished. Looks like they gutted it and put it back together again," Ada Lynn said while pointing toward the roof and new paint job.

My eyes scanned the exterior. It certainly looked a lot better. I wouldn't miss the ugly boarded-up windows and yard full of tall grass and weeds.

Just then, a large truck with Markley's Furniture gracing the side in large black, fancy letters, pulled up in front of the house.

"Well, guess we won't be waiting long to meet the new neighbors, huh?" Ada Lynn said, nodding at the truck.

"Things have been the same for so long now, the change will be weird. I hope they're not assholes," I muttered under my breath.

"I heard that," Ada Lynn chided me. Most of the time she was cool about me swearing, but I guess she felt it was her adult responsibility to get onto me occasionally.

A navy-blue BMW pulled up behind the truck. My eyebrows knitted together, and I shot a curious look at Ada Lynn. Her mouth parted slightly as she leaned forward. Both of us equally nosy.

"Must be the realtor who sold the property," she said.

A tall, handsome man wearing a black suit stepped out of the car. He waved at us, then walked toward the house.

Minutes later, a deep red Lexus four-door pulled up behind the BMW.

"Are they having a party or something?" I asked, my curiosity growing.

I leaned forward in my rocking chair, eager to see who was in the car. Possibly our new neighbors.

When the driver emerged, my heart skidded to a halt. Tall, dark hair, broad shoulders, jeans hugging all the right places. And, despite the sunglasses covering his eyes, I recognized him immediately.

"Holy fuck," I yelped. "It's Hendrix."

Ada Lynn's mouth dropped, and she quickly closed it again. She didn't even chastise me for dropping the F-bomb.

Hendrix slipped off his sunglasses and ran his other hand through his hair. He turned, stared at us briefly, gave a little wave, and walked toward the house, disappearing behind the truck.

"That boy has some balls." Ada Lynn eyed me, a big grin on her face.

I'm not sure what high blood pressure feels like, but I'm pretty sure mine shot through the roof the minute I saw Hendrix step out of the car. There was no other reason he would be at the house across the street unless he'd just bought it. What the hell? He and Mac both had issues with boundaries. The library table was one thing, but moving in across the street from me in Louisiana was insane.

Ada Lynn remained quiet. My simmer began to turn into a full boil. I stood when BMW dude came back.

I hurried across the street, my fists clenching while I tried to contain my temper.

"Hi, are you the realtor?" I asked politely.

"Jim Johnson," he said, extending his hand. "Do you have a home you need to sell? I'm happy to help."

I fought the urge to choke on the scent of his overly strong, sweet cologne.

"No, not me. However, I am wondering about our new neighbor. It's a pretty tight community, so we like to check out the new folks."

Jim gave me a grin like he knew exactly why I wanted to know about the young man I'd just seen walk into the house.

"Lucky for you he's single," he started.

My body bristled. Single? Seriously? Heat spread up my neck and cheeks.

"I'm sorry, miss. I didn't mean to embarrass you."

"It's fine. But, did you sell the house to him or is he renting it and the owners updated it?"

"Oh no, he bought it. Paid cash and had it remodeled. It's beautiful inside. I'm sure he wouldn't mind showing you around. He seemed like a really nice guy."

I turned and strolled up Ada Lynn's porch and resumed my position in my rocker.

"He bought the house," I muttered.

"Told you he loved you," Ada Lynn said quietly.

Chewing on my thumbnail, I silently steamed over the situation. Finally, all the trucks and cars left except the shiny new Lexus.

I peeked at Ada Lynn. I wanted to see her expression for this next one. "Did I mention he's rich?"

"Hmmm, makes the pot a little sweeter so to speak." She chuckled at her own joke. "It would explain all the changes to the house. He probably bought the house dirt cheap, and now he's made money overnight. Sounds like a smart young man."

I huffed. "Seriously? That's all you have to say? Hendrix moved across the street to keep tabs on me, and you're talking about how intelligent he is?"

"You're assuming a lot. Granted, I do think he wants to be near you, but there has to be more to it. Guess you won't find out until you ask, huh?"

Sitting back in the rocker, I glared at the house. I hoped he could feel my stare burning holes through it.

"Gotta go," I said. "I'll see you later." I hurried to my house and slammed the door behind me.

"Sorry," I said to Dad as he shot me a dirty look from his recliner. He'd not shaven in days and wore the same grubby blue housecoat and dirty T-shirt for the fifth day in a row. If he didn't shower soon, I would have to hose him down. Between the body odor and the beer, it was enough to kill the plants Mom had around the house.

"New neighbor?" he asked as I passed him on the way to my bedroom.

"No idea."

For the next three hours, I stayed in my room, pacing. I fought the urge to text Mac to see if she knew Hendrix had moved here, but I didn't want to bother her with it. She was going to have enough of an adjustment living in Louisiana without me jumping down her throat about her brother. On the other hand, there's no way Mac could have kept that secret for weeks. Although she didn't talk a ton about him, she still brought him up on occasion.

It was almost nine in the evening, and I couldn't take it anymore. I pulled on my emerald green shirt, brushed my hair, and changed into the cutest jeans I owned. If he was going to be this close, then I wanted to look good enough to make him hurt. Grabbing my jacket, I tiptoed by my passed-out dad and slid out the front door.

10

My nerves jangled while I stood on my front porch, working up the courage to confront Hendrix and demand some answers. Apparently my feet had a mind of their own, and I suddenly found myself ringing his doorbell.

My breath hitched when the door opened almost immediately, and Hendrix stood before me, his hair wet. My eyes traveled from the white T-shirt that hugged his chest and biceps, down to the gray sweatpants riding low on his hips. My focus lingered, recalling what was underneath them. Realizing I was undressing him in my mind, my eyes shot back up to his face.

"What. The. Hell?" I asked, my hands on my hips.

"I figured it wouldn't take long before you showed up. Do you want to come in?" He grinned his panty dropping smile at me, and heat pulsed straight through me. This had to stop.

"No! I don't want to come in, Hendrix. Why are you here?" I snapped. "You have no right."

"I'm sure you're forming a lot of conclusions in that beautiful head of yours, but there's more to it."

"More than you not giving me the space I asked for?"

"You'll have your space. I promise. I won't bother you, and I won't be here all the time, either," he replied and leaned against the door frame.

"What exactly does that mean?" My anger was calming the more we talked. Regardless if I liked it or not, he had that effect on me.

"I'm leaving, Gem. When you didn't come back, I accepted a concert gig. But, I only agreed to tour in the southern states for now. I didn't want to be across the country in case you needed me."

I couldn't help it, I literally gawked at him. "You're finally getting your dream, and you want to start it in the South?" My pitch stepped up a notch at his ridiculous decision. "How about California or New York?"

"I made my choice." He folded his arms, emphasizing it was no longer up for discussion.

"Fine, does your sister know you're here?" I asked, tilting my chin up in defiance.

"No. I'm going to tell her, but please don't mention it to her yet. You know she'll come to you when she finds out."

"Why wouldn't you tell her? I mean, obviously you're really good at keeping secrets, but this is new. Thought you and Mac were super close?"

Hendrix rubbed his jaw. "She's going through some stuff right now. She needs a break from Asher, and there's been a lot going on at home lately. I know she'll be happy I'm closer, but I'm out of here in a few days, and she needs to focus on school. I don't want to be a distraction."

I chewed my lip, trying to ignore the urge to open the screen door and step inside his house. It would be so easy to wrap my legs around him and talk him into showing me his new bedroom. My head dropped so he couldn't see the flush creep across my cheeks. I took a deep breath and looked up at him again. Then I remembered *why* I couldn't throw my arms around him and kiss his lips. And in one fleeting moment, I was pissed again.

"How's Andrea?" I asked, venom lacing my words.

"I'm working on it, Gem."

"Don't call me that. I'm not your Gem anymore."

"Fine. Gemma, I'm working on proving my innocence and having the case thrown out. Andrea can't possibly have any evidence since I didn't rape her, but we have a private investigator on it to figure out why she's lying."

The struggle against believing him and walking inside his house, going back to the way we were, was real. I was about to fall to pieces right in front of him. Couldn't he see this was wrecking me? If I didn't leave now, I was going to say something mean that I couldn't take back. Lately, my emotions had blasted through me, taking charge of what flew out of my mouth. But this time, I didn't want to say something I might regret.

"Have a nice tour." I spun around on my heels and marched back across the street. I didn't bother to look back, but I heard Hendrix's door close behind me.

My first impulse was to text Mac, but I couldn't. Even though I had mixed feelings about Hendrix being close again, I didn't want to hurt her. There was a good possibility she'd be upset he hadn't talked to her about moving here first. Or had he just told me that so I wouldn't tear poor Mac to pieces?

The weight of the circumstances smothered me as I reached my house. Gasping for air, I sank into the porch swing and attempted to calm my anxiety. I hadn't sat there since Hendrix had slept on it. Grief stirred inside me, wishing yet again Mom was here for me to talk to. We'd never had the opportunity to discuss guy problems before, and I was struggling to find my footing without her. Frustration and anger twisted inside my stomach, realizing how different my life should have been. How I should have had normal teen conversations with Mom about dating, birth control, and prom. Not only had I lost those years, but I'd also lost her now, too.

Apparently, Mac staying for a few weeks helped me slip into a routine again. It wasn't much, but I got up, made coffee and breakfast, showered, opened the windows, started laundry, and kept the house picked up even after she was gone. Dad slept until late afternoon and then made a beeline for the alcohol. He'd jumped from beer to the hard stuff, and my concern blossomed into full-fledged worry.

It was after lunch by the time I went next door, and relief spread through me when I didn't see Hendrix's car parked in his driveway. Guess he really wasn't going to sit there and keep an eye on me like I'd initially thought.

"Hey," I said, hopping up Ada Lynn's porch steps. She was already in her rocker, drinking iced tea.

"Afternoon, how's your day so far?"

"Meh, ya know, samie same."

"I've noticed you have a good day now and again, and I'm hoping you're starting to heal a bit about your mom."

"I think it's like the ocean. Sometimes it's far off in the distance, and suddenly the tide comes in and knocks me off my feet unexpectedly."

Ada Lynn nodded, then said," I've got an errand to run. You should go with me."

"Sure, it will get me out of the house for a bit."

"Alright, let's go."

Ada Lynn stood, patted her pocket, and held onto the railing as she cautiously descended her porch steps. I frowned and followed.

She walked past my house, looked up and down the road, and crossed the street. My eyes narrowed. What in the world was she doing? I hurried to catch up with her while she opened Hendrix's mailbox and pulled out the mail.

"What in the world are you doing?" I asked.

She peered at me and opened his front gate. "You sure have gotten sassy since you've been in Washington."

I sighed, exasperated.

She kept going, up the stairs to his porch.

"He's not home." I tucked a strand of hair behind my ear and waited for her to turn around and go back to her house.

"I wouldn't have checked his mail if he'd been home." She smiled at me. "Hold this." She handed me the few letters while she fished around in her front pocket until she produced a key. I rolled my eyes as she slid the key in the lock and opened the front door.

"Don't just stand there, come on." She motioned for me to follow her.

"What are you doing?" I stepped foot into the house, the familiar smell of his cologne lingering in the air. My pulse raced into overdrive. It was strange being in his personal space again. This house was different than the one in Spokane. Simpler, but still elegant. A part of me wondered if he was about to pop out from around a corner and yell surprise. But I knew he wouldn't do that and scare the shit out of Ada Lynn.

Dark hardwood floors ran through the living and dining area. The white leather furniture and beige walls accented the room perfectly. A gas fireplace was framed by a beautiful oak mantle. My eyes widened as my attention drifted toward the pictures on the wall. One in particular caught my attention immediately. A large sketch hung over the mantle. Me. In the drawing, I looked over my shoulder, smiling with my floppy hat and sunglasses in my hand.

Tears welled in my eyes. Hendrix had been the reason I'd had the courage to remove my hat and glasses. No matter what I wore, he showed up every day and asked nothing of me. Whoever had drawn it did a fantastic job. I looked better in the picture than in real life.

I strolled into the dining room where a four-person table sat in the middle of the room. A matching hutch held delicate blue and white china, each strategically placed to showcase the intricate design. I opened the glass door and peered inside.

"It's beautiful," Ada Lynn said, approaching me from behind.

"Yeah, but he had great taste in Spokane, too."

I closed it and wandered into the kitchen. An unpredictable ball of emotions churned inside me. The decor similarities to his Spokane house were unsettling, bringing back the memories of our time together I'd worked hard to push away. Where Mac, Hendrix, and I ate and drank screwdrivers together. Where Hendrix and I made out like teenagers until he carried me to his room and made love to me. Where we discussed my pregnancy test.

Agony speared through my heart. He'd brought all of those special moments from the past with him. Even though I'd refused to allow him in my life, he had kept me with him every day.

I left Ada Lynn in the kitchen and continued to snoop. I located the bathroom, poked my head in, and then passed by it. There were three additional doors down the hall, and I opened the first one on the right. It was a nicely decorated guest bedroom with a queen bed and matching dresser. The black bedspread was nearly covered with white and black throw pillows. A worn, light brown, slightly dirty teddy bear rested against the headboard. Frowning, I approached it. My heart two-stepped with the realization the teddy bear might have been Kendra's.

Suddenly feeling as though I was invading his privacy, I slipped out and closed the door behind me. The next door I opened was his bedroom. A four-poster bed and dresser filled the new space. It was similar to what he had in Spokane. A small but nice master bath joined the bedroom. Water beaded the walls of the shower, the smell of his soap and cologne still in the air, filling me with longing. All I wanted was to crawl into his bed and pull the covers over my head, inhaling his scent. How was I ever going to get over him now that he was so close?

I hurried out of the bedroom, afraid I would break down and cry.

There was one room left, and I slowly peeked inside the door. This room was so dark I couldn't see inside of it. My hand searched the wall for a light switch. Finally locating it, I flipped it and gasped, gawking in awe. Hendrix had a recording studio put in the house. A new mixing console, mics, and a decent sized recording space occupied this end of the house. Everything he needed in order to work on his music was right here. I walked over to a chair and sat down, taking it all in.

"This is where the magic happens, huh?" Ada Lynn asked while she sat next to me in the other chair.

I nodded. "We recorded together," I said sadly, sliding some of the controls on the panel up and down.

"You did?"

"Yeah, we were goofing around one night, and all of a sudden, I started harmonizing with him. It shocked me, I wasn't even sure where it had come from. I hadn't sung since the night of the—"

"You don't have to say it." Ada Lynn reached over and squeezed my hand.

I swallowed hard. I wondered if I would ever sing with him again. My mind toyed with the idea that maybe he'd built this for us and not just a place to record while he was touring in the South.

"I need to go." I hurried out of the studio and into the kitchen, but the memories were everywhere. His smell, his touch, his lips. It was consuming me with every turn. I darted out the front door and straight back to Ada Lynn's. It used to be my safe place, but now all I saw was him when I sat on her porch, when I looked out my living room window, or when I went out to check the mail.

Tension knotted my neck and shoulders as I waited for her, the creak of the weathered rocking chair breaking the afternoon silence.

Ten minutes later, Ada Lynn returned.

"Come on in, we need to talk."

My brows knitted together. This was serious. Something was wrong.

Ada Lynn refilled her glass with iced tea and made one for me, too. She pulled out her chair and nodded for me to have a seat at the kitchen table with her.

"What's wrong?" My voice cracked with fear. It wasn't like I'd gotten a lot of good news lately.

"Now don't you worry, nothing is wrong, we just need to talk is all. No one else is dying, no one has been hurt, this is just some old lady business." She picked up a stack of papers from the table and thumbed through them while she peered at me over the top. After a moment, she laid the papers down, placing them strategically where I couldn't see them.

I slumped in my chair, relief flooding through me. If I lost her, I'm not sure I'd be able to come back from it.

"Hendrix left early this morning, and he stopped by before he did. He said he'd be in Texas performing multiple shows and asked if I could keep an eye on the house and check the mail for him. Since you were just over there with me, you already know I agreed."

"Okay? I'm confused why any of this has anything to do with me."

"He brought over legal papers for me, and we had a long heart to heart talk."

"Legal papers?" What the hell?

11

*E*ven though Ada Lynn had said nothing was wrong, this didn't seem right. I couldn't figure out why in the world Hendrix would be bringing legal papers to her.

"I just want to preface this conversation with this—what he said made sense, so I agreed to it."

"Ada Lynn, you're torturing me. What's going on?" Heat traveled up my neck and face, a sure sign of my anxiety.

"Gemma, calm down. It's okay." She patted my hand, and I grabbed hers, holding on as though she were life itself.

"You remember when you chatted with the handsome realtor?"

I nodded.

"Hendrix did buy the house, and we just saw what he did on the inside of it."

"Yeah," I motioned for her to get to the important stuff.

"He sold the house today."

I blanched. "What? That doesn't make any sense? I thought he was staying for a while."

My pulse double-timed with the thought of him leaving permanently. I pushed it to the side, unwilling to allow my thoughts to dwell on him right now. Ada Lynn was trying to tell me something important.

"He said he wanted me to have the house, Gemma. I paid him a dollar and signed the papers he brought over this morning." She patted the stack she'd just thumbed through.

"You own the house we were just inside of? Is he leaving?" I sputtered.

"I do own the house, but there were a few stipulations I had to agree to before we finalized the deal."

My brow arched in question. He had better not be messing with my Ada Lynn.

"First, that he be able to live there and come and go anytime he wanted to. Second..."

"Oh my God, this is like pulling teeth!" I groaned. "Just say it, please."

"Second, that I leave it to you in my will. Basically, Gemma, he bought that house for you. He knew you wouldn't accept it outright, so he bought it for me to give to you when I move on. Sooner if you needed somewhere to live. He said you could sell it and finish school or live there, whichever worked best at the time."

I sat there speechless as I attempted to wrap my mind around what she'd just told me.

"He's worried you won't have somewhere safe to go if anything happens to me. I don't think he's too impressed with your father. I suspect you told him how your dad handled the rape and your pregnancy?"

I nodded, embarrassed he'd shared with her. "But why the house across the street?"

"He said when he was looking for property here he wanted to be close to you, be there if you needed him. He hadn't intended on buying the abandoned house across the street, but he couldn't find anything else in the area. Guess the market is tight right now. When the realtor mentioned this one, he snatched up the opportunity. Not only is it paid for, but it now has equity, which also increased everyone else's home value on the street. Hendrix figured it was a way to help everyone in the community."

"It helped everyone?" I asked, softly. It was so like him to try and help people.

"Yeah, and you'll always have a home no matter what."

Tears brimmed in my eyes.

"He'll keep it maintained and the taxes paid. There's nothing for us to deal with except keep an eye on it. I'll check the mail and go in once a day, and make sure the house is secure, and no water pipes have broken or anything."

"That's nice of you to help."

Ada Lynn chuckled. "It's my house, actually, so I need to do my part."

I smiled, fidgeting with the hem of my shirt.

"You do realize all of this is for you, Gemma? He truly loves you. Even when he's not around, he wants to keep you safe."

I bit my lower lip, trying to process everything. The house wasn't mine yet, but it would be someday, and until then I was grateful Ada Lynn had a backup in case she needed it. If an emergency happened, he'd let her live there and find somewhere else to stay. It's just how he was. My heart ached for him, but once again Andrea's image and words popped into my mind, fucking me up all over again.

"One more thing." Ada Lynn got up from the table and made her way to one of the kitchen drawers. She returned with a plain white envelope, my name neatly written on the front of it.

"He asked me to give this to you and make sure you opened it."

I stared at it like it was a poisonous spider.

"Go on, I'm growing older by the second over here."

Slowly, I reached for it and tore the end of it open. I tilted it up, and two items fell into my hand. A key and a thumb drive.

"We agreed that if you chose to, you could use the studio and have some quiet study time while he was gone."

I frowned. "I won't use it."

"No matter, keep the key just in case."

I shoved it into my jeans pocket and stared at the thumb drive, twirling it between my fingers.

"He said to watch it. You can use my computer if you'd like, but I was to make sure you got it and didn't throw it away or whatever else you might do."

I huffed loudly. "I don't need a babysitter."

"Then do as he asks this time, and I won't have to. He said he'd know when you did. Don't ask me what that means." Ada Lynn shrugged. "You know where my computer is."

I rolled my eyes at her. "No, I'll take it home and use mine."

She nodded as I stood up, shoving the thumb drive in my pocket along with his key.

"I think I need a little time to think," I said.

"Understandable."

I walked over and hugged her.

"Love you, my blue-eyed girl," she said, patting me on the back.

"Love you, too." I placed a kiss on the top of her head.

I hurried next door, my mind churning through every possible scenario of what was on the thumb drive.

"Hey," Dad said, slurring his words. "Where the hell ya been? You're never home anymore." Sadness filled his eyes.

"I was just next door helping Ada Lynn with some stuff. Have you eaten? I can make you some food."

"That'd be good. You need to finish the laundry, too."

I wasn't sure if I should be hurt or pissed that he'd noticed our clothes and not bothered to toss them in the dryer, but maybe he was too drunk to stand without tossing his cookies everywhere.

"Thanks," I muttered and strolled into the utility room. After I started the dryer, I rifled through the fridge and heated up some leftover spaghetti. I toasted the garlic bread and took Dad his dinner.

"Where's the cheese?" he asked, eyeing the plate of food.

I swallowed my irritation and returned with the container of grated parmesan cheese.

"I have homework to do so I'll be in my room." I didn't wait for him to answer. Instead, I turned on my heel and stomped off. He'd not even offered a thank you.

I locked my bedroom door behind me in case he drunkenly barged into my room while I was watching whatever the hell Hendrix put on the drive.

Sitting down at my small desk, I inserted the drive and waited. A moment later a video popped up, Hendrix's face frozen in time. Frowning, I reached for my headphones and plugged them in, then pushed the play button.

"Hi, Gemma." He gave me his panty-dropping smile. I scanned the background and recognized the new studio from across the street. "I know you haven't read any of the letters I've sent, or you would have known about the house. I figured this was the best way to talk to you since you either have me blocked or you've turned your phone off."

Shit, he'd figured out I'd blocked him.

"I didn't want to leave without saying goodbye, but I need your help as well."

What in the world did he need me for?

He ran his hand through his long brown hair. A pang of misery assaulted me, and I reached out, touching the screen.

"I've not been able to write any music since you left, Gem. I'm not begging for you to come back so, please don't stop listening to the video. I was hoping that you might be open to the idea of collaborating with me on a new song."

"What?" I asked out loud.

"I'm visualizing your reaction right now, but please, just hear me out. You might not like me, or you think I've done some horrible things, and you're right. I have."

My heart jumped into my throat. Was he about to confess about Andrea?

"My biggest failure was not keeping you and Kendra safe." He paused, glancing down briefly. "I'm so sorry for letting down the two people I've loved more than life itself."

A tear snuck down my cheek.

"Losing your mom...losing someone in your family is devastating. After Kendra, I felt as though there was nothing left of me, much less anything to give to anyone else. Some days were so bad I felt like I was being buried alive, suffocating. The one thing that began to heal me was my music." He tucked a strand of hair behind his ear and continued to stare at the camera, his blue eyes filling with compassion and pain. "I have a dual purpose with the request. First, I need your creative input. We don't have to see each other. You can go to the studio when I'm gone, listen to the tracks I've laid down, add, tweak, sing, write it all out, and leave it for me. I'll see it when I'm back. I'll work on it some more, and then when I'm gone, you can return to the studio and listen to the changes. Second, it's the only thing I know of that might help you feel a little bit whole again. On the days you think you can't make it and there's only a shell of a person walking around on this earth, I want you to reach for a place that brings you some peace. I think your mom would want that for you, too, and it's the best way I can help you without overloading you at the same time."

I shook my head, overwhelmed by his suggestion. How could I even think about music right now? All it did was bring back the agony of losing him and her. Or was he right and it might be the thing that helped me stay sane? Plus, I didn't have to see him at all. My focus returned to the video as he paused and looked around the studio for a minute.

"I hope you'll do it. I miss us working on music together. You're so talented, and it's such a waste not to use it. Not only are you breathtaking when you're writing and singing, but your entire soul lights up. I miss being able to see you happy, touch you..." He cleared his throat. "One other thing, then I need to leave for Texas. I'm close to having the proof concerning Andrea. I'll update you when I have it all, but just know I love you. Every minute that passes by, and you're not next to me is ripping me to pieces. No one has ever owned my heart like you do, and I'll do everything in my power to get you back. I love you."

With that, the video stopped. Hot tears streamed down my

cheeks, the salt burning my slightly chapped lips. I wiped them away with the palm of my hands, but they just returned. I stared at the screen, taking in every beautiful thing about Hendrix. His piercing blue eyes, his hair that I missed running my fingers through, his soft lips. I couldn't help but wonder what Mom would think about all of this. Would she like him if she were here?

Exhaustion seeped over me, and I closed my laptop and removed my headphones. I snuggled up on my bed and allowed sleep to take over, relieving me of all the pain in my life.

12

*H*endrix filled my dreams. I woke flushed, my sheets soaked with sweat. The feeling of his hands and mouth still lingered on my body. I flung the covers off and sat on the edge of my bed, gathering my groggy thoughts. The video. His house.

Stifling a yawn, I stumbled into the kitchen and turned the coffee maker on. I needed to work on homework assignments before I met up with Mac at the library later, where I planned on plying her with a million questions about her new roomie and classes. If I allowed myself to admit it, I missed attending college in Spokane. I missed my life there—Mac, Hendrix, the library, our music, and even the stupid little dorm room. Refusing to dwell on those thoughts for long, I filled my cup and rubbed my eyes as I walked into the living room. My nose wrinkled at the stale smell of alcohol and body odor. Setting my mug on the coffee table, I jumped when Dad rolled over on the couch. He hadn't even made it to bed. I scanned the floor around him and spotted an empty whiskey bottle laying on its side. I quietly picked it up, then tiptoed across the room to crack open a window. Disgusted, I chewed on my bottom lip and stared at him while he snored. His rumpled clothes had food stains on the front, his blue and gray bathrobe threadbare and wrinkled. Every day, I took the time to clean up, cook, and make sure he ate. You'd think the least he could do was shower. Guilt wasn't far behind my thought when I realized I'd done the same after my pregnancy. The only difference was that I didn't bury myself in a bottle of booze.

After I discarded the whiskey bottle, I took a long, hot shower. Hopefully, the smell of my citrus soap and apple shampoo would help the stink in the living room dissipate quicker.

Refilling my coffee cup, I settled in at the desk in my bedroom, ready to get some homework done. My attention landed on the thumb drive, my pulse quickening thinking of what Hendrix had said. Although he'd smiled while he talked, his eyes were filled with sadness, and dark shadows had settled beneath them. I wondered if he really missed me that much or if he'd been up late struggling with writing. Twirling the thumb drive between my fingers, I opted to watch it one more time before I studied. This time I didn't bother with the headphones. Dad was out cold, and I wouldn't have the sound up very loud, anyway. I just wanted to see him again, hear his voice. I leaned back in my chair and watched Hendrix flicker to life on the screen, my heart pounding against my ribcage, threatening to burst. My reaction was always a surprise. I never knew if I'd want to run to him or run from him.

Emotions were a pain in the ass, so I shoved them aside when the logical part of my brain once again reminded me that not only was Andrea a problem, but there was nothing left inside me after Mom's death. All I'd do is hold Hendrix back from achieving his dreams. There was no way I was good for him. The best thing I could do was let him go.

Clicking the pause button, I opened my browser, blocked Hendrix out of view, and logged onto the college website. Although I'd considered taking two classes, I'd opted for one. Ada Lynn and Mac had insisted I do something to keep my mind engaged even during the days that were drowned out by the grief. But today, between the stench of my father and the rapid fire emotions concerning Hendrix and Andrea, I was grateful for the distraction.

Before I knew it, four-thirty had rolled around, and it was time for me to meet Mac. I gathered my books and backpack. Searching around for anything else I might need, I headed for the door. Dad was no longer on the couch, so I peered into the kitchen.

"Hey," I said to his back.

He leaned on the kitchen counter and grunted at me as he took a drink from his glass.

"I'm off to meet Mac at the library. You can call my cell if you need anything."

"That girl is strange, but she's okay," he muttered and refilled his tumbler.

"She's got some issues like we all do, but she's a good person." I wasn't sure why I explained this to him since I highly doubted he really cared.

"Take my Jeep. It's just sitting there, anyway."

"Are you sure?" I asked, frowning. He'd never offered me his car before, but I never went anywhere when I lived here, either.

"Keys are on the table." He nodded in the general direction.

"Thanks, Dad. I appreciate it." My heart softened toward him. Every once in a while, I'd see glimpses of the man I called Dad. I walked over, stood on my tiptoes, and kissed his cheek. "I'll be home late, so don't worry, alright?"

"Be safe." His focus cast down to the floor. I wondered if he was remembering the last time he saw Mom. My stomach lurched with the idea. At least he'd seen her that day.

"I will." The keys jingled in my hands while I hurried out of the house and to the car. I'd never driven it before, and I wanted to adjust the seat and get my Spotify ready. The car purred to life effortlessly. It was only three years old. My eyes fluttered closed with the memory of the day he'd bought it. He'd actually asked if I liked the white or the black Jeep Compass better. I'd surprised him when I said neither and suggested the dark green Cherokee. A few hours later he and Mom had pulled into the driveway with it. We'd never owned a brand-new car before, but Dad had just received a raise, and the Chevy Cavalier had been limping along on its last leg.

If I could still the noise inside myself, I could almost hear Mom's laugh as they walked into the house that evening, the keys in Dad's hand. He'd twirled her around the living room. It was one of the few happy memories I had of them together. Of any of us. They knew I wouldn't leave the house to celebrate the raise and car, so they'd brought home my favorite, a supreme pizza with cheese filled crust.

I forced the tears away and flipped through my Spotify list. The sound of Billy Raffoul filled the car as I backed out of the driveway and drove toward the downtown library.

With Mom's accident so fresh in my mind, I was hypersensitive to the cars around me. I kept the music low, my focus between the mirrors and the other vehicles on the road. Fortunately, the traffic wasn't heavy. Tension snaked down my neck and in between my shoulder blades. Maybe this wasn't a good idea. I hadn't driven anywhere since Mom's accident. Anytime Mac and I left, she drove her new car.

It felt like hours later when I pulled into a parking spot at the library and clicked the button on the key fob, locking the car behind me. Relief washed over me the moment I stepped into my sanctuary filled with books. Humming softly under my breath, I texted Mac to let her know I'd arrived and made a beeline for the fiction section. Since we planned to meet here a few times a week, maybe it would help my mood to check out a few books.

My fingers ran over the spines as I eyed the titles on the large shelves and quickly pulled down *Twilight* by Stephenie Meyer. Mom and I had both loved this book. We'd babbled nonstop about the series while we read it together. It was one of the first books I'd picked up after the rape and the year from hell.

"Yo, bestie!" Mac whisper yelled at me.

"Hi!" The way we were acting, people probably thought we hadn't seen each other in years. It'd only been a week.

We hugged and then settled in quickly at a table, facing each other. Her smile lit up her features. She looked happy. Her big brown eyes twinkled with mischief, and her usual braids had been replaced with soft, shoulder-length waves.

"Tell me everything," I whispered and patted the table.

"Gem-ma. You're so fired for not telling me how fucking hot the Southern dudes are. Like what the hell?"

Someone from another table shushed her, and she sank into her seat, covering her mouth with her hand and giggling.

"You're in a good mood over hot guys?" I asked, shaking my head. This was new. The months we'd shared a dorm together, she rarely mentioned any guy she thought was good looking.

"Like muscular, and totally swoon-worthy. They have manners, too."

"Well, I would hope so, but didn't Asher have manners?" I wrinkled my nose the moment the words passed my lips. "Shit, sorry. I know you're trying to move on."

"It's okay." Her attention dropped to her feet and back up again. "On the bright side, the guys so far don't even care that I babble."

"That's really awesome, Mac." I knew she was self-conscious about her ADHD. People in the past had dismissed and criticized her as annoying and dumb. Mac could definitely be annoying, and we had some run-ins in the beginning. But the worst was when she'd shoveled pie into her mouth at Ada Lynn's and spilled too much information. We'd been fine since then.

"I have a date tomorrow night," she said, leaning toward me.

"You do?" I clapped my hands together quietly for her. As hard as I tried, I felt nothing inside, though. Grief was weird. I was okay one minute, and the next my feelings would simply fade to black, leaving only an inky residue in a hollowed-out shell.

Mac didn't miss it.

"Are you not happy for me?" she asked, her lower lip jutting out.

"Of course, I am." I grabbed her hand and gave it a squeeze. "Tell me about him. His name would be helpful."

"Are you sure? I haven't even asked about you or Ada Lynn."

I brushed her off. "She's good, but it's all the same. Nothing new to report here." Apparently, Hendrix hadn't talked to her yet.

"Jeremiah. Isn't that like the best name ever?"

Holy shit. She was majorly crushing on this guy. I would need to meet him soon. Hell, Hendrix would want to meet him, too. I wrapped a lock of my red hair around my finger while I realized I didn't have that type of relationship with him anymore. I couldn't just text him or meet him in the library to talk about Mac. Or anything for that matter.

"I met him at the student center. He and his best friend, Gregg, were playing pool. He's about six one, so he dwarfs me, and he's a junior. Only one and a half more years before he's off being a brainiac somewhere. He's majoring in aeronautical engineering. Like, what the hell do you even do with that? The dude is seriously smart, but his brain works as fast as mine does!" Her eyes widened with the delivery of the information.

"He has ADHD?"

"No, ADD, but he found his thing. So he not only gets me, but he's told me once I find whatever my thing is, I'll be able to focus on it."

I frowned, I wasn't following.

"So, let me see if I can explain it. Oh, he said it's video games for his brother. He can focus for hours and hours. It's like the stimulation is so intense it holds his attention."

"And aeronautical engineering is the same for him?"

Mac nodded. "Right? It's amazing. For the first time, I have some hope I might find something I can focus on. Something special I can really love doing and my brain won't bounce around like a fucking ping-pong ball. Totally unlike right now, because I'm pretty sure I was talking about Jeremiah, then ADHD, then ping-pong," she said and snickered.

"Do you have any idea what it might be?"

"No damned clue, but it's okay. I think Jeremiah might be the perfect distraction for now." She wiggled her eyebrows at me. Suddenly, a sharp yearning for Hendrix tugged at me.

"Be careful. Take your time and get to know him. And bring him to the library next time if the date goes well. I would love to meet him."

"You would?" she asked, her leg bouncing.

I placed my hand on her knee.

"Of course, I would."

"If you're sure. I know you and Hendrix had a bit of a run in the other day—" She slapped her hand over her mouth.

She knew.

"Don't worry about it, Mac. He made me promise I wouldn't say anything until he had a chance to talk to you. At least you know he's in Louisiana when he's not on tour."

"Yeah, but he said you weren't happy about it. Like. At. All."

"It's nothing you need to concern yourself with, nor do I want to talk about it. Tell me more about Jeremiah. Is he from here?"

And just like that, I was able to redirect her away from her brother. Honestly, I was relieved Hendrix had told her. If something happened with him or Andrea's case, I would need someone to talk to. Mac and Ada Lynn were my only friends.

"He's an army brat, and they landed here after his father retired. They've lived everywhere, including Europe! Do you know how exciting that is? I want to go to Europe so bad."

As any best friend would, I kept her focused on Jeremiah and plied her with questions. All I wanted was for her to be happy and for a guy to love Mac for who she was. We all had our shortcomings. Mine was being emotionally unavailable, hers was talking nonstop and blurting shit out. But when it came to her heart, I wouldn't trade her for anything in a million years.

"How's your new roomie?"

She took a deep breath. "Rarely there and when she is, she comes in and passes the hell out. The girl goes to every party on and off campus. I have no idea how she will actually graduate, but as long as Rachel leaves me alone, it's not my problem. Right?"

I grinned. "So no one will take my place anytime soon?"

"Girl, please. No one can ever take your bestie status." She wrapped her arms around me and gave me a big hug.

"I miss you," I said, softly. "It's pretty quiet at home."

"How are things with your dad?"

I shrugged. "He's graduated to the hard stuff." My lips pursed with the information. "I think I lost both parents when Mom died in the accident."

"Oh, Gemma. I'm such a bad friend. I should have just shown up on your doorstep again this week."

I laughed and blinked away the tears that were beginning to form. "It's your first full week here, Mac. I know where you are, and Dad let me drive his Jeep tonight. You and I are super close now, and I can visit you on campus, too."

"Oh, yeah!" She bounced in her chair with the thought.

"I want you to get settled in. It's important, okay?" I arched my brow at her. She needed to know it mattered to me.

She stopped bouncing and nodded. "All right. I think I'm going to like it here okay, but it's not the same without you."

"I get it. I feel the same way."

We talked for another hour. Well, Mac did most of the talking, but that worked for me. I needed the distraction to take my mind off Mom, Dad, and Hendrix. Mac agreed to text when she was ready to meet again, and then we walked to our cars together. With Jeremiah taking up the majority of the conversation, she hadn't brought up Hendrix again. I already owed Jeremiah a favor for that alone.

Traffic was minimal on my way home, and I parked the Jeep in the driveway a little after ten. Gathering my books and phone, I locked the car and hurried inside.

"Where in the hell have you been?" Dad roared the moment the door clicked closed behind me.

I shrieked, my hand flying to my mouth. He stood in the entryway of the kitchen, a half-empty bottle in his hand, his eyes flashing with anger.

"I met Mac at the library, remember?" I leaned against the front door for support, my body shaking uncontrollably. Had he drank so much he didn't remember?

"Liar!" His voice thundered through our small house.

"Dad, you said I could drive your Jeep." I attempted to keep calm and levelheaded.

"I'd never tell you something like that. Where are my goddamned keys?" His words were slurred, and he looked like he might fall over any second.

I held them up. "I'll put them on the table." I shuffled slowly toward the table and put them down. As long as I stayed calm, maybe it would diffuse the situation. I'd never seen him so angry before.

"I should have called the cops on you. You're nothing but a little thieving bitch. Not to mention a slut." Venom dripped from his words, and my stomach clenched with fear.

"What?" I gasped. He knew I'd struggled after the rape, thinking that it was partly my fault...I shouldn't have walked home after dark, or I should have been with a friend. But he had never laid blame or said anything hurtful like this.

"So now my daughter is having online sex? Your mother would roll over in her grave." He stopped long enough to take another drink.

"What are you talking about, Daddy?" I asked, bile rising in my throat. I hadn't called him Daddy since I was little, but I hoped it might break through the alcohol-induced brain fog he was in.

"The video you left up on your computer." He ran the back of his hand across his forehead, slurring his words.

Oh, my God. I'd not removed Hendrix's thumb drive. He'd watched it? Even if he had, why in the world would he think I was having sex online?

"Dad, it's Mac's brother. I'm not having sex with anyone." My voice remained calm, the exact opposite of how I felt. I mentally kicked myself for leaving the drive in my laptop, but the college website had also been open. Which meant in order for him to see Hendrix's image on my screen, Dad must have snooped and seen it not long after I'd left. Otherwise, my computer went to sleep after an hour.

"Mac?" He ran his hand over his hair, swaying as he did. He reached for the counter to stabilize himself.

"You like her, remember? She stayed with us for a few weeks? She's going to college now, just a few minutes away from here. I was with her tonight. She said to tell you hi."

"Her brother?" His face softened while he struggled to fit all the pieces together.

"Yeah, that's all it is."

He staggered toward the recliner, and I remained smashed against the front door. I was afraid to move in case he lunged at me, and I needed to make a fast exit. Ada Lynn would most likely be asleep by now. She'd always said I could come over if I needed her, though. Is this what she'd been referring to those times she'd urged me to go back to Spokane?

"There better not be a boy touching you," he spat, the fire in his eyes reigniting momentarily.

My body shuddered while he plunked down in his recliner and picked up the remote control. He flipped through channels as he squinted at the TV.

"Dad?" I asked cautiously, testing the waters. He seemed to have calmed down some, or at least forgotten why he was angry. I wasn't picky, either would work.

"Huh?" he grunted, scratching his bulging stomach.

"Are you hungry? I can make you something."

"Sure."

And with that, I quietly made my way into the kitchen. I made him some peanut butter toast as quickly as I could and set it on the coffee table next to him. He didn't even acknowledge my existence, and I wasn't going to complain.

The moment I was in the safety of my bedroom, my knees buckled, and I sank to the floor. Burying my face in my arm, I shuddered, then the tears broke free. Suddenly, I jumped off the floor and moved my computer mouse. The screen came to life, Hendrix's expression taking up every inch of it. Anger pulsed through me, and I pulled the thumb drive out of my laptop, throwing it across the room.

"I hate you!" I screamed. Crawling onto my bed, I scrambled under the covers, expecting Dad to pound on my door after my outburst, but he never did. In the back of my mind, I knew the lock on the door wouldn't hold for long. But if it ever came to it, it might give me enough time to sneak out my bedroom window.

13

The deep rumble of thunder woke me the next morning. I massaged my temples, the residual of my crying jag looming over me like a hangover.

I loved storms. Tugging aside my curtains, I peered outside at the now brown and haggard garden Mom had worked so hard to take care of.

Fat raindrops began to splatter against my window as I cracked it open, inhaling the fresh smell of the rain and wondering if I would be around to clean up the garden in the spring or if the weeds would just take it over. I leaned my forehead against the cool glass, my mood slipping further into the darkness. The last day I'd had with mom was outside, digging in the dirt and chatting about nothing of any importance. I would never have that time with her again.

Concern and fear broke through my melancholy, goosebumps rising along my arms as I recalled Dad's outburst last night. He had never acted like that before, but he'd also never drank this much. At least that I was aware of. Maybe he had, and I was too young to notice or too immersed in my depression.

I turned away and shoved the loneliness and grief down. Peeking out of my bedroom door, I looked for Dad, but he was nowhere in sight. I walked into the hallway, my socked feet silent on the wood floor as I rounded the corner into the kitchen and stopped short at the stench that assaulted my nose. I'm not sure what Dad had been doing last night, but the room was a mess. Shaking my head in disgust, I started the coffee, opened a couple of windows, and quietly began to clean every surface possible. I discovered the source of the awful smell when I glanced at the trash can in the corner. Apparently, Dad had decided to clean out the freezer and throw away all the left-over casseroles from Mom's funeral. Unfortunately, his aim was hit and miss. Now thawed potatoes, pasta, chicken, and gravy lay in a wet pile all over the floor. Mom would be pissed if she saw how he'd left her favorite room in the house. But then again, she'd be pissed about the drinking and his behavior last night. Deep down, I hoped it was a onetime deal with his temper, but I wasn't stupid. Each day that passed, I watched the drinking progress. If he kept going at this rate, he wouldn't be standing up most of his day.

I wiped down the counters one last time and dried my hands as the coffee finished brewing, then filled my cup and walked outside to sit on the porch swing. The rain had started falling faster, and I inhaled deeply. The sound of the drops against the roof was almost as nice as listening to music. I snuck a peek at Hendrix's house, my pulse stepping into overdrive. Longing and anger intertwined themselves inside me. Logically, I knew it wasn't his fault Dad went on a rage after seeing the video, but it gave me something to further justify pushing Hendrix away. At the same time, if Hendrix had heard my dad yelling at me, he'd have laid him out. One punch would have sent him to la-la land.

No one could know, though. It was better Hendrix not find out about it. And there was no way in hell I would tell Ada Lynn. She was under enough stress with Mom's death and worrying about me. At least for now, I could deal with Dad.

A flash of lightning split open the dark gray sky. Maybe the storm would last all day, and I could snuggle up with a good book. Then it dawned on me, I hadn't checked one out while at the library.

Struggling to find a comfortable position on the swing, I looked across the street again toward Hendrix's house. I had a key, and I was restless. Maybe hearing his ideas for the new song wouldn't be a bad thing. A roll of thunder smacked me back into reality. Frustrated with myself for even considering it as an option, I stood to go inside. My phone buzzed, and I pulled it out of my pocket, eyeing the message.

Library tonight? You can meet Jeremiah.

I chewed mindlessly on my fingernail and eyed Dad's Jeep. There's no way I'd put myself through that again. I'd need to borrow Ada Lynn's car to meet Mac. Maybe meeting new people was what I needed. Mac would be with us. Although my life had slipped into a dull routine, I didn't want to become my Dad and never leave the house or bathe.

My fingers tapped against my phone screen.

I would love to meet him. What time?

Heart emojis lit up my screen. Honestly, I wasn't sure if I even cared about meeting Jeremiah, but it was an opportunity for me to be there for my best friend and make sure she wasn't getting into too much trouble without her brother around. Shit. When would I stop thinking about him every second? I gave a nasty look at his front door as if it cared. If he hadn't bought the stupid house, everything would be different. I barked out a laugh. Sometimes the lies I told myself were flat out stupid.

6:30?

Sounds good. See ya then.

Thank God Mac was close, so I had something to do other than drown in my emotions. By the looks of it, if it kept raining this hard, I would be drowning in it, too.

14

I waded through the puddles on the sidewalk and made my way to the front door of the library. Thoughts of Hendrix and I running through the rain together popped up, and I swatted them away.

I shuddered as I entered the lobby of the library and attempted to wipe some of the water off my face with the sleeve of my shirt. The rain hadn't lessened any, and I'd left a little early so I could take my time driving.

I'd just sent Mac a quick text when her characteristic giggle rippled through the otherwise quiet space. My phone buzzed with a response and her location.

Rounding the aisle to the back of the library, I spotted the back of Mac's noggin and who I assumed was Jeremiah, sitting across from her. From where I stood, he looked gorgeous, which didn't surprise me. Mac was beautiful, she just had no idea. His messy light brown hair flopped into large, dark brown eyes. His smile lit up his entire face while he reached for her hand. When she giggled again, I realized Mac was in trouble and falling fast. Which meant I had to step into stern best friend mode and scope him out. When I was only a few feet away, the chair next to Jeremiah moved, and another guy settled into the seat.

I scowled. Mac hadn't said anything about anyone else. I stopped and ducked behind a large bookcase, my heart beating wildly against my rib cage. It was one thing for me to meet Mac's boyfriend, but to have another guy's attention on me freaked me out.

I willed my wobbly legs to behave. I was jumping to conclusions and needed to take a deep breath. Maybe he had just run into them when they had arrived. Slowly, I peeked around the corner again. Whatever was going on, I would never figure it out from behind the bookshelf.

I sucked in a fast breath, smiled, and walked toward the table. Apparently, hottie Jeremiah had a hottie friend. Swearing under my breath, I wiped my sweaty palm against my pants. Thank God I'd picked out a cute emerald green shirt and acid wash boyfriend jeans.

"Hey," I said, approaching Mac and the guys.

"Bestie!" She jumped out of her chair, pulling me in for a big hug.

My heart melted a little. Meeting Jeremiah was super important to her. If nothing else, I was glad I came to show her how much I loved her.

"Let me introduce you." She beamed at me. I'd never seen her so happy.

"This is Jeremiah and Alexander. Guys, this is my bestie, Gemma."

Heat traveled up my neck and cheeks while Jeremiah and Alexander stood, extending their hands to me. I shook them and grinned like an idiot. What in the world was wrong with me?

We settled in at the table, and I shoved my backpack beneath it, accidentally bumping Alexander's knee with my hand. Mortified, I pulled away and placed them on top of the table. "Sorry," I mumbled, my cheeks warming to an uncomfortable level.

"No worries," he said, grinning. He ran a hand over his short, light brown hair. His eyes were a pale blue, his gaze holding mine. He was intensely hot, but what was more shocking was the fact that I'd noticed and cared.

Forcing my focus toward Mac, I gave her my best smile.

"I didn't realize someone else would be joining us," I said, arching my eyebrow at her.

"Oh, ma gosh. So, Alexander had texted Jeremiah right before we were leaving. Then I'm like dude, bring your friend so he can meet my friend and we can all be friends together."

Mental images of my fingers wrapped around Mac's neck flashed through my mind. I was sure her intentions were good, but Alexander probably thought it was a setup.

"You can never have too many friends, right?" I asked, looking back and forth between Alexander and Jeremiah. An awkward silence hung in the air as the guys stared at me. My lack of experience in social situations was showing its ass.

"Mac mentioned you're majoring in aeronautical engineering," I said, hoping to shift the focus to what the meet up was really about. Mac and I would definitely be discussing this afterward.

"Yeah, what about you? What are you getting a degree in?"

I wasn't prepared for questions. Any. I swallowed hard, fumbling for something intelligent to say.

"She's undecided," Mac chimed in. "Personally, I think she should major in music. Girl's got a voice that is amazeballs."

Shit. Although Mac was trying to help me not feel so intimidated and insecure in a new social situation, her words had the opposite effect.

"Really, you sing?" Alexander said, leaning forward in his chair. "Do you play or compose as well?" His questions came at me like rapid fire, and I wasn't sure how to handle them.

"Um, well, I sort of sing—" Hendrix's image flashed into my mind along with our first real conversation in the library when he'd shrugged off the fact he could sing well. I swallowed hard, forcing the memories to the side.

"Sort of my ass," Mac said, giggling.

"Yeah, I do sing, and I've collaborated on a few songs with a band. Not a big deal, but ya know, being in the studio was really awesome."

I discreetly nudged Mac with my elbow, signaling for her to dial it down a bit.

"Maybe I'll get a chance to hear you sometime," Alexander said, flashing a smile that reached his eyes. Butterflies fluttered in my stomach.

I nodded, attempting to not full on swoon like a giddy teen. Where had Mac found these guys?

"How did you two meet?" I asked Alexander, my focus bouncing between him and Jeremiah.

"School," Alexander replied. "I kicked his ass at pool the first day of freshman year, and we've hung out ever since."

"We're actually roommates, too," Jeremiah said.

Sadness pulled at me. I missed my college days in Spokane.

"Us too!" Mac wrapped a lock of brown hair around her finger while she talked. "I scared the shit out of poor Gemma the first day. She had no idea what to do with my bundle of energy, but soon, I won her over," she said, rather proudly.

I laughed softly. "It was good, though. We were great roomies."

"That was in Spokane?" Jeremiah asked. Mac must have already told him this, and he was just continuing the conversation.

"As in Washington?" Alexander asked, brushing his hair off his forehead.

"Yup, Gemma is from Louisiana, but we met in Washington."

"So why are you both here?"

I shot Mac a look, and for once she understood it. I needed to drive this part of the conversation.

"I had to come back home," I said softly. "My mother was killed in a car accident a few months ago, and I'm taking care of my dad for now." A lead ball dropped into the pit of my stomach, the weight of my words almost doubling me over with grief. But I couldn't fall apart. Not here. Not in front of complete strangers.

"Shit." Alexander leaned back in his chair. "I'm so sorry. I had no idea." Sadness flickered through his gaze.

"Me either, Gemma. I'm really sorry," Jeremiah said, reaching for Mac's hand.

"It's why I'm here," Mac added. "When I realized Gemma wasn't coming back to Washington right away, I came here for a while. Just to help and be there when she needed me. It's what besties do, right?" She looked at me, searching for some kind of reaction. She probably wondered if I was mad the subject came up, but I wasn't. It just happened.

I reached over and squeezed her other hand. "Right."

The small talk continued over the next hour, and as hard as I tried to keep it going, my temporary infatuation with Alexander had left the moment I talked about Mom.

"I should go," I said, pushing my chair back. I reached under the table and grabbed my backpack. This time I didn't accidentally grab anyone's leg.

The guys stood, and without realizing it, my focus traveled up and down Alexander. His well-built frame straightened up to what I guessed was six foot two. His muscled arms were huge, and I briefly wondered if he had worked on a farm growing up. For some reason, he gave the impression he knew what hard physical labor was all about.

When Mac insisted everyone walk me to the car, I was relieved. It hadn't even crossed my mind it would be dark out.

The rain had finally stopped. Once we were outside, Alexander walked next to me while Mac and Jeremiah hung back a bit.

"I enjoyed meeting you tonight," he said, shoving his hands in his front jean pockets.

"You too," I said, trying to smile, but my heart wasn't in it.

"Will you be in Louisiana for a while or will you go back to Washington soon?"

"I have no idea," I said, glancing up at him. "Plans for the future are a bit of a blur right now."

Alexander's gaze softened, and then he stopped walking. I turned toward him.

"Well, if you want to hang out sometime that would be cool." He rubbed his jawline, his finger tapping nervously against his chin.

My heart sank. Although he was uber hot, I wasn't ready.

"I'll keep it in mind," I said, nervously tucking a strand of hair behind my ear.

"Fair enough." He began to walk again, and I led us toward Ada Lynn's car. Mac and Jeremiah were behind us, Mac talking a mile a minute.

"She's a good friend." He nodded toward Mac.

"The best. Not many people would uproot everything to hang out with their best friend like she has." She and her brother both, I realized sadly.

We reached the car, and I pulled the key fob from my jeans pocket.

"Well, I hope to see you around soon. We can always hang and shoot pool, nothing big, just friends. Maybe it would help some. Hell, I don't know. Does anything really help when you've lost someone close to you?" His eyes filled with compassion.

I hesitated. "I'm pretty new at this grief stuff, but my answer is no. At least not yet."

He nodded as Mac and Jeremiah caught up with us, holding hands.

"Can you give me a few minutes with Gemma?" Mac asked, directing her question to Jeremiah.

"You bet." He leaned down and gave her a quick kiss on the mouth.

"Later," Alexander said, giving me a small wave.

We watched them walk away, then Mac turned toward me. "Let's get in the car so we can talk."

I nodded and unlocked the doors. After we settled in, Mac pulled her legs underneath her and faced me.

"I'm sorry about springing Alexander on you, Gemma."

"It turned out alright. I was just caught off guard," I said, turning the key and cranking the engine. I flipped the heat on, ready for it to warm the inside of the car.

"I didn't really think when I invited him to come along. Are you mad at me?" Mac's face filled with anxiety as she waited for me to reply.

"I was at first. Not because you invited him, but because you didn't tell me. Plus, did he think it was a setup?"

"No, I didn't present it like that at all. Just friends hanging out. I thought it might be good for you to join us sometimes, get you out of the house. You're not attending classes on campus, and I don't want you to fall back into old habits where you never leave your room. I really thought it would help. Besides, you seem like you're really not going to give Hendrix a chance at getting you back, so maybe a date wouldn't hurt. Maybe a one-night stand, ya know, scratch the itch so to speak." Her eyebrows wiggled at me.

"Mac!" I said, swatting her shoulder. "You know I don't do one nighters."

She rolled her eyes at me. "You've now been properly broken in, so we'll see how long you can go without some relief."

"Not happening," I said, shutting her idea down.

I shook my head and stared out the window. The guys were waiting beneath a large oak tree. At least they wouldn't let Mac walk to her car alone. Maybe they were decent people and not just after a piece of ass.

"I wasn't really prepared to meet Jeremiah either, so when the questions started. I—I wasn't sure what to do."

"I know it was hard for you, but I love you even more for it."

"What do you mean?"

"I know what you've gone through, I know it's hard on you in new social situations, especially with the dudes. You came out tonight when you didn't want to and met Jeremiah for me. It means a lot. I just wanted you to know I recognized it."

"You're my bestie. What else would I do?"

Mac grinned and then sighed. "As much as I want you to come back with us, I need to go. If you change your mind and want to hang out with everyone let me know."

"He asked me out," I blurted.

"Wha, what?" Mac bounced in her seat, a mischievous grin spreading across her face. "And did you say yes?"

"No. I said no. Basically. Sort of."

Mac stopped bouncing, her expression filling with disappointment. "Maybe it would be good for you? Help you move on from —stuff."

Unable to stop it, I smiled. "Nice save." For once, she thought about what she was going to blurt out. "I wouldn't go anywhere without you, Mac. Which means that if I change my mind, you'll be the first to know."

"Deal." She leaned over and hugged me. "Text me later."

"Stay out of trouble and don't let Jeremiah scratch your itch too soon." My eyebrow raised at her.

She giggled as she got out of the car and made a mad dash across the library lawn back to the guys.

My heart ached, yet at the same time I was happy for Mac. I had no idea what was going to happen with Hendrix and me, but I couldn't live with my dad much longer. It was time to figure out what I wanted to do with my life.

15

I slipped inside the house quietly, relieved to see Dad asleep on the couch softly snoring, which meant he was passed out for the night. It shouldn't be this way. I shouldn't have to watch him stagger around drunk all the time and worry if his cancer might return. Not only was that in the back of my mind, but his mood swings had gotten worse, and I constantly tiptoed around him. My chest tightened. I missed my dad. He'd continued to slip further and further away, and I wondered if I would ever get him back.

A high-pitched giggle broke through the quiet. I frowned and moved toward the living room window, pulling the curtain to the side just enough for me to see where the sound had come from.

My heart skidded to a stop. Hendrix was on his porch with a girl. Not just any girl, but a beautiful one. Her perfectly straight blonde hair cascaded over her shoulders, and she definitely had curves in all the right places. Another giggle erupted from her while she hung all over him, and he opened the front door. His laugh echoed through the night, and her arm snaked around his waist. White hot anger shot through me as I watched him guide her inside his house.

Tears welled in my eyes, and I let the curtain drop back into place.

I refused to cry. I'd told Hendrix I didn't know when or if I might be ready to resume our relationship.

My hands fisted at my sides as I made my way to my bedroom, slammed the door behind me, and flopped into my bed. Hendrix had moved on. It shouldn't have come as a surprise, seeing how I'd shoved him away and refused to hear him out about Andrea. My actions may as well have screamed, I think you're a rapist! God, what was wrong with me? Even he knew I was too broken to wait for.

I sat up slowly, head pounding, and eyes swollen from my cry fest last night. I eased my legs over the side of the bed and paused. Standing up too fast seemed like a bad idea. The sun barged in through a gap in my curtains and made a beeline for my sensitive eyes. Obnoxious asshole. I wanted nothing to do with all of its *happy* this morning.

What I needed was coffee, a long, hot shower, and a heart-to-heart chat with Ada Lynn. She would help me make sense of this mess. The events of last night looped through my mind on replay. Thank God Dad hadn't been awake to yell at me for who knows what when I got home. My attraction to Alexander had completely caught me off guard, stirring up confusion and a heavy dose of guilt. Until anger took over when Hendrix ushered some flirty giggle box into his house right before my eyes. How had life turned from amazing to shit? One minute I was in Spokane, packing to move in with my boyfriend, and the next I was in Louisiana, watching him bring another girl home.

Coffee cup in hand, I made my way over to Ada Lynn's. My attention automatically drifted across the street, but Hendrix's car was gone. A part of me was relieved he wasn't home. Although I'd pushed him away, seeing him with someone else speared right through me. I just didn't understand why he would display another girl in front of me like that. Had touring changed him so much he went for busty, shallow girls now?

Maybe Mac was right and I needed to hang out with her and the guys. Alexander seemed like a good person, but in no way was I ready to date. I would have to be crystal clear with Mac about it, too. In fact, I still struggled to hang out with any guys other than Hendrix. Mac would be with me, though, so I would be safe. There was also a good probability that Mac would blab the details to Hendrix, too. Maybe then he would have an inkling of how I felt last night, but somehow I doubted it. He'd apparently done what I couldn't. Moved on.

If Mac agreed to stick next to me, I would hang out with them and see how it went. My heart jumped into my throat with the mere idea of hanging around guys again. It seemed my past snuck up on me when I least expected, and I didn't want to embarrass Mac if I needed to leave. But I was willing to try. I would text her later and see what she thought.

My knuckles rapped against Ada Lynn's door, and I waited for her to answer. Sometimes it took her a while, but it seemed longer than usual. I knocked again, an uneasy feeling gnawing at me. I tried the handle, but it was locked. Pulling my key out of my pocket, I inserted it and turned the knob.

"Ada Lynn," I called and stepped inside. It was unusually quiet. Typically, the TV was on, and the aroma of coffee was in the air, but not this morning.

Receiving no answer, I hurried into the kitchen. She wasn't there. Shit, this wasn't right.

"Ada Lynn, it's Gemma." Anxiety coursed through me when there was still no answer. I felt like I was invading her privacy, but I shoved the nagging feeling aside and bolted down the hall.

"Ada Lynn!" I flung the bathroom door open and checked the shower. Nothing. "Ada Lynn!" I screamed, my stomach clenching with fear as I rushed to open the next door. Her guest bedroom remained untouched, and my fear stepped up another notch. Breathless, I'd reached her bedroom. I cautiously opened the door, terrified of what I might find.

Time stood still as my attention landed on Ada Lynn. Unmoving. Eyes closed. On the floor.

"No! No! No!" I hurried over and kneeled next to her. "Don't you leave me. Don't you dare," I whispered while I felt her neck for a pulse, trembling with relief when I found it. "Hang in there Ada Lynn, hang on." Pulling my cell out of my back pocket, I dialed 911 and gave them her address.

Anxiety hummed beneath my skin, and I sat next to her, holding her hand. I brushed the hair off her forehead and focused on the soft rise and fall of her chest. As long as she was breathing, I had hope. The ambulance was taking forever, but I didn't know what else to do. All I knew was that I couldn't lose her, too. Mom had just left us a few months ago, and my heart couldn't take losing Ada Lynn. Not now. Not ever.

The front door banged open, and the EMT's hurried into the house.

"Back here!" I screamed.

The nightmarish reality sank in while I watched the EMTs in action and moved out of their way. I willed the tears back as they gently picked her up and placed her on the gurney.

"Are you the granddaughter?"

I nodded. If they knew the truth, I wouldn't be allowed to ride in the ambulance with her.

"You can ride with us," a male EMT said.

"Is she going to be okay?" I asked, near hysteria.

"We're taking her vitals now. Hang in there." He patted my shoulder as they hauled Ada Lynn out of the house and into the ambulance. I jumped up behind them, and then the EMT closed the door. The sirens began to wail, and my body lurched to the side with a quick turn out of her driveway.

I held her hand and willed her to be okay.

"I know you."

"What?" I asked, staring at the guy who had just spoken to me. I frowned and wiped my stuffy nose with the back of my shirt sleeve.

"I delivered a car to your friend, Mackenzie," he said.

"Josh the Kia driver?"

"Yeah, but it's only part-time."

I nodded, grateful I sort of knew someone else and wasn't entirely alone. "Ada Lynn helped raise me, she's the closest thing I have to a parent now." I choked down a sob. "My mom just died."

"I'm sorry. The loss of a parent is so difficult." He paused and glanced at Ada Lynn. "Does she have anyone else? A daughter?"

"Nope, just me." My hand trembled as Josh continued with the conversation. It took me a minute to realize he was distracting me from the real issue, Ada Lynn.

An eternity later, we arrived at the hospital.

16

I paced the busy waiting room, a strange feeling of numbness and detachment washing over me. It was as if I were watching myself in a dream, knowing I would wake up soon and Ada Lynn would be at home, safe and sound. Unfortunately, this wasn't a dream. And I needed my best friend to help get me through this. Pulling my phone out of my back pocket, I texted Mac.

Sup bestie? Mac replied.

I quickly filled Mac in, my hands shaking while I typed.

Holy Fuck! I'm on my way.

Mac was the only person I would have left if Ada Lynn didn't make it. Dad was no longer reliable, and Hendrix had found someone new. A quiet fury stirred inside me at the cruelty of the situation. How could God do this? Didn't he know I had already surpassed my limit of bullshit? If Ada Lynn left me now, I would never recover. I might as well join my dad and stay drunk. Maybe it would offer some relief from the constant pain that stabbed me in my heart over and over.

"Hey," a male voice said.

My head snapped up. "Hey, Josh. Do you have any news?"

"No," he said, gently. "They won't tell me anything now that I'm here on the inside. I just wanted to check on you."

"Thanks. I haven't heard anything yet. The waiting really sucks, ya know?"

He nodded. "By the time people are here at the hospital, their hands are tied. All they can do is wait and pray for some good news. It's why I like being out there." He nodded toward the front doors of the hospital. "If I can get to someone in time, I can save a life."

Looking up at the ceiling in order not to cry, I blinked a few times and collected my nerves. "Thank you. And thanks for not ratting me out that I'm not a blood relation." I said, making eye contact.

He patted me on the shoulder. "No problem. Often times, our real family isn't blood-related at all."

"Very true."

"I gotta run. Good luck." He gave a little wave and walked away.

Maybe there were still some good people out there, filled with compassion for others. Josh seemed to be one of them.

Loud footsteps from behind me broke my thoughts. I turned in time to be tackled by Mac.

"Bestie," she said, hugging me hard. "Have you heard anything? I got here as soon as I could. Oh my God, I can't believe this. But listen, I'm here, right here with you—every step of the way. You're not alone, got it?" Mac's voice hitched while she talked.

I hugged her back, my tears landing softly in her hair.

"I didn't have anyone else to call."

"Hey, we're family forever and always." Mac let me go and wiped her own tears away with the pad of her thumb. She grabbed my hand and led me to the chairs along the wall.

"What happened?"

I shrugged, recalling running through Ada Lynn's house searching frantically for her.

"Don't know. She was out cold on the floor of her bedroom when I found her." My jaw tightened with the image that flickered across my mind again.

"Have you told your Dad? I know Hendrix will want to know."

I flinched with the mention of his name.

"Mac, Hendrix is with someone else," I whispered, barely able to choke the words out.

"What? No, he isn't, he would have told me."

"He is. I saw them walk into his house. Some blonde girl was hanging all over him." Unable to control my crying, I buried my face in my hands, curling up in the chair.

"Gemma, I'm so sorry. I didn't know. Are you sure? Have you talked to him at all?"

My gaze narrowed at her. "Mac, you can't say a word to him," I pleaded. "I mean it. I'll let him know about Ada Lynn when I know something."

"Fine. I promise, even though I don't like keeping things from him. I just think he would want to be here with you."

"Ms. Thompson?"

I jumped up at the sound of my name. "Yes?" An older doctor approached me, compassion filling his hazel eyes. He extended his hand toward me, and we shook. Then he folded his arms over his broad chest and smiled gently.

"I'm Doctor Finch."

"Is she?" I couldn't finish.

"She's going to be okay for now. She had a heart attack."

Once I heard the official diagnosis, my sobs shook my shoulders.

"She's alright, though," he said, attempting to calm my near hysterics. "She went straight from the emergency room to the catheterization laboratory or Cath lab as we call it, where we deployed a stent in her blocked artery. We moved her to ICU for now, and afterward she'll need to be in a regular room for at least twenty-four hours. We'll run some additional tests tomorrow to make sure, but if all goes well, she'll be back home in a few days."

"Can you fix it? If anything else is wrong?" Mac asked, bouncing on her tiptoes.

"I'll need to see the results, but most of the time we can. It just depends on what we're looking at. We may have already fixed the problem so try not to worry," he said, kindness in his expression.

I nodded. "When will we know, and can I see her?"

"We're scheduling the test for first thing in the morning. And yes, you can see her. Follow me."

Mac squeezed my hand.

"I'll be right back."

"I'll be right here," she said, sitting in her chair, her leg bouncing. She needed her brother. He would be the best thing for her right now.

I followed the doctor down the hall, then he stopped in front of a door. Ada Lynn's name was scrawled on the tag above the room number.

"Go on in."

I took a deep breath while he strolled away.

Peering into the room, I searched for Ada Lynn.

"Come on in my blue-eyed girl." She smiled softly. Her thin skin was pale, dark half-moon circles beneath her eyes. The soft beep of her machines filled the otherwise quiet room.

"Hi," I said, choking back the tears. "Guess I got to you in time."

She patted the bed next to her, and I sat down, taking her hand. "You scared the shit out of me," I mumbled.

"You and me both."

"The doctors told me they are going to run some more tests to make sure you're okay."

"Yeah." She grew quiet. "I might be here for a while, Gemma. You'll need to check on Hendrix's house for me."

I nodded, unwilling to argue why that wasn't a good idea at present. It didn't matter, anyway. The only thing that was important was Ada Lynn getting better and coming home.

"You can't leave me yet," I said, my voice hovering above a whisper.

Ada Lynn reached up and stroked my cheek.

"You realize I'm eighty-three, right?" She grinned. "I'm old, Gemma."

"No," I squeaked out, dropping my head and allowing my hair to fall over my face. "I've lost Mom, Hendrix, Dad—you're all I have left, Ada Lynn."

"Oh honey, I'm going to have to go sometime."

I peered up at her. "Just not yet. I still need you," I pleaded.

Tears slipped down her cheeks.

"Come here," she motioned.

I curled up in the bed next to her, and she wrapped her arm around me while I cried.

After the tears slowed, I peered up at her through swollen eyes.

"I realize you've just started to calm down, but you need to know this," she said.

Tension ran down my neck and shoulders as I waited for her to continue.

"If the test results come back with anything else and it requires surgery, there's a chance I'm too old."

"No," I said, sitting up. "Why are we even talking about this?" My voice climbed up a notch.

"Because I don't want you to hear it tomorrow and have it push you over the edge. Granted, I'm the one in the hospital bed, but you're the one I'm worried about. I know what you've lost, Gemma, but please don't go backward. And for God's sake, make things right with Hendrix. Life is too short. You know this."

I looked away from her. I couldn't do this right now. It was too much.

"I need some air," I said, standing. "I also need to update Mac. She's here, too."

"She is?"

"Yeah, do you want to see her? She's super upset. She's been a bundle of bounce since she arrived." A smile pulled at the corner of my mouth.

"Go get her, then. Just tell the nurses she's my other granddaughter," Ada Lynn said, smiling. "And don't feed her any pie." Her soft chuckle filled the room.

"I'm going to update her and let her fall apart before I bring her in."

Ada Lynn nodded. "See you two in a few."

I hurried out of the room, unable to breathe. I needed air.

"Mac," I called to her while I hurried toward the front door. She could join me outside.

"Is she okay?" Mac asked as we rounded the corner of the hospital. White outdoor tables filled a small patio, the towering oak and maple trees shading it. Multi-colored tulips and roses surrounded the perimeter. If I'd not been so upset, I would have thought the area was beautiful.

"She is for now, but she wants to see you."

Mac's mouth parted in surprise. "She does?"

"Yeah, but I need to talk to you first." I paced across the patio, attempting to control the ball of emotions that were on the edge of erupting.

"What is it?"

"There's a chance the tests may come back saying she needs surgery...she might not be a candidate due to her age."

"No," Mac said, shaking her head violently. "No, she's going to be okay." She pointed at me for emphasis.

I sank into a chair and watched Mac pace, her fingers massaging her temples.

"You've been through enough, Gemma. It's going to be alright. If she needs surgery, then it will be okay." Mac's tears slipped down her cheeks. "You need to come out with me tonight. Just take a break from the shit called your life. We can shoot pool and hang out with Jeremiah and Alexander."

"I can't, Mac. I need to be here with Ada Lynn."

"You. Need. A. Fucking. Break. In fact, I'm going to ask Ada Lynn what she thinks about it."

"She can't make me go." I huffed and folded my arms across my chest, my gaze narrowing at Mac.

"Fine, then I'll call Hendrix right now and you and I both know he will be on the first plane home. So unless you want to see him tonight while you're all covered in snot, then go out with me. It's just for a few hours. I'll pick you up and bring you home. Her tests aren't until the morning, anyway. She's in the safest place she can be."

"You can't call Hendrix," I said, steel in my tone. "I'll text him when we hear the test results tomorrow."

"Then you're going with me tonight." She placed her hands on her hips, her toe-tapping against the patio. "It's your choice, Hendrix or the guys."

"You're a brat." There would be no winning this with her and deep down, I knew she was right. Ada Lynn was safe, and they would call if anything else happened. Until then, this might be the only time I'd get out of the house for a while. After Ada Lynn came home, I'd need to be there to take care of her.

"Fine. Maybe it will help me not obsess over Ada Lynn."

Mac's shoulders slumped with relief. "Honestly, Gemma," she said softly, walking over to me, "I'm scared you're going to lose your shit. I need you with me, so I know you're alright tonight."

Searching her face, I realized she was just as scared as I was.

"I'm scared, too. Mac, I've lost so much. My teen years were taken from me, I lost Mom and—the first guy I've ever loved. Now Ada Lynn's life is hanging in the balance. I'm afraid to get close to anyone anymore. In fact, I don't think I can. You're it for me. Life has beaten the shit out of me, and this is as good as it's going to get."

"Don't say that." Mac engulfed me in a hug.

She was it. I couldn't risk losing anything else, even if it meant keeping everyone at arm's length.

"Let's get inside and spend some time with Ada Lynn," I said, rubbing my face with my hands.

Mac nodded and followed me to see Ada Lynn. The moment Mac saw her, she bolted across the room and threw her arms around her.

I stood back, struggling to stop the tears. A part of me wondered if this would be the last time I'd see my two best friends together.

17

Second thoughts warred inside me while I showered and got ready for Mac to pick me up. I should have been with Ada Lynn, but I couldn't deal with Mac alerting Hendrix. The only alternative I had left was to hang out with Jeremiah and Alexander for a few hours.

I straightened my hair and applied makeup, hoping it would help me feel a bit more human. I backed up and took a critical look in the mirror. No matter what I did, I looked like hell, but everyone would just have to deal with it.

An hour later, Mac texted me she was waiting outside. I grabbed my purse and searched for Dad, locating him in the kitchen eating a sandwich.

"I'm leaving for a while," I said from the entryway.

"With who?" he asked around a mouthful of food.

"I'll be with Mac. Don't wait up," I said, my voice clipped.

Before he could reply, I turned on my heel and walked away. If he wasn't going to act like a father, he didn't get to tell me what I could and couldn't do.

I hurried out the door and got into Mac's car.

"Geez, I still can't believe you manhandled me into going," I said, shutting the door behind me.

"You need a break, and if you lose your shit, then I need to be there to take care of you."

I glanced at her and buckled up. "I'm not your responsibility, Mac. You have enough going on."

"The hell you're not. Besides," she said, pulling out of my driveway, "you need to let loose for a bit and forget everything that's going on. Play some pool, have some drinks, whatever you need to do. And if you want to drink, it's totally cool. I'm driving tonight, so I'm not going to."

Maybe it wouldn't hurt to knock the edge off and try to have a little fun. There was nothing I could do for Ada Lynn tonight, anyway. Plus I had a ride home.

"Yeah, okay."

"Really? You'll have a few drinks to knock the edge off? I think it'll help. I don't mean drunk, just relaxed. Ya know, like we did with Hendrix." Her mouth clamped shut, and she groaned. "I'm sorry."

Nostalgia tugged at me. "I know, Mac. It's impossible for you not to talk about your brother. I get it." And I did. He was a huge part of her life, and I would have to learn to deal with it.

It wasn't long before Mac pulled into the driveway of a large, white colonial house. I didn't recognize the neighborhood, but then again, I didn't frequent the upscale areas, either.

"Where are we?" I asked.

"At Jeremiah's friend's house. He's out of town, so Jeremiah is house sitting. The dude has a pool table and a liquor cabinet you wouldn't believe. Come on," she said and motioned for me to get out of the car.

I followed her inside and into a breathtaking marble entryway with triple crown molding. A crystal chandelier hung gracefully from the ceiling.

"Holy crap, is he rich or what?" I asked, wondering how much the entryway alone had cost.

"Right?" Mac asked, locking the door behind us. "You've gotta see this house."

Mac led me into the living room.

"Wow," I said, noting the dark hardwood floors and the same marble tiling from the entryway around the fireplace. I resisted the urge to sit on all four pieces of gold and brown Victorian furniture.

Mac continued toward the kitchen.

"Holy shit," I said, glancing at her. "This dude is for real."

"I know!" Mac nodded emphatically.

I ran a finger along the pristine marble countertops, wondering what I'd cook in here and how in the hell I'd keep from flinging food all over the white cabinets.

"The guys are upstairs," Mac said, making her way toward a hand-carved, curved staircase.

With every step, my feet sank into the carpet.

"I've never been in a house this nice," I said quietly.

"Me either," she replied. "Hendrix has, though." She wrinkled her nose. "Sorry."

"It's fine," I said, trying to reassure both of us.

We reached the top of the stairs and walked down a long hallway. Mac knocked on the last door and then opened it.

"We're here," she called out, taking my hand and pulling me inside behind her.

"Hey," I said, and waved to Alexander and Jeremiah. My flight syndrome threatened to kick in, and I took a slow and steady breath while I scanned the room. The pool table sat in the middle, and a few cocktail tables were lined up against the wall. A well-used dartboard hung above the full bar, and music floated through the stereo system. The lights were dim, but not so much you couldn't see everything.

"Hey," Alexander said, stepping forward. "Glad you could make it." A genuine smile spread across his handsome features and for a moment, I forgot about all the drama I'd left behind me.

"Yeah, thanks for inviting me to hang out," I said, smiling.

"Would you like something to drink? We've got a full bar."

I hesitated, glancing at Mac. She nodded and shooed me toward the alcohol.

"She'll take a screwdriver," Mac said, grinning. "She definitely needs to chill for a while."

Jeremiah smiled, sadness flickered across his face. I assumed Mac had told him about Ada Lynn. I'd hoped they hadn't blabbed to Alexander, but they probably had.

"Come on," Alexander said, motioning for me to follow him.

I sat at the bar and watched him make our drinks, refusing to allow my mind to conjure up the last time I'd had a screwdriver and with whom. It was in the past, and tonight was about moving on with my future, even though it was looking pretty damned bleak.

Alexander slid my drink over to me, and I glanced over my shoulder. Mac was comfortable on Jeremiah's lap, making out like a teenager. Heat traveled up my cheeks. I hoped no one expected me to make out with Alexander.

"Those two, they're hard to pry apart," he said, nodding toward Mac and Jeremiah.

I wondered if he could sense my unease.

"Yeah? They're like that all the time?" I asked.

"Pretty much. Well, unless you're around."

"What do you mean?" I tilted my head in question.

"Mac wants Jeremiah to make a good impression on you, so they keep the making out to a minimum." He poured some vodka in his glass and topped it off with orange juice. He raised it in the air. "To friends."

"To friends," I replied and raised my glass to his.

I took a long drink and welcomed the tingle it sent through my body.

"You play pool?" Alexander asked, nodding toward the table.

"Never."

"What? You've never played? We have a rookie in the room?" His pale blue eyes danced with mischief.

"Nope. Never." I took another drink and heaved out a large sigh.

Not only was I a major lightweight, but I'd not eaten today, and the alcohol was hitting me fast and hard.

"Long day, huh?"

My nose wrinkled. "You have no idea."

"How about I top off your drink and teach you to play?"

Butterflies fluttered in my stomach. I'd seen enough TV to understand what teaching a girl to play pool was really about. The guy always smashed up against the girl, bending over her, and swearing he was only assisting with her aim. My pulse two-timed at the thought of being that close to him. Before I knew it, I nodded and shoved my glass his way to refill.

Alexander made his way past Mac and Jeremiah who hadn't come up for a breath since I'd left her. Grabbing two pool sticks, he then handed one to me. I took another drink and then set it on one of the small round tables against the wall. The alcohol traveled through me and all of the tension eased from my shoulders. Popping my neck, I self-consciously tucked my hair behind my ears, focusing on Alexander racking up the pool balls. I watched him as he sauntered around the table. He picked up the little blue square and chalked the tip of his stick, his attention never leaving my face.

I smiled, then he took the first shot, sending the balls flying in every direction.

"You ready?" he asked, rounding the table toward me.

My breath hitched as he grew closer, and my attention traveled down his black, well-fitted polo shirt that hung outside his jeans. Levi's had never looked better on a guy than right now. They fit him in all the right places. My stomach flip-flopped. No other guy had been this close to me since the incident other than Hendrix. Except—Brandon. Chills shot through me with the memory.

"You cold?" Alexander asked, frowning.

"No, I'm fine. I'm ready to learn." I swallowed hard, pushing the thoughts of Brandon away. Alexander positioned himself next to me and showed me how to hold the pool stick. I attempted it on my own, but I failed miserably.

"Can I?" he asked, his expression serious.

"Yeah," I whispered. Alexander bent over me from behind and placed his hands on my pool stick, his spicy cologne intoxicating. He felt good, warm, comfortable. I wasn't sure if it was the alcohol or if it had just been a while since I'd had sex, but suddenly every part of my body came to life. Shit. Mac was right.

We laughed when I finally made a shot by myself and missed every ball on the stupid table. Warmth filled my cheeks when his gaze lingered on me a little longer than normal.

For the next few hours we drank, and he helped me learn to play. But honestly, I didn't even care about pool anymore. Every time I took a shot, Alexander offered to help. His body next to mine was causing some serious throbbing between my legs. I wasn't the only one, though. Alexander was making it crystal clear he was willing to play. But was I?

My attention drifted over to Alexander's well-defined body as he stood by the pool table. The alcohol had definitely kicked in full throttle, and I was feeling brave. When it was my turn, I bent over the table in front of him and gazed over my shoulder. "Ready?" I asked. When he leaned over me, I backed up, tentatively rubbing my ass against him. He was wonderfully hard, and a small moan escaped me. I dropped the pool stick on the table, whirled around, and stared up at him. I cupped his erection through his jeans, surprising both of us with my boldness.

"Shit," he muttered. His fingers traced my cheek, and I leaned into his touch. Every part of me craved him. Craved something to make me feel normal and alive.

"You want to find some privacy?" he whispered in my ear.

I nodded, and he took my hand. I cleared my throat loudly, gaining Mac's attention.

"Be right back," I said, smiling.

Mac wiggled her eyebrows and grinned. She was probably proud of herself for helping me scratch my itch.

A few doors down the hall we stopped.

"This work okay?" Alexander asked, opening the door and flipping on the light switch. "It's a guest bedroom."

A queen-sized bed with a floral print comforter and matching pillows sat in the corner. The antique dresser and vanity matched the bed. My fuzzy brain wondered if this was where grandma slept when she visited.

Nerves tugged at me briefly, and I swallowed hard, pushing them aside. He closed the door behind him and wrapped his arm around me, bringing my body flush to his. His finger tilted my chin up, and his lips tentatively met mine.

"You sure about this?" he asked, his other hand running up my back.

"Yeah," I replied breathlessly.

Our lips parted, and his tongue caressed mine. Heat spread through my body, and I slipped my fingers beneath his shirt, grazing his skin. He moaned into my mouth as I explored his chest and stomach.

His soft kisses trailed down my neck, and I tilted my head, allowing him better access. He slid a hand underneath my shirt and ran his fingers up my side. I sighed and arched into him.

Somewhere in my alcohol clouded brain, my mind was saying no, but my body was telling it to fuck off. Drunk Gemma was insisting I vent my anger at Hendrix for waving that blonde bimbo right in my face. And Alexander was the guy to help me. I stepped back and pulled my shirt off.

Alexander's eyes darkened with need as I stood before him in my bra. I flipped open the button on my jeans and unzipped them. His attention remained on me, his tongue darting across his lower lip as I slowly walked toward him. "This is in my way," I said, tugging on his shirt.

He hastily removed it, revealing rock hard abs and tanned skin. My nails grazed down his broad chest and stomach, pausing at the top of his jeans. I slipped my fingers beneath the waistband and realized he was commando. Drunk Gemma was cheering me on, but was this what I really wanted? Even if Hendrix and I never got back together, this wasn't right. I was acting out of anger.

"You're amazingly beautiful," he said, his voice deep and husky.

He kneeled down and took hold of the waistband on my jeans, tugging slightly. His breath tickled me as he planted a kiss on the sensitive skin of my stomach. I moaned the second his warm mouth made contact.

Alexander glanced up at me, his eyes filled with lust, as he gently pushed me backward onto the bed and continued kissing my stomach, moving toward my breasts.

"Oh, God." My head dropped back, my eyes fluttering closed as I lost myself to the familiar touch.

"That feel good?" The deep voice seemed to float in the air.

"Mm-hmm." I nodded, my eyes still closed.

"Don't stop," I murmured, visions of beautiful brown hair tucked behind a shoulder and piercing blue eyes holding my gaze while he brought me to the edge, made the sweet sensation inside me grow stronger. I had missed this. Missed him. I felt a single tear slip down my face.

"Hendrix," I whimpered.

"Gemma," A deep voice that wasn't Hendrix's jolted me into reality.

"Shit," I said, sitting up and pulling my legs to my chest. What the hell had I just done?

Alexander sat on the edge of the bed.

"Gemma, I know you're going through a lot. And, as crazy as it sounds, I don't think I can have sex with you. You just called out some other dude's name, which tells me you're in love with him. Being with you tonight, if it pushed you over the edge with everything you're dealing with. Well—it'd be fucked up. I couldn't live with that."

Guilt gnawed at me, and I closed my eyes, attempting to regain my composure. After a deep breath, somehow, I managed to look at Alexander.

"I'm so sorry." I scooted off the bed, zipping my jeans and grabbing my shirt. "I'm not normally like this. It must be the alcohol. This is the first time I've even been drunk. I've been with one guy in my entire life. One-night stands aren't my thing. And I think you're a nice guy, but you don't want me. I don't have anything I could possibly give you."

Alexander reached for his shirt, his attention never leaving me.

"It's okay. I think you're just in a dark place right now."

"I should probably go home and sober up. I have to be at the hospital early for tests. I mean, Ada Lynn's tests. I'm sorry," I said, my lips pursing together.

Alexander opened the door and led me back to the game room, then surprised me with a quick hug and a kiss on the cheek. "I'm sure I'll see you around." He gave me a kind smile, and then I made my way over to Mac and Jeremiah.

"Hey, Mac, I need to get home."

She broke away from Jeremiah and peered at the clock. "It's only midnight," she replied.

"I know, but I need to be with Ada Lynn in the morning."

"Yeah, guess you're right." Mac gave Jeremiah a quick kiss and got off his lap.

Jeremiah stood with her. "Keep us posted, Gemma. Let us know if you need anything."

"I will, thanks." My focus darted toward Alexander, my cheeks warming from humiliation. What in the hell had I been thinking tonight? I gave him a small wave and led Mac out of the room, down the stairs, and outside.

"You feeling better?" Mac asked, grinning as we climbed in her car.

"Apparently I have another side to me when I'm drunk."

"Yeah? Did you go all wild on him?"

"Oh my God. We didn't have sex," I blurted.

"Well damn. I thought that's why you left the room." She shot me a confused look as she turned right and drove toward my house.

"He kissed me, then I called him Hendrix." I groaned, realizing the alcohol was still manipulating my actions. No way would I have ever shared that with Mac if I were sober.

"Holy fuck!" She screeched. "Oh my God. You know what this means, right?"

I cringed, Mac was way too excited.

"No," I said, looking at her for some clarification.

"You're still in love with Hendrix. You want to be with him, Gemma. Like, that truth stared you right smack dab in the face tonight, girlfriend. No way you could possibly deny it now."

I leaned back against the headrest, watching the trees and houses pass as Mac drove.

"It doesn't matter," I whispered and choked down the emotions the alcohol had brought to the surface again. "He's with someone else."

"So! We'll just take her out and toss her to the gators. Right? Isn't that what you all do down here when you don't like someone?"

"Mac," I said, rubbing my temples and wishing all of this would go away. "We can't ambush her."

"I still think you should ask him. I know Hendrix, and this doesn't sound like something he would do."

"I need to pull it together as much as I can and stay focused on Ada Lynn. She is going to need me when she gets home from the hospital."

"I know," Mac replied, a hint of sadness in her tone.

We rode in silence the rest of the way to my house.

"Thanks, for tonight," I said.

"You going to be alright tomorrow? I can skip classes if you need me to be at the hospital with you guys."

My heart swelled with gratitude.

"I'll be fine, but I promise I'll text you the minute I know anything."

Mac gave me a quick hug, and then I hurried into the house.

I peered through the dark living room at the couch, but Dad wasn't there. Maybe he'd already gone to bed. Silently, I made my way to the kitchen for some water. Flipping on the light switch, I jumped, and my purse clattered to the floor.

18

"Where you been?" Dad growled.

"Dad? What are you doing? You scared me half to death." I bent over to pick up my purse, and that's when I saw it. Letters and photos scattered across the table.

"What's all of that?" I asked, approaching him.

"You know it was your fault, right?"

"What was?" I asked, my forehead creasing. I gasped, the pictures coming into full view. "Where did you get all of these?" I placed my purse on the table and picked one up, flipping it over. *Jordan, six months old* was scrawled on the back. "Six months?" I asked and sank into the kitchen chair next to Dad. Shocked, I scanned the letters and numerous pictures of my son.

"A little girl only gets raped if she asks for it," he said, slurring his words.

Horrified, my eyes met his. But I wasn't looking into the eyes of the father I'd known. This man terrified me. Anger and disgust twisted his facial features into someone almost unrecognizable.

"No, how can you say something like that?" I asked, choking on my fear. "No girl asks to be hurt. Ever." The hair on the back of my neck stood with my words.

"You wore that short little dress that day, and you were already developed."

"It wasn't short," I fired back. I swallowed hard, trying to control my mouth. Drinking tonight had been a bad idea.

"You were too goddamn beautiful! What man wouldn't have wanted you?" His fist slammed down on the table, his eyes filling with lust as he scanned my body.

Unable to control it any longer, I trembled violently.

"Dad," I whispered. "Please tell me the alcohol has screwed you up. Please tell me you didn't just admit you looked at your own daughter like that." I flew out of my chair, barely reaching the sink in time to vomit. Leaning against the counter, I turned on the cold water and rinsed my mouth.

"You asked for it, and God punished you with the pregnancy," he said right behind me.

I turned slowly, my gaze making contact with his.

"You're fucking sick," I spat. "Don't you dare talk to me like that. I never asked to be brutally raped or to have Jordan."

Before I realized it, Dad grabbed my arms, his fingers digging into my skin while he shook me. He tossed me down like I was a rag doll, and my skull bounced off the kitchen floor. I whimpered, and nausea swirled in my stomach while I tried to regain my bearings.

"Little bitch. You messed up everyone's life!" He roared before his foot came into contact with my ribs. My gut-wrenching cry broke free with the contact. I curled up into a ball, fending him off the best I could while his foot made contact again. My mind scrambled for some type of help, but my phone was in my purse across the room, and Ada Lynn wasn't next door. No one could hear my screams while my father beat me.

Tears slid down my cheeks and landed on the kitchen floor. At some point, Dad had lost interest in me and wandered off, but I was too sore to get up off the floor. Although my brain wasn't fully engaged, I finally understood. This is what Ada Lynn had been worried about...my father going off the deep end. She suspected he was violent, but I don't think she had any idea he was a sick fuck, too. I should have gone back to Spokane immediately after Mom's funeral like Ada Lynn had begged me to.

My alarm on my phone blared. Terror shot through me as I pulled myself up off the floor. If Dad was asleep, I didn't want to take the risk of waking him. I grabbed my side, hobbled toward my purse, and located my phone. It was a little after seven in the morning. Apparently, I'd laid on the floor for hours.

I sank into my chair and mentally took inventory of my pain level. Digging through my purse, I located the Advil, popped four, and swallowed them without any water. Somehow, I needed to make it to the bathroom. I had to pee like crazy. Then I needed to get the hell out of here. If I was lucky, Dad would sleep most of the day, allowing me to pack and slip out of the house undetected. I would have to stay next door. I wasn't sure if I'd be safe there, either, but my options were seriously limited.

Glancing at the clock, I remembered why my alarm had gone off. Ada Lynn was in the hospital, and I needed to get my ass there to be with her.

Willing the Advil to hurry and take effect, I stood on shaky legs. I needed to suck it up and grab what belongings I could. I would have to shower at Ada Lynn's. There was no way I could take a chance he would wake up. I grabbed my purse, ensured all the critical items were in it, and shuffled to my room.

I locked my bedroom door behind me and went to my closet and scooped up my duffel bag. As quietly as possible, I eased open the dresser drawers, pulled out my clothes, and stuffed them in the bag. My heart ached when I picked up Hendrix's shirt and letters. I placed the shirt against my face and inhaled as deep as I could before the pain in my side took over. No longer able to stop them, tears streamed down my cheeks while I finished packing. I picked up my laptop and frowned. Shit, I'd almost forgotten about the thumb drive. I'd been super pissed and threw it across the room. I lowered myself slowly on the floor and peered underneath my bed and desk, but I didn't see it. I groaned with exasperation when I spotted it in the back corner under my dresser.

"Dammit." I bit my lower lip so hard it drew blood, but it diverted my attention away from the blinding pain in my body. I stretched my arm out, my fingers grazing the drive. Panting, I gave it one more stretch and finally wrapped my hand around it. Now to get off the floor and out of the house.

Ten minutes later, I was packed. Thank God I only had to carry it next door. It was heavy as hell. I wondered if I'd even be able to make it down the porch steps. Deciding to save my energy, I pulled on the strap and dragged it down the hallway to the living room, swearing at the loud scraping noise it made across the floor. Out of breath, I stopped and rested my hands on my knees. A tiny prayer formed on my lips, begging whoever might be listening to help me get out of the house alive.

Finally, I reached the door, flipped the locks, and swung it wide open. Freedom was just on the other side.

"Hey there," a female voice said from my porch.

"What the hell?" I asked, my mouth dropping open. "You gotta be fucking kidding me."

19

"*I* don't have time for this. Step back."

I didn't wait for Andrea and Hendrix to move out of the way before I heaved the bag in front of me and tossed it on the front porch. It landed with a heavy thud. I doubled over in pain, grabbing onto the door for support.

"Gemma," Hendrix ran over to me.

"Don't touch me," I whispered sharply. "Just close the door for me."

Worry filled Hendrix's expression, but he did as I asked and pulled the door closed behind me. Eventually, I stood up, my vision blurring.

"Jesus, what happened?" Hendrix ran his hands up my arms.

"Nothing." I pulled away from him. He couldn't know what Dad had done.

"This doesn't look like a good time, Hendrix. Maybe I should wait until she comes back to Spokane. I mean, I don't want to miss my plane," Andrea said, eyeing me.

Finally, a little clarity of who was in front of me sunk in.

"What are you doing here?" I snarled at her.

Andrea's hands rose slowly in surrender.

"Hang on, Andrea," Hendrix said. "What happened, Gemma." His jaw tensed, waiting for my reply.

"Nothing. You two need to go. This is a really bad time. I have to get my bag next door and leave."

"I'll get it," he said, picking up the duffel. "Andrea." He motioned for her to walk in front of him. She glared at him but walked down the steps. I held onto the railing and slowly made my way next door. Hendrix and Andrea remained beside me.

I dug around in my purse for the key and opened the door. Although I didn't really want Hendrix here, I was grateful he'd brought my bag over. I would have passed out from the pain. Hendrix closed the door behind me.

"Where's Ada Lynn?" he asked, glancing around for her.

"Hospital. I need to go, so whatever you two need, make it fast." I leaned against the wall for support.

"What?" Hendrix asked. "Is she okay?"

"I have no idea. I'm stuck here with you two when I need to be with her. She's having tests run this morning. It's all I know," I said exasperatedly.

Hendrix let it go for the moment, which told me they were here with something equally as important.

Andrea's gaze dropped to the floor and back up to mine.

"We need to talk," she muttered.

"Now?" I asked, astonished she had the guts to show up on my porch in the first place. Good God, they needed to leave before my father woke up and came looking for me. After last night, I couldn't imagine what he would do next time. I couldn't put them in danger, too.

My breath hitched, and I grabbed my side.

Hendrix stepped toward me, his fingers tilting my chin up, forcing me to make eye contact with him.

"I'm not going anywhere," he said firmly. "You're not okay. Let me help you to the kitchen and I'll make some coffee. Plus, I flew Andrea in from Spokane. She needs to tell you a few things. I'll have her in and out in a few minutes." His expression filled with worry. "Then,

I'm taking you to the hospital to see Ada Lynn and find out what's going on with both of you."

"Nope, I've got this. Ada Lynn is my responsibility, not yours." I clenched my fists together, willing the unrelenting pain to go the hell away. I couldn't fall apart now. Ada Lynn depended on me. "You have five minutes," I said. "Just make sure the door is locked for me." The best thing I could do at the moment was give in. Hendrix wasn't going anywhere.

He leaned around me, turned the deadbolt, and slid the chain into place. Hendrix slipped his arm around my waist and helped me to the kitchen. I groaned, sinking carefully into the chair. Andrea pulled out the seat across from me, and Hendrix made the coffee. He knew where everything was, which told me he'd visited Ada Lynn more than once without my knowledge.

"What do you want?" I asked, my gaze narrowing as it landed on Andrea.

She wrung her hands together and took a deep breath. "I lied to you."

My brows spiked upward.

"Hendrix never touched me."

Her shoulders slumped in relief with the confession. My attention traveled to him. He stared at her intently and leaned against the counter, rubbing his chin. Anger flashed in his eyes.

"Keep going," he ordered.

Andrea cringed a little. "I know I really messed things up with you two, and I'm sorry."

"Why in the hell would you do that?" My tone was on the edge of hysteria. Hendrix made his way over to me and gently rubbed my back. It was working, and I calmed a little with his touch.

"One day after classes, some random guy approached me and handed me an envelope. There was a note inside that said if I pressed charges against Hendrix for rape, I'd get paid ten thousand dollars. Whoever sent the note knew about my mom, too. She has cancer, and we couldn't afford the treatment anymore..." She paused, sadness flickering across her expression. "The delivery dude stayed with me while I read the note. I asked who sent him, but he wouldn't budge with any information. He said his job was to deliver the envelope and get my answer. Obviously, I said yes."

I wasn't sure if it was the pain or my anger, but black dots danced before my eyes.

"So you wrecked our lives to save yours?" I spat, the reality of her words crushing me beneath it.

"I know, I'm sorry." She glanced down and back up to me, her facial expression changing on a dime. "Let me ask you something, though. If you could have saved your mother from dying, what would you have done for her?"

Her words slapped me in the face, and I flinched. She knew my Mom was dead. How could she look me in the face and say something so horrible? Hendrix's hand moved up to the back of my neck, his fingers massaging the tense muscles. I pulled his hands away.

"Who? Who paid you to lie? You have to know where the money came from," I demanded.

Andrea shrugged. "Honest to God, I don't know."

I shook my head. "I can't believe you. You're all nonchalant about ruining someone's life. Do you know what would have happened to Hendrix if he'd been charged? Jail. Do you even care that you ripped us apart?"

"Honestly, it wasn't about you. It was about my mom. I did what I had to. I'd do it again, too."

In one swift motion, I flew across the table and grabbed her by the collar of her shirt, jerking her forward. Searing pain shot through me, but I ground my teeth together and ignored it.

"You and Hendrix do whatever you have to and clear his name. For now, get the hell out of my house before I fucking ruin you." I growled. I let her go and sank into my seat, my forehead beaded with sweat from the effort.

"I'll just wait out front for my Uber," she said, scooting the chair away from the table, and scurrying away like the coward she was.

The front door closed, jolting me back to reality.

Hendrix sat down next to me and took my hand.

"She signed papers that released me from all the charges. We decided, in exchange for coming forward, we'd protect her. My attorney said it would be best if she said it was a case of mistaken identity."

I stared at him speechless. It was too much. He was going to help protect her even though she'd lied.

"Gem," he said softly, his fingers caressing my cheek.

I leaned into his touch. I was so tired. Anything else I'd had left inside had been beaten out of me with my father's drunken confession last night. I couldn't ruin Hendrix, too.

"Can we work things out, now?"

I straightened, and his hand dropped to the table. Fear and sadness flickered across his face.

I stood, grabbing my side.

"You said if I gave you proof, you'd come back." His features clouded with confusion. "I don't—I thought."

I stared him straight in the eye. "You already have a girlfriend. There's not enough room for the both of us." I was too exhausted and overwhelmed to have this conversation right now.

Hendrix's mouth gaped open. I hobbled as fast as I could for the front door and located my purse. Fumbling for the keys, I felt his presence next to me before I saw him.

"Gem, let me explain."

"Hendrix, I have to go. Ada Lynn is the only thing I can deal with right now. Lock up when you leave."

And with that, I opened the door, hurried down the steps, and to Ada Lynn's car. Thank God the Advil had finally kicked in.

"Gemma, wait!" Hendrix yelled from the porch.

I started the car, shifted into reverse, and headed toward the hospital.

20

*A*fter the conversation with Andrea, I shut down hard. There was no way I could even begin to process what she'd said. Besides, Ada Lynn needed me right now. Anything else was officially moved to the back burner until I knew if she was okay or if she required surgery. She was the one person that hadn't let me down, and I owed her everything.

My chin quivered with emotion as I chewed on my bottom lip in an attempt to make it stop. No way would I cry before I saw her. God, I was so tired of crying.

Even though the Advil had helped, my body still ached and throbbed. Refusing to think about last night with my Dad, I pulled into the hospital parking lot and parked near the entrance. I didn't have to walk very far to the front doors, but making it to Ada Lynn's room was another story.

I let out a long hiss when I closed the car door. Agony shot through my entire body with the movement. How in the hell would I be able to hide this from Ada Lynn? Straightening up, I willed myself forward.

The hospital doors whooshed open, and I dropped my arm from my side and stood straight. I could at least act like I was okay for a few minutes, right?

"Miss?" a friendly female voice said from behind me.

I turned my head in her direction.

"Miss? Are you okay?" A nurse in blue scrubs approached me, worry lines creasing her forehead. Her hand shot out toward me, guiding me by my arm.

"I'm here to see my grandma."

"Someone is here for you?"

Puzzled, I stared at her.

"You've been admitted?"

"What?" I gasped. What was she talking about?

"Let's get you into a wheelchair." She wheeled a chair over to me. "Sit down, hon."

Nausea rolled in my stomach, and I sank into the chair, no longer caring.

"Ada Lynn," I muttered, clutching my side again. Tears flowed down my cheeks as my body folded in on itself.

"Hang on, sweetie. I'm nurse Hallsworth. You're checked in right?"

"What?" I asked, unable to catch my breath. Panic speared me. I reached for the nurse, digging my fingers in her arm, struggling to breathe. "Can't breathe," I managed to choke out.

"I need assistance over here!" she called.

Black dots floated across my vision as I was lifted from the chair onto the gurney. Searing pain rushed through me, clouding my thoughts. When the mask landed on my face, I clawed at it weakly.

"Emergency contact?" the nurse asked.

I couldn't understand what she was saying. I didn't understand what was happening. The next thing I knew, everything went black.

An annoying beep pulled me from my safe oblivion. I squinted against the light, looking around me. Where was I?

"Hey," a warm voice said.

I tried to speak, but my throat was to dry.

"Take this."

A cold piece of ice parted my lips, trickling down my parched throat. I groaned as the room came into focus.

"You're all right. They have you on some pretty strong meds."

"Hendrix?"

"Yeah, babe, I'm right here."

I choked on a sob, then the pain ripped through me. Clutching desperately at my side, I tried to control the ever-growing panic inside me.

"Ada Lynn," I whispered, frantically.

"She's fine. She knows you're here."

I grabbed his hand, digging my nails into his skin. Fear shot through me. I didn't understand. I didn't remember anything.

"Gemma, calm down. A few of your ribs are broken." He smoothed my hair while he talked.

Between his touch and my meds, I began to relax a little bit.

"I...I need to get to her. She can't find out, Hendrix. No one can know the truth. There's no way she knew..." My voice trailed off, exhaustion seeping deep inside me. Sleep wrapped me in its arms, and I allowed myself to drift off again.

L arge, worried brown eyes hovered directly over me when I woke up.

"Hi, bestie," she said softly.

"Mac?" My vision was blurry. "What are you doing here?"

"I've been here all day. The moment Hendrix called me, I jumped into my car and broke all of the speed limits."

I grinned.

"You're still on strong meds, so you're probably feeling a little loopy."

"Nothing hurts for the moment. In fact, I'm feeling pretty good." I tossed the sheet off me and sat up. "Shit," I said, grabbing my side. "What the hell?"

"Gemma, sit back." Mac gently pushed me back against the bed. "What happened?"

"I dunno," I replied, frowning. "What did happen?"

"Dammit, you're still too out of it. I figured this was the only way you were going to tell me the truth."

"Damaged." I swallowed hard, my throat scratchy.

"What is?"

"Me. Everything is ruined. I'm ruined."

"Gemma, you're not making a lick of sense."

I barked out a laugh. "You said *lick of sense*."

Mac frowned.

"It's a Southern expression."

"Your focus is as bad as mine," she muttered, rubbing her tired face with her hands.

"I dreamed Hendrix was with me." I smiled. "He looked so good. I miss him, but I don't think his girlfriend would like it if I told him that."

"He's here, actually. He's visiting Ada Lynn. There was no way in hell he was leaving your side until I told him she needed an update and I'd stay with you."

"Ada Lynn. Man, this shit is crazy. I can't stay focused. Is this what it's like for you?" I leaned forward, staring at Mac until the pain forced me to lay back again.

"She's going to be okay. No surgery," Mac said, giving me a big smile.

"Really? She's going to be okay? She's not leaving me?" My voice caught in my throat with my words.

"Nope. You're stuck with her."

"Oh good, we can take care of each other, then. Especially since we're roomies now." I smiled. "How's Alexander?"

Mac's mouth dangled open. "Um, yeah, he's good."

"Who's Alexander?" Hendrix asked, entering the room.

"A hot dude that did *not* fuck me while I was drunk. Oops," I said, covering my mouth with my hand.

"Shut up, Gemma!" Mac's tone was sharp. "Leave Hendrix. Now is not a good time."

I glanced over at him, veins popping out of his neck. "Did he do this?" Hendrix asked, his hands clenching and unclenching at his sides.

"Not. *Now*," Mac said sternly, jumping in front of him, but still leaving me a front and center seat of the action. "She's out of her head and not only that, you're dating someone so why are you even here?"

"What?" His focus darted away from me toward Mac. "Why does everyone think that? You've got it all wrong."

"Hmm. Might have something to do with the girl you took home. But that's for another time. So out. We'll figure this out later, but for now she needs to get the pain meds out of her system without hurting anyone's feelings."

Hendrix's shoulders sagged. "You're right. I'm probably the last thing she needs right now," he mumbled.

"Give her some space for a little bit. Let her get better. A whole lot of shit just went down, and she needs to feel safe. You have my word, the moment she's ready, one of us will let you know."

Hendrix's jaw tensed, his expression twisting into remorse. "I love her, Mac. I can't lose her for good. Andrea screwed everything up. But whoever did this to her—"

"I'll never tell," I whispered hoarsely.

"Go." Mac physically turned him around and marched him out the door.

"You're spunky for being so little," I giggled.

Mac closed the door behind Hendrix, then sank into the chair next to my bed and took a deep breath.

"Not that you'll remember any of this, but I don't think there was another girl. My bright idea of having you hook up with Alexander might have done more damage than good." Her shoulders fell with the confession.

"We didn't have sex."

"I know, but there were other things."

I fell into silence, my brain scrambling to assemble the broken bits and pieces and put them back together again. It wasn't going to happen, though, at least not right now.

Mac turned on the TV, and eventually, I slipped into a fitful sleep.

"How are you feeling this morning, hon?" Nurse Hallsworth asked.

"Like shit," I replied, blinking against the unnecessarily bright light.

"The doctor is on his way. I think you get to go home today." She frowned. "But I need to ask you some questions first."

I nodded, rubbing the sleep from my eyes. I glanced around the room. Mac wasn't anywhere to be seen, and neither was Hendrix.

"Are you safe at home?"

Shit. Did they know? Did I say anything while the drugs were making me crazy?

"Yeah. I'm good."

"You sure? Do you remember how you got here?"

I stared out the window, my mind scrambling to recall the events.

"Some of it. I came in to see a patient here. Then I doubled over from pain. You were there, but that's all I remember."

"It was a good thing I caught you. Your lung collapsed."

"What?" I pushed myself into a sitting position, grimacing.

"You also have two broken ribs."

"Ugh. That explains why I feel like I got run over by a truck." I gingerly touched my side.

"We took x-rays, too. Your entire side is purple from whatever happened. With this new information, I'm going to ask again: are you safe at home?"

Hesitation tugged at me. My father had broken my ribs. But I wasn't telling them what happened.

I pushed myself up again and stared at her, our gaze locking. "I. Am. Safe." My gut tightened with the bold-faced lie.

"Here's a hotline you can call twenty-four hours a day and seven days a week. They never close. If you ever find yourself in trouble, this is a safe place for you to go."

Nodding, I accepted the card.

Nurse Hallsworth gave me instructions for care. Shortly after she finished, a doctor came in, checked me out, and gave me a prescription. I struggled to focus as he reviewed exercises and care over the next several weeks.

"You have a ride home?" he asked, patting my arm.

"Yeah. I'll text my best friend."

"You were lucky this time. Please take care of yourself. No one ever deserves to be hurt like you were."

Turning away from him, I stared out the window. According to my father, I deserved everything I got.

"Thank you." I glanced his way again.

"Sure thing."

He turned and left the room, and for the first time in a few days, I was utterly alone and coherent. Reaching for my phone, I pulled up the Uber app and ordered a ride home. There was no way I would bother Mac. She had classes, and I'd pulled her out of school enough already.

Ten minutes later I was dressed and on my way toward Ada Lynn's room. I hadn't seen her since the night with Alexander.

My stomach churned with thoughts of Alexander and what I'd done while I'd been drunk. But it was nothing compared to my father's words and the impact of his foot that broke my ribs.

"Hey," I said, peering around Ada Lynn's door. She sat up on the bed, dressed.

"My girl," she said, a tired smile easing across her features. "Come on over. I've missed you."

I stood as straight as I could and walked over to her.

"Are you discharged yet?" I asked, sitting gently on the side of her bed.

"Not yet. Are you on your way out of here?" she asked, a mix of regret and worry filling her face.

"Yeah. I um, my stuff is at your house."

Ada Lynn placed a shaky hand over her mouth, tears forming in her eyes. Her suspicions had just been confirmed.

"We don't need to talk about it." My gaze fell to the floor and then slowly drifted back up to her.

She nodded. "When Hendrix told me, I knew what had happened. And yes, we will talk about it, but not now. I'm supposed to reduce the stress, so I don't end up with another heart attack. The doctor gave me a long list of things to do and not to do. Not to mention more meds." She actually rolled her eyes with her last comment.

"I'll help as much as I can," I offered. "But you're okay? No surgery? And the doctor didn't say you needed surgery, and you're not telling me?" I arched my eyebrow at her and gave her a stern look.

"Nope, the stent fixed the problem."

I patted her hand. "Good. Let's not do that again."

She smiled. "Let's not."

My app indicated my Uber was here.

"My ride is here. I'll see you at home."

"Yeah. I'll see you in a little while."

I stood gingerly and walked toward the door.

"Gemma?"

I stopped, carefully turning back toward Ada Lynn.

"You be careful and get yourself into the house quickly. Do you understand me?"

My heart ached for her, for me, for the situation. "Yes, ma'am." There was no way I'd argue or question her. This time, I understood.

21

"**C**an you wait for a moment and see that I get inside the house safely?" I asked the female Uber driver.

"Of course," she said, offering an understanding smile.

Unfortunately it took a few minutes to make it up the stairs and into Ada Lynn's house. Even though it was almost three in the afternoon, I made some coffee. Exhaustion pulled at me as I filled my cup and sank into the chair. Was I safe here? Would Dad come over, looking for me? He had to know I was next door. There was nowhere else for me to go.

A few hours later, a loud click gained my attention, and I carefully got out of my chair. I grabbed my side and waited anxiously. Did Dad have a key? Was it Ada Lynn? My feet rooted themselves in place, my panic teetering on the edge.

"Here ya go," Hendrix said, guiding Ada Lynn to her recliner.

"Shew, this fiasco sure did leave an old lady tired." She sat down, flashing him a grin.

My body wilted, and relief spread through me. I shuffled into the living room.

"Thanks," I said to Hendrix. "For bringing her home."

He nodded. "Can we talk?" His body tensed with his question.

"Sure. I just made coffee." I was too weak to protest, and he was already here.

"Sounds awfully good, but I guess I have to switch to decaf now," Ada Lynn said with a slight whine in her voice.

"That sucks," I replied from the kitchen. "I'll have to figure out how to get you some."

The sound of the TV filled the house, and I realized Ada Lynn was trying to give us some privacy. I selected a cup from the clean dishes next to the sink and filled it for Hendrix.

"You don't have to serve me," he said, cautiously turning me toward him.

"I know," I whispered, placing the steaming mug on the counter.

He gently pulled me to him, and I sank against his body, my head resting on his chest.

"It's over, Gemma. All of this shit with Andrea is over."

I looked up into his blue eyes. He had no idea how wrong he was. Maybe Andrea had confessed she'd lied, but we still couldn't be together. It was too dangerous.

"Honestly, I don't know how you're keeping it together. You just lost your mom, and then the bullshit with Andrea—I'm surprised you're not drinking right along with your dad."

I bristled against him, pulling away.

"Mac told you?"

"Yeah. She just said he was hitting the hard stuff now."

Silence filled the small space between us.

"Did he? Did he do this to you?" Hendrix asked softly. "You can tell me."

My nostrils flared with anger at the situation. I was trying to protect him.

"You need to stop. Leave it alone." Now that I'd experienced first-hand what my dad was capable of, I needed to keep Hendrix as far away as possible.

"How do you expect me to leave it alone?" He ran a hand through his hair, his expression pleading with me. "I love you, Gem. Can you imagine what I'm feeling? Just for a minute? I mean, they call me from the hospital and tell me you're there with broken ribs and a collapsed lung."

"There is no way your girlfriend would appreciate you being here right now. You need to go," I said.

"Dammit. I don't have a girlfriend. I'm not seeing anyone, and I'm not screwing anyone. Are you happy now?" He swallowed visibly and released a huge sigh of frustration. "She's my producer's daughter. The only reason she was at my house was to pick up some papers for him. If you'd waited, you'd have seen her leave by herself a few minutes later."

I clutched at the collar of my shirt, processing the information he'd just given me. He didn't have a girlfriend. He hadn't replaced me. My insides quivered. Shit. What was I going to tell him when he wanted us to be together again?

"Oh," I whispered.

His eyes searched mine, and then, "I'm not sure who Alexander is, but are you dating someone?" His voice cracked with the heaviness of his question.

I turned away, shame washing over me. I'd never intended on telling Hendrix anything about Alexander. How ironic that the moment I mentioned his name to Mac in the hospital, Hendrix walked in.

"No," I said softly. I kept myself busy grabbing some coffee while I recovered emotionally, then turned back toward him.

He blew out a breath. "Okay." He paused for a moment, his eyes never leaving mine.

Although I wanted to take him to his house and show him how much I still loved him, I couldn't. Dad would go after him if he even suspected I loved him. I would never forgive myself if anything bad happened.

"The band and I are off to Texas and after that Nevada. Mac said she would stay here at Ada Lynn's on the weekends if you needed her. She promised she would take care of you, and text me if anything went wrong. But if you say the word, I'll stay."

More than anything in the world, I wanted him to stay. But I'd only drag him into the pit of hell with me.

"You should go. Your band depends on you. This is a huge deal for your career, Hendrix. Take it."

His expression fell, his shoulders sagging.

"Before I go, do you believe me about the girl you saw?"

I mentally reviewed everything he'd said. Now that Andrea had admitted she was lying, it served to confirm what my heart had known all along...Hendrix had always been honest with me.

"I do." I set my coffee on the counter next to his.

"I'll be back in a few weeks."

My body tensed. I didn't want him to leave at all, much less weeks at a time.

"I love you. Come back to me, Gem," he whispered.

He carefully wrapped his arms around me, and I melted against him. I grabbed his shirt, clutching it, never wanting to let him go. But I had no choice. I couldn't leave Ada Lynn, not now when she was recovering from her heart attack. And if Dad saw Hendrix, caught wind we were together...I didn't want to take that chance. I needed to keep Hendrix safe.

Hendrix tilted my chin up, his lips brushing against mine. My hand slid down his back, noting every muscle along the way to his waist. His hands cupped the sides of my face, his kiss growing more intense. Losing any will to maintain my control, my lips parted. I moaned against his mouth, his tongue gently caressing mine.

My other hand threaded through his hair. I pushed against his hips, feeling his erection through his jeans. Hot tears spilled down my cheeks, falling between our mouths.

"Did I hurt you?" he asked, breaking our kiss, our foreheads meeting.

"No," I said quietly, my voice shaking.

"What is it?" He asked, wiping my tears away gently. "Baby, please. Talk to me."

At that moment, I chose to do the most unselfish thing I'd ever done in my life. And it was going to fucking kill me.

"Don't come back," I whispered, repeating the very words Ada Lynn had said to me. "If you love me, don't come back."

He stepped away, shock flickering through his expression.

"You should know by now I don't give up easily. Not only will I be back for you, but I'm not done with Andrea, either. We're investigating further to find out who paid her to lie."

With that, he walked out of the kitchen, said goodbye to Ada Lynn, and waltzed right out the front door. I'd forgotten that when he was upset, raw power radiated off him. It was the hottest thing I'd seen.

Raising my hand, I touched my lips where his had just been.

"Don't come back, baby," I whispered under my breath. "I can't keep you safe."

"Aren't we a pair?" Ada Lynn asked.

I settled into her couch the best I could.

"Hendrix and I picked up your prescription." She reached into her purse and produced a bag.

"How did you know?"

"I told the doctor I was your grandma and needed to pick up any medications for you on my way home."

I opened the lid and dumped one into my hand. "I'd hoped I wouldn't need it, but thank you. Obviously, I do." I winced with the pain and then swallowed the pill.

"You and Hendrix figure things out yet?" Ada Lynn asked, eyeing me.

"Nothing to figure out," I sighed, my hand automatically reaching for my ribs.

"Who are you trying to protect?"

Dammit. She knew me too well.

"Him," I said, staring at the ceiling unable to look at her. If she saw my eyes, she'd realize there was something more I hadn't told her.

She shifted in her seat and waited until my attention returned to her. "I'm so sorry. I should have done more to get you to go back to Spokane. I tried to keep you safe, but you've been so heartbroken over your mom. Plus I was just a selfish old fool. I thought I could protect you when you said you needed to stay and take care of your dad."

"It's not your fault. But swear to me, Ada Lynn. Swear to me that you won't breathe a word of this to Hendrix or Mac. No one can know the truth."

"Honey, they already know."

I leaned forward, blanching at the mind-blowing pain. "Maybe you're right, but there's a difference between suspecting and looking the truth in the face."

She stared at me. I realized her wheels were turning.

"What are we going to do about Mac? I know you're worried about Hendrix, but that boy can take care of himself. In fact, I would almost pay to see him whip your father's pathetic ass."

My eyes popped open wide. "Ada Lynn! I've never heard you say anything like that."

"Well, he's got his comin'."

"I hope so," I mumbled under my breath.

"Mac mentioned she's dating someone new," Ada Lynn piped up.

"Yeah, his name is Jeremiah. He seems like a nice guy, but I don't know for sure yet. It's too soon." I frowned. It seemed I missed a lot of conversations while on the painkillers. Shit. I just took another one. I hoped I wouldn't start rambling off at the mouth again. Now paranoid, I snatched the bottle and peered at it. "Is this?" I asked, my voice trailing off.

"Tylenol three. It's not the same stuff you had in the hospital." Ada Lynn said, grinning. "I heard you were rather chatty."

Palming my forehead, I groaned. "Oh God. I'm not going to ask." I placed the bottle back on the coffee table. "I guess when Mac wants to visit, I'll tell her to bring Jeremiah. He's a solid guy, so if there are any problems from next door, he'll keep Mac safe. It might be a good time to get to know him better, anyway."

"I think that's a good idea. And I've seen a few things in my years. I'll spot a jackass a mile away. If this boy is no good for Mac, then I want to know."

I snickered. "I'm so glad you like her. I wasn't sure after the pie incident."

"Poor kid, she sure did get herself in some hot water, didn't she?"

"Yeah, she did. But we got through it, and she's never allowed to even glance sideways at sugar again."

"I sure am proud of you. I would kick myself if I died and didn't tell you that at least one more time."

I covered my mouth with my hand, willing myself not to cry.

"You got yourself out, moved across the country, and even though you struggled with Brandon, you kept going forward. Nothing stopped you."

"I couldn't have done it without Hendrix and Mac. They helped me," I said, the impact of my words pulling on my heartstrings.

"We need a plan, now." Ada Lynn paused for a minute. "You can't stay here too long."

"Where am I going to go? It's going to take up to six weeks for me to heal. I don't have anywhere else to live," I said, panic lacing through my words.

"You're not safe right next door to him so the minute you're able, you have to go back to Spokane. I don't want you to go anywhere without Mac or Hendrix, either. You carry your pepper spray and don't you dare hesitate to use it on your dad. I don't give a flying flip if he's your father or not. Let the bastard have it." Ada Lynn stopped, struggling to take a deep breath.

I leaned forward, ignoring the sharp pain in my side. "Calm down. It's okay. Do you need meds?"

"Nitroglycerin. It's in my purse."

I hurried over to her bag, locating her prescription. I popped open the lid and shook one out into my palm. "Here."

She placed it in her mouth. I waited, standing next to her to see if I needed to call 911.

"I can't leave you like this," I said, reality crashing down on me.

"You could have died the other day. If I'm not here, there's no one to look after you."

She fumbled for my hand and squeezed it. A minute later, she visibly relaxed.

"Sit back down, I'm fine now. Thank you, but you have to go."

"How?" I stammered. "You tell me how I'm supposed to leave you and I'm out of here in six weeks, but if you can't—I'll have to take my chances."

"You're a stubborn, stubborn, girl." Ada Lynn gave me a disapproving look.

"It doesn't matter right now anyway, I'm here while I heal. We'll see after that." I folded my arms and winced from the pain. Never in my wildest dreams did I think I would be sitting on Ada Lynn's couch with broken ribs my father saw fit to give me.

22

---

*A*fter I tucked Ada Lynn into bed, I struggled to get comfortable in her guest bedroom. I'd rarely spent the night in the past, but now it was my new home.

Unzipping my duffel, I stared at my clothes. I didn't have the energy to unpack tonight. It would have to wait until tomorrow. However, I needed my pajamas.

I rooted around in my bag and searched for my sleep clothes. Suddenly, my hand brushed against the stack of envelopes from Hendrix. I pulled out his shirt and buried my face in the soft fabric. His kiss, still lingering on my lips. The most unselfish thing I'd ever done was to let him walk out the door. He needed to tour, I could never hold him back from his dream, but even then, my world was too dark. He would want to step in and save me.

Flipping through the stack of letters, I looked at the postmarked date for each one, arranging them in order. If Ada Lynn's heart scare had done nothing else, it had reminded me that life was short. It was time to read them.

I let out a soft sigh and sat on the bed, tearing off the end of the first one. Pulling a piece of paper out, I unfolded it. Only three words filled the page.

I love you.

I tore open the next one. Only four words.

I'll never leave you.

I continued, ripping them open as fast as I could. Five words.

You take my breath away.

The next, six words.

Nothing could ever break us apart.

Then, seven words.

You are the song inside my soul.

I stopped, my heart pounding against my rib cage. Disbelief swirled inside me. Each letter had a reminder that no matter what the circumstances were, he loved me.

The next to the last letter was longer. I twirled a strand of hair around my finger and began to read it.

Dear Gemma,

I hope you've read the letters, but I have no way of knowing for sure. What I do know is that your world turned upside down, shaking you to the core of your existence. I should be there with you, holding you every night, making love to you, making sure you eat and, getting you out of the house. But instead, I'm two thousand miles away, drowning in my own grief over losing you. I can only pray that someday, fate will see fit to bring you back to me. Until then, you hold my heart in the palm of your hands.

Forever Yours,

Hendrix

My breath hitched in my throat. I massaged my temples, trying to clear all the crazy emotions that swirled inside my mind.

After a minute, I reached for the last letter.

Dear Gemma,

You're going to be mad, but I've made up my mind. I don't know if you're okay or not. Mac is incredibly worried about you, too. I have nothing to go on except the crazy thoughts looping through my mind. Each one worse than the one before it. Not knowing if you're okay is tearing me apart. So I bought the house across the street from you. I won't bother you, I promise, but knowing you'll have a safe place to run to if anything happens to Ada Lynn brings me a little bit of peace. Maybe I'm overprotec-

tive, but my gut says otherwise. You'll have a key to get in whenever you choose.

On the other hand, I'm close to being able to prove to you that Andrea is lying. I think I know who is behind all the bullshit with that nonsense. It goes back to Kendra. If I'm right, you'll need to stay in Louisiana. You'll be a target simply because I love you.

A cry escaped me with the last sentence. What in the hell was he talking about? How would I be safer here in Louisiana?

I folded the letter and slid it back into the envelope, tucking them gently between the clothes in my bag. I gently slipped off my shirt and put his on. His smell enveloped me as I cried into the soft fabric. Uncanny how I was trying to protect him from danger in Louisiana, and he was trying to protect me from danger in Spokane.

The only thing I knew at this moment was that my body hurt like hell, but my heart ached even more as I swore I'd protect him, even if it meant losing him.

I turned off the lamp and stretched out in the bed, praying for sleep to come. Unable to even toss and turn, I picked up my phone, the light illuminating the otherwise dark bedroom.

You awake? I can't sleep.

I waited for Mac to text me back. I stared at the screen, hoping. Finally, little black dots flickered across my screen.

I'm here bestie. You made it home okay? I'm hurt you didn't call. I would have been there for you.

I know, but I didn't want you to miss any more classes due to my screwed-up life. You deserve someone who isn't so needy, that can give something back to you.

I chewed on my lip, wondering if she would understand I was trying to be a good friend to her, keep her safe.

Do not make me come over there and smack you senseless.

I laughed and winced at the same time.

My thumbs moved across the screen, typing my next message.

I love you. I feel like I've let you down.

Are you smoking crack, or some other fucked up shit? You're not making any sense.

Are you? I text back, deflecting her question.

Nope. I'm lying naked next to Jeremiah who is snoring softly. He's so damned hot.

Forgetting about my pain, I shot straight up in bed. My fingers flying across the keyboard.

What? You're sleeping with him? Is he good? Are you happy? Were you two safe?

Oh my God with the questions already. lol

You're not getting out of it that easy. Spill.

I shut my eyes, hoping Jeremiah was a good guy. Asher had ripped her heart out and stomped all over it. If Jeremiah did the same, Hendrix and I would have to deal with it.

Dude's got a dick! And holy wow does he know how to use it.

I could feel myself flush with her words.

TMI. TMI.

You asked. But, seriously, for a few minutes...he makes me feel like I'm the only person in the world who matters. I haven't felt like that in a very long time.

I took a minute, collecting my thoughts before I replied. I knew exactly what she meant.

You deserve to feel like that every minute of every day.

Love you, bestie.

You too, Mac. :)

Hendrix said he finally had a minute to explain about the bimbo you saw.

I literally laughed out loud.

He did.

And?

I understand. I jumped to conclusions.

What did ya learn?

I wished more than anything we were in the Spokane dorm room, facing each other while having this conversation. I missed her so much.

To ask?

Most definitely. Are you two getting back together? He sounded sort of happy for the first time in months.

Tension snaked down my neck and shoulders. I couldn't tell her that not only was I too broken to give him what he deserved, but his safety was now an issue. Dad would kill him and me too if he caught us together. I wouldn't be the only one in danger. I would willingly bring others into my nightmare, and I couldn't. I loved him too much.

I need to stay focused on Ada Lynn and my own recovery. He needs to focus on his music and his career.

You both suck.

I know.

Finally feeling tired, I grabbed my headphones, flipped to my Spotify playlist and located some music for sleep.

The incredible aroma of breakfast woke me the next day. I'd always made it for Dad and myself, so this was a nice change.

"Hey," I said, walking into the kitchen. It was weird being at Ada Lynn's full time. But at least she was alive, and I wanted to enjoy every day we had together.

"Did you sleep any?" she asked.

"Not really," I said, filling my cup and joining her at the table. She flipped open the newspaper in silence.

"You read the paper this early in the morning?"

"Yup, most of the time before you ever showed up, ya know, when it was nice and quiet."

I cracked a grin, taking the hint.

Ada Lynn finally put the paper down and looked at me.

"How are you feeling?"

"Meh," I replied.

"Do you want to tell me what happened?"

No, of course, I didn't, but she would push until we talked about it. I might as well do it now and get it over with. "You have your nitro-glycerin nearby?"

"You can get it out of my purse, but I don't think I'll need it."

I took a sip of my coffee, daring to revisit that night. "I'd been out with Mac, Jeremiah, and a guy named Alexander," I started.

"Oh?" Ada Lynn gave me a look full of curiosity.

"I'm not interested in Alexander, so don't worry." I glanced around the kitchen, uncomfortable with the conversation, but recognizing the need to have it. "I got home late, and of course Dad was drunk, but...this time was different. When I walked into the house, he had pictures of Jordan strewn all over the kitchen table." I hesitated for a moment, my words lodging in the back of my throat. "And letters. I had no idea the adopted mother had been writing with updates of him. For some crazy reason, she thought it was a good idea." I frowned. "I don't know what she was thinking, Ada Lynn. Did she not know the circumstances of how Jordan came into this world?" My hands wrung together in a vain attempt to deal with the situation. "How did I make it through that?" My focus turned back to her, finding myself suddenly breathless. "And now..."

"You're safe now, honey." Ada Lynn reached across the table, grasping my hand between hers.

"For how long, though?" There, I'd said it. But she already knew. I was just thinking out loud.

"One thing at a time," Ada Lynn said, attempting to calm me down.

I glanced at our hands, reminding myself I had people who loved me. I didn't have to stay in the same house with Dad, and for the moment I was safe.

"The moment I walked in the door, he was ready for me. He started to yell. He said horrible things like I'd asked to be raped because my dress was short." I stopped cold, unable to say the rest. Squeezing my eyes shut, I attempted to gather my emotions, and then I stared blankly at my steaming cup of coffee.

"It's not true," Ada Lynn shook her head adamantly. "He's a drunk and an abusive bastard. Don't you dare listen to him. You were a young lady. You weren't sexy or advertising. Nothing was wrong with the way you dressed. Damn him." She smacked the palm of her hand against the table. "Hell would be too good for him."

In that split second, I wondered if she knew. Did she know what I couldn't repeat out loud? I couldn't ask, though. It would just solidify what he'd already said, and a part of me realized I was grasping at straws, but he'd been drunk when he told me. Couldn't a small part of me still hope I was wrong?

"It just escalated from there. He called me names, and at first, I argued with him. Then, I got sick..." Shit. I hadn't meant to share that information. "I think the stress had gotten to me." I hadn't lied, I just didn't want her to know I'd also been drinking. "He came up from behind me, threw me on the floor, and kicked me," I blurted.

For some screwed up reason, relief flooded me as I told her what had happened. It was liberating sharing my secret. At least part of it.

Ada Lynn coughed into her hand, trying to cover up the fact she was crying.

"Do you need anything?" I asked, trying to fix the mess I'd made again. The last thing I ever wanted was to cause her pain.

"No, I'm okay. I just should have insisted you live here."

"Did you—please, tell me the truth. Did he hurt Mom? He was never like this when I was younger was he?"

This time, instead of deferring my question, Ada Lynn cringed. "I always kept an eye on you, Gemma. You were over here every day after the...after your attack. You were so exhausted, so drained, but the nightmares haunted you. Your mom was up every night with you. And, not knowing what else to do, she would occasionally slip you a sleeping pill in your dinner to help. She always told your dad which I found odd, but she had this unhealthy compulsion to tell him everything. He had a sneaky, underhanded way of controlling her. Anyway, I suspected it was those nights he'd lose control and I'd hear her scream. I showed up a few times, breaking up the fight. I'd hoped it was just stress, but it got worse over time. There were never any signs he laid a hand on you, though."

My gaze averted from hers, and I stared at the white ceiling...struggling with what she was saying.

"There's something else," she said, her voice shaking.

"What?" I asked.

23

"What is it?" I leaned forward, my elbows on the table, willing her to tell me whatever she'd been hiding from me.

"I can't be sure, Gemma, it's why I've not said anything before."

"What?" I barked, then calming down, "I'm sorry, I didn't mean to be rude."

"It's about your mom."

My heart literally stuttered in my chest.

"Not a word to anyone, do you understand?" She was firm in her request.

I nodded.

"The police questioned your father after your mom's accident."

"What?" I cried, covering my mouth with my hand.

"You know firsthand how good this town is at covering up and hiding problems. Well, after the autopsy...Your mom had a concussion. Apparently, she was driving herself to the doctor when she lost consciousness at the wheel."

"I don't understand. What are you telling me?" I swallowed hard, trying to hold it together.

"I think your dad had gotten a hold of her, Gemma."

A sob erupted from me. "He killed my mom? He fucking killed my mom?" I yelled, standing so fast my chair went flying across the small kitchen.

Silent tears streamed down Ada Lynn's face. "We don't have solid proof, but that's what the police suspect."

"How? How do you know all of this?" My hands fisted at my sides, ready to tear everything around me into tiny little pieces.

"I have a longtime friend on the force. He paid me a visit since I lived next door." Her voice faltered.

I needed air. I whirled around, stomped my way through the living room and out the front door. Something horrible inside me sprang to life, and I dared him to see me from next door. I welcomed him to come over here. I would be waiting for him. After he had spewed religious bullshit at us for years, too! Rage flared hot inside me. He was a total fake. A liar. If it were the last thing I did, I would make him pay for his choices.

"Gemma, get back in here," Ada Lynn demanded from the front door.

No matter where I was inside myself, I did what she said most of the time. Except, except— the time that would have saved us all. Instead I'd chosen to stay in Louisiana and watch over a sick, twisted man. My father.

24

February had finally arrived. Between taking care of myself and laying low, it had seemed like an eternity.

"Can Mac and Jeremiah visit? I'm going stir crazy. Even the years I stayed at home, I could at least go outside and come over here. Now, I'm just *here*."

"Are you up to it? I know you're tired of being inside, but your safety is my main concern. Don't forget, we agreed you're not to leave here without someone with you. Since your ribs are almost better, I'm sure Mac would be okay picking you up and getting you out of the house next week, too."

I nodded. It had been three weeks, and I was itching to see other people. One more week and I'd be back to normal. Whatever normal was. I still had to stay out of sight, and I couldn't be around Hendrix for fear of Dad killing him. Or maybe it'd be the other way around if Hendrix ever confirmed Dad had hurt me. Nausea filled my stomach with the mere thought of it.

"I would love to see her and meet this young man," Ada Lynn said, pulling me from my mental torture chamber.

"Me too. I mean, I want you to meet him, too. I want to know what you think of him."

I grabbed my phone off the coffee table and texted my best friend.

Come over. Bring Jeremiah.

Really?

Yeah, Ada Lynn wants to meet him. :)

Shit. Should I be scared?

Always. I grinned, knowing she'd be nervous.

What time?

I asked Ada Lynn what would work for her.

5? She said she'll cook dinner. No pie, though. Sorry.

Haha. You're so not funny. Okay. We'll see you then.

As silly as it seemed, I was excited. I was ready to see my best friend. She'd offered to visit sooner, but I'd made excuses I was still tired and healing. She had no idea I needed to make sure I was healthy enough to protect her in case my father wandered out of his house in a drunken stupor and threatened us. At one time in my life, I would have never even thought that way. Now I would put nothing past him.

It took longer than forever for five o'clock to roll around. I'd helped Ada Lynn cleanup, but overall we had kept the place pretty clean.

The doorbell rang, and I practically ran for the door.

"Don't you remove the chain until you're sure it's them," Ada Lynn called from the kitchen where she was cooking crawfish, cornbread, black-eyed peas, and collard greens. I thought it would be fun to give Mac a real southern meal. Not the frozen variety she'd grab at the store to pop in the microwave.

Peeking through the few inches between the door, I closed it and removed the chain.

"It's them!" I called to Ada Lynn.

I swung the door open and literally jumped up and down as Mac pulled me to her for a gentle hug.

"I'd give you a bear hug, but I wasn't sure about your ribs."

"Almost healed, so I'll be hitting you up next week to get me the hell out of here."

Mac frowned. "You can't drive to meet me? Not that I mind picking you up at all. It's an excuse to see Hendrix if he's in town, and of course Ada Lynn. I'm kind of confused."

Shit. I hadn't thought it out very well.

"Yeah, the doctor said still no driving, but I can at least get around better." It was a flat-out lie. I could drive now, but Ada Lynn and I had agreed I shouldn't be alone since Dad was right next door. Every time someone rang the doorbell, I practically jumped out of my skin, wondering if he'd finally decided to come over and drag me home by my hair.

Mac leaned in close. "You still owe me an explanation of what happened. I've not pushed since you're healing, but your time is almost up. I told Jeremiah that you fell down the stairs, by the way," she said under her breath.

Ignoring her, I turned my attention to her boyfriend.

"Come in." I ushered them inside, realizing Mac, Jeremiah, and I were standing on the porch in plain sight. I was already taking a chance with them here, but at least Jeremiah was a muscular guy. Although he didn't know it, I'd use him as a buffer if I had to. But honestly, Dad hadn't been seen in weeks. Only with that information had I decided it would be safe to have Mac and Jeremiah over.

"Hi, Miss Ada!" Mac hurried past me and into the kitchen.

I laughed. "Hey, Jeremiah. Thanks for coming over."

"You bet. I was excited when Mac mentioned it." He flipped his bangs off his forehead and grinned.

The dreaded blush crept up my neck as I looked at him, Mac's conversation about his male anatomy popping into my brain. Dammit. It was so not okay. She couldn't provide those kinds of details if she expected me to keep a straight face when I saw him. I cleared my throat while Jeremiah stared at me, concern flickering across his face.

"Sorry. Sometimes the pain comes out of nowhere." There was no way in hell I would share what I'd been thinking.

"You doing better? Mac told me you fell down some stairs and broke a few ribs. That's a shit day." He rubbed his chin, his big brown eyes filling with compassion.

"Yeah, it was stupid how it all happened." Internally, I heaved a big sigh of relief. I'd been so wrapped up in my own crap, I hadn't even thought about asking Mac what she had told Jeremiah. She did well. I owed her.

"Have a seat," I said, motioning to the couch. "Ada Lynn is cooking, but the kitchen is tiny, so we'll be more comfortable out here. Can I get you some tea or coffee?"

"Coffee sounds great if you have it," he said, sinking his long, lanky frame into the couch.

"Black, milk, sugar?"

"A dash of milk is perfect."

I offered him a genuine smile. Since Mac's mom was in Spokane, Ada Lynn and I were the closest to family she had. Other than Hendrix, but he was touring so much he was rarely around.

Grabbing coffee for us, I joined him in the living room while Mac and Ada Lynn continued to chat in the kitchen. Mac was helping her with dinner, which was good. It allowed me to get a read on Jeremiah. He'd been tough to figure out, but in all fairness, I'd only been around him once at the library, and the night I got drunk. My face burned crimson. Had Alexander told Jeremiah what had happened? Mac knew some of the specifics, but I wasn't sure what kind of guy Alexander was and if they shared intimate details. I did leave Alexander with a massive case of blue balls, which I still felt guilty about, but more than that, I should have never been with him in the first place.

"Alexander said to tell you hi, and he hoped you were feeling better."

Dammit, could he read minds?

"Oh, that's sweet. How is he?" My hands fidgeted in my lap. I wished Mac would hurry up and help me with the conversation, but then again she might make it worse. Never mind, she needed to stay in the kitchen with Ada Lynn.

"Good, studying a lot."

"He seems like a good guy." Uncomfortable would be an understatement for what I felt right now.

"He is. I don't know what happened the night you two were shooting pool, but he seems to care about you."

Uh oh.

"He didn't tell you?" I asked, hopeful he'd kept it between us.

"Nah, he's not a kiss and tell kind of guy. The only reason I know about the kiss is because you two were going at it in the same room Mac and I were." A slow grin eased across his features.

"Mm-hmm," I squeaked out.

"Anyway, I do know he would be happy to see you again."

My brows knitted together. Seriously? Me calling out some other guy's name hadn't deterred him? Maybe he'd chalked the whole night up to grief and alcohol. Regardless, I felt guilty and mortified at my behavior.

"Hey, hey," Mac said, entering the living room interrupting the conversation. "Are you keeping up with your online class okay?"

"Yup. Thank God I've had something to keep me focused. Staying inside and healing has been brutally boring. How are your classes going?"

"Gem-ma," she said slapping her leg while plunking down next to Jeremiah on the couch. "I have not one, but two A's right now. Can ya fucking believe it?"

"Language!" Ada Lynn hollered from the kitchen.

"Sorry Miss Ada," Mac replied, cringing. "I'm not used to worrying about my swearing." She glanced at Jeremiah and me, shrugging innocently.

"That's really awesome, Mac. I'm excited for you. What about your other classes?"

"Cs and one D. But before you say anything, Jeremiah is helping me pull it up so I don't lose my scholarship."

"Scholarship?"

"Yeah, good ol' stepdad helped me figure all of that out."

"Franklin seems like a good guy," I responded, happy he'd been able to help Mac.

"Yup, when he's sober, he's great. Plus I think he's got a lot of guilt about those years, and he's trying to make up for it."

"Jeremiah, what about your parents?" Ada Lynn asked from the kitchen doorway.

"Both of my parents are retired military." He stood, walked toward Ada Lynn, and extended his hand. "Thank you for having me for dinner ma'am."

Ada Lynn grinned like a little kid. "I gotta make sure you're treating my Mac properly."

Jeremiah's face fell for a split second, and then he recovered. I pursed my lips together, stopping a giggle from slipping out.

"Aw, you're super awesome Miss Ada. Thank you," Mac said, beaming at Ada Lynn.

Jeremiah waltzed back over to the couch and settled back in with Mac, draping his arm around her shoulder.

"What branch did they serve in?" Ada Lynn asked.

"My father is a retired marine and Mom was in the army."

"You tell them thank you for serving our country and keeping my loved ones safe."

"Yes ma'am, I will. I wish our military men and women heard that more often. So many of them risk their lives, give up families, and even go to war. Then they aren't taken care of when they return home."

"I couldn't agree with you more. Their families should be taken care of until they die in my opinion. They're the heroes, fighting in the underbelly of hell to take care of us. Well if I had a say, I would change a few things in that area."

"You and me both. My mom's best friend committed suicide after returning from Iraq for the third time. It devastated all of us. It really put some things into perspective, but she should have been better taken care of. When you're fighting on the front lines, you don't come home the same person. From what I've seen, some of them don't know anything else except the men and women in their battalion and fighting to save them. When they get back here, that's all gone, except the nightmares of what they've seen."

Thank God I had the manners to sit there and not let my mouth hang open. Although I appreciated our military, the thought of serving, or of a loved one serving, would be more than I could handle.

"I might like you already, young man. But hold on, I need to pull the cornbread out of the oven."

"I'll help." I hopped up from my chair, the fastest I had in weeks and joined her.

"You like him?" I asked, whispering.

"So far. I'll get a better take on him during dinner."

Ada Lynn and I finished cooking and set the table. I peered into the living room, catching Mac and Jeremiah in a searing lip lock.

I cleared my throat, "Food's ready." Although I would have snuck in a kiss with a special someone, I was glad Ada Lynn hadn't been the one to catch them.

After a quick prayer over the food, everyone dished up. Mac's eyes were as big as saucers as she tasted her first crawfish.

"Oh. My. God. Amazing!" She grinned at Ada Lynn. "You're such a good cook. And these are so much better than crab. Your fingers don't smell like pussy afterward. Shit." Mac slapped a hand over her mouth, cringing.

Unable to stop it, I barked out a laugh. "Are you serious? Crab smells like—that?" I couldn't bring myself to say the word in front of Ada Lynn. Gingerly peeking toward her, she continued to eat like Mac hadn't blurted out something highly inappropriate at the dinner table.

Mac looked at everyone, surveying the situation. When no one jumped on her, she continued, cautiously. "Yeah, it's seriously gross." She screwed up her nose. "After the one time I had it, I swore I would never have a three-way."

My head dropped into my hands. I was afraid to see Ada Lynn's expression.

"Babe, maybe we should change the subject," Jeremiah said, wrapping his arm around her shoulder.

I peeked at him between my fingers. He was rubbing Mac's back gently, soothing away the anxiety I'd seen firsthand after she stuck both feet in her mouth.

"I can honestly say I've never had a conversation like this at the dinner table before." Ada Lynn's voice was stern, but not critical as she dabbed her mouth with a napkin and set her fork on the side of her plate.

"Sorry," Mac said, her leg bouncing so hard the table shook.

"Mac," Jeremiah said softly. "Look at me."

Mac turned toward him.

"It's okay. Take a deep breath and tell me what you're grateful for."

Mac nodded and looked at all of us. "I'm grateful for all of you. You're my family," she said softly.

The moment she said it, the entire mood shifted, the earlier faux pas forgiven. I wasn't sure about anyone else, but Mac was right. We had to focus on what was important, and that was each other, not Mac's slip-ups.

"Are you majoring in Psychology?" Ada Lynn directed her question toward Jeremiah.

"No ma'am, my degree currently is aeronautical engineering, but I've started to reconsider."

My brow shot up, and I gave Mac a look. She smiled, shyly. "I'll tell you later," she mouthed.

"Sometimes a little time away and the opportunity to gain some real-life experience can help you along the path," Ada Lynn suggested.

"I'd agree, Miss Ada," Mac said. "Even the few months I've been here, I've loved learning about another culture and state. I've only ever lived in Washington, so I think it's really helped me."

"I'm glad to hear it," I said, guilt nagging at me. She'd given up so much to be with me, I just wanted her to be happy. So far Jeremiah seemed to be helping, too. He certainly understood how to calm her, just like Hendrix. Chiding myself for thinking about him, I moved on with the conversation.

"Will you stay to finish the year or move back to Spokane in the spring?" Ada Lynn asked.

Mac slowly turned toward Jeremiah, their gaze zeroing in on each other. "I don't know yet," she said in a hushed tone.

What in the world had we just witnessed? My stomach fluttered with unease. Mac said she would update me later, but it wouldn't be soon enough.

"Dessert?" I asked, standing and gathering dinner plates.

25

"No thanks, I'll pass on any sugar," Mac said, smiling. Her cheeks dusted pink with her words.

Ada Lynn reached over and patted her hand. "I have something special for you," she said, winking at her.

Mac lit up like a Christmas tree. "You do?"

"Yes, and if it doesn't work and we have another episode, well, then we won't do it again will we?" Ada Lynn smiled gently. "I have a friend who owns a bakery, and I told her I had a granddaughter who was allergic to sugar. Apparently a lot of people are avoiding sugar these days because she showed me the sugar-free section."

"What?" Mac asked, bouncing in her seat and clapping her hands.

"Yes, ma'am. So Gemma and I got out of the house today and picked you out a few small treats to test."

Confusion clouded Jeremiah's face.

"We had a bit of a hiccup one time after I fed Mac some sugar. She...well, let's just leave it at that. How do you feel about being a guinea pig, Jeremiah?" I asked, grinning.

"No one is worse than my brother. I've seen and heard it all," he laughed, leaning over and giving Mac a quick peck on the forehead. "I'm game."

"Gemma?" Mac asked, her gaze holding mine. "I screwed up with you the worst last time. Are you sure?"

I paused, holding the plates, looking at my best friend. No matter what happened, this girl had an awesome heart, and if a little chocolate brought her happiness. I was there for her.

"Yup. Ada Lynn took me with her, and I picked out a few things for you to try."

"Omigosh! What is it?" Mac asked, bubbling over with excitement.

Ada Lynn's chuckle filled the room.

"I'll be right back, but no peeking," I said and walked to the corner of the kitchen. I returned with three plates of apple pie a la mode.

"Hang on," I said, grinning at Mac. If I didn't hurry, I was worried she'd burst from her giddiness. Ada Lynn and I had stashed her treats in the cabinet, and it only took me a minute to grab them.

"Here," I said, putting a plate down in front of her.

Her mouth gaped open.

"This is a turtle," I said, pointing. "This is a chocolate cupcake, and the other two are obviously taffy."

Mac picked up the turtle, eyeing it suspiciously. Even though she was excited, I figured after the last time she was also nervous.

She took a little nibble. "Wow, tastes like a regular one." She took another bite and chewed slowly. She smiled at Jeremiah and placed the half-eaten chocolate on the plate. "I'll give it a few minutes to see. Don't wait on me though, you guys enjoy. I know how good Ada Lynn's pies are." She flashed us a toothy grin.

"Wow, this is fantastic," Jeremiah said after chewing his first bite.

"Thank you," Ada Lynn replied proudly.

He quickly looked at Mac and frowned. "You would hate it. Really. Your chocolate looks way better." He wiggled his eyebrows at her.

Mac giggled and punched him lightly on the shoulder. He feigned pain and rubbed his arm while we all laughed. It seemed as though Jeremiah really cared about Mac. Plus it was nice getting to know him a little better. I wondered what Ada Lynn was thinking, but I would find out soon.

Mac successfully managed her new treats. We were all thrilled she could enjoy dessert with us and not feel like a freak because she couldn't tolerate sugar. It wasn't her fault, but we couldn't have her running around wild, either.

After dinner, we moved into the living room and played a few hands of five-card stud. Ada Lynn kicked our asses consistently. Jeremiah teased her about marking cards, but she just waved him off, grinning.

It had been a long time since I'd laughed and enjoyed being with friends. And for a little while, I forgot about all the madness around me.

By eight o'clock, Mac said they needed to get back to the dorm. I figured that meant Jeremiah's bed, but I wasn't about to ask.

"I'm going to walk them out to the porch since it's dark," I whispered to Ada Lynn as Mac and Jeremiah took turns using the bathroom before they left.

"No farther." She gave me a stern Ada Lynn look I couldn't argue with.

Mac hugged Ada Lynn goodbye, and Jeremiah shook her hand, thanking her profusely for dinner and the wonderful company.

"We'll see you again, soon. You two stay out of trouble."

"Man, do we have to?" Mac asked and giggled.

"Yes, you do." Ada Lynn replied, her hand on her hip.

I followed Mac and Jeremiah onto the porch and closed the door behind me. Scanning the area through the darkness, I didn't see anything of concern.

"Can you start the car for us, babe?" Mac asked, handing the keys to him.

"Thanks, Gemma. It was fun. Hopefully you'll be back to hang out with us soon," Jeremiah said, smiling.

"Night. Get her home safe, please."

"Isn't he amazing?" Mac asked the moment he was out of earshot.

"He seems like a good guy. I'm glad I got to know him a little better tonight. But what were you going to tell me?"

Mac began bouncing up and down on her toes. Whatever it was, it was significant.

"We're getting married," she blurted.

"What the hell?" I blurted right back at her.

"Shh, we haven't announced it yet."

My stomach lurched. "Mac, it's only been, what...five weeks?"

"Six. But listen. We're going to take our time with a long engagement. Like at least six months."

I was completely speechless. Never in a million years had I seen this coming.

"Besides, he's going to drop out of college and enlist in the army."

"What?" I said, my hands grabbing the side of my head, preventing me from blowing my lid. "You're going to be a military wife? Mac!"

"Gemma, I know it's fast, but you don't understand. He gets me. My ADHD doesn't faze him a bit. He can manage me better than Hendrix can. I'm crazy about him, and he loves me."

"Mac, I don't——. I need some time to absorb all of this. You're so young. Are you sure you're not rebounding from Asher?"

Mac's face flamed red. "Really? You're my best friend, and I thought you'd be happy for me."

"Shit. I'm sorry. But Mac, if he's right for you, what's the rush?"

"Because after six months, the military will ship him off, and I'm either with him, or I'm left behind."

Suddenly, I got it. She would rather jump in with both feet, blindly, than take the chance of losing him altogether. A part of me understood. The other part of me wanted to slap her. Hard.

I wrapped her in a big hug. The only thing I could do right now was show some support. "I guess I'll be busy helping you plan a wedding."

She pulled away and looked up at me. "Really?"

"Really," I said, giving her my best smile.

"Thank you!" She jumped up and down. "Okay, I'll talk to you tomorrow, then. This will be so much fun."

Then, something dawned on me. "Mac," I said, softly. "What about Spokane? What about us going back?"

Her face fell. "Gemma," she said, averting her eyes. "I won't be going back." Her words were tinged with guilt.

My heart dropped like a lead ball into the pit of my stomach.

"I understand," I whispered, tears threatening my eyes.

"I'm sorry." Her shoulders slumped forward with her confession.

"Nothing to be sorry for. You uprooted your entire life to be near me. If you're happy and he's good to you, then I'm on board. I'll figure it out. I did it once, and I'll do it again." Nothing in me genuinely felt that way, though.

Mac and I hugged goodbye, and I slipped back inside, locking the door behind me.

Stunned, I looked at Ada Lynn. "What did you think?" I asked, my voice cracking with concern for Mac.

"I think we're off to a good start, but he sure was coy about his plans for the future. I didn't miss the avoidance which concerned me a bit, but I can't put my finger on it quite yet."

"They're getting married," I sputtered. I cringed. I hadn't meant to tell her like this, but the heaviness on my shoulders was more than I could take right now.

Ada Lynn's eyes narrowed in thought, then her expression grew serious. The ticking of the kitchen clock could be heard in our silence.

"You know what you have to do," she said quietly.

I nodded.

Although it was the right thing to do, I was kicking and screaming the entire way. Mac was going to hate me, and I couldn't lose the only friend I had who was my age.

Ada Lynn had gone to bed, but I couldn't sleep. Mac's news

weighed too heavily on me. Her need to fit in and be loved was about to cause her to make a major mistake. But was it my responsibility to do what I could to stop it, or should I shut up and support her? After I had lived with Mac and learned more about ADHD, I knew making impulsive decisions without understanding the consequences was something she did often. Unfortunately, it meant she had to learn the hard way, and I didn't want her to this time. Jeremiah could be stationed in Iraq, and she'd be a million miles away from him. I was a selfish brat. No way could I stand the thought of her dealing with that. Honestly, it was more than that. As I'd recently found out myself, people could be different behind closed doors. Combat and serving in the military changed people. What if her knight in shining armor turned into a nightmare and she was so far away I wouldn't know? A chill shot through me.

Finding a comfortable position on the bed, I reached for my phone, my pulse racing. It was after one in the morning. A few taps on the screen later, the phone rang in my ear.

"Gem?"

"I woke you," I said softly. "I'm sorry."

"No, it's fine. Are you alright? Do you need me to come back?"

I could hear him rustling around, and imagined him tossing off his covers, sitting on the side of his bed. His hair would be beautifully messy and his blue eyes sleepy. Swallowing, I attempted to stay focused on why I called instead of what he looked like without a shirt and in his boxer briefs.

"It's not me. I'm not calling for me, Hendrix."

"I don't understand."

"It's Mac."

Silence followed my statement.

"I'm awake now. What's going on?" he asked, his tone sounding brotherly and protective.

"I—I'm worried about her. I shouldn't be calling you. This is a bad idea. I should let you go."

"Gemma, don't hang up. If you called me, it's big. Please. What's going on?"

"She's getting married," I whispered.

A loud clatter filled the phone and then Hendrix swore a blue streak.

"Are you still there? I dropped the phone," he said.

"Yeah. She can't under any circumstances know I told you. She's my best friend, and if you're able to do anything, she can't know I instigated it."

"I know. Shit. How did this happen?"

I gave him the quick and dirty version of everything I knew.

"I can cancel the tour."

"No!" I said, sitting straight up in bed, my side punishing me with the quick motion. "There's nothing here for you to come back for."

I could hear his breathing through the phone. I felt like shit for saying it, but he couldn't stay here.

"You're there, Mac is there, Ada Lynn is there. I have plenty to come back for," he snapped.

I cringed, I'd not only woken him up, but I'd just reminded him we weren't back together.

"Listen, I know you're back and forth between touring and Louisiana, but—" I wasn't sure I could say it. But then the memory of Dad's angry face and kick to my ribs reminded me it was for his own good. For mine, too. "Get Mac, and you both get the hell out of here," I said. "Don't ever look over your shoulder. Just keep going."

With that, I ended the call. I folded in on myself. Hendrix deserved someone better, he deserved someone who didn't have a fucked-up past. He sure as hell didn't deserve a sick, twisted fucker looming over him. The best gift I could give Mac and Hendrix was to get them out of here and let them live their lives.

26

*D*epression had become my closest friend. No matter what I did, she refused to leave, wrapping me up in her cold arms.

Even though I'd tried to recover from Mac's news about the marriage, she'd pulled away from me. This wasn't the first time in my life a friend had practically disappeared when I'd expressed my concern over a guy. She made up every excuse possible not to hang out over the next several weeks. No matter what I did, she continued to keep me at arm's length.

Ada Lynn insisted I go with her to check on Hendrix's house, but I refused. I'd made it clear in the last phone call he needed to leave. Typically, he didn't take no for an answer, but I hadn't heard anything from him. Secretly, I hoped the tour was going so well he would forget all about me. But I also knew I was full of shit, merely attempting to make myself feel better.

Some days, I spent a lot of time at Ada Lynn's living room window, staring across the street. Maybe it was self-torture. Today, when I parted the curtain and looked, I jumped. His Lexus was parked in his driveway. If he was here, I suspected he would stop by and check on Ada Lynn. He always did.

Like an idiot, I hurried into my bedroom, grabbed fresh clothes, and hurried to the shower. He couldn't see me looking like crap.

Forty-five minutes later, I was dressed, makeup on, and my wavy red hair straightened. Maybe I'd cook and invite him for dinner. No, I couldn't. I'd told him to leave. Shit. Maybe I was bipolar. I wanted him one moment and not the next, but that wasn't actually true. I wanted a better life for him. I wanted him to have the career of his dreams and someone who could emotionally be there for him. It wasn't me. My shoulders dropped, the depression beckoning me to wallow in it a while longer.

The anger wasn't far behind, and I stomped into my bedroom, grabbing my phone and flopping onto my bed.

I tapped the screen and listened to the phone ring. I'd had enough. It was time I put my foot down.

"Knock it off," I said.

"What?" Mac asked, feigning astonishment.

"You're full of shit, Mackenzie Worthington. Since the moment I freaked out on you about the wedding, you've brushed me off. You rarely call, we haven't hung out since that night, and you're lying about being too busy to see me."

Silence filled the line. "You don't have anything to say? I find that incredibly hard to believe."

"That was mean," Mac snapped.

"Talk to me, Mac. We're best friends...or we were," my voice trailed off.

"Are," she replied, softly. "I...I just didn't know how to deal with your disapproval. I have three people I love more than anything in this world, and one of them doesn't approve of my decision. It tore me in two."

I flopped back in my bed. "Then stop. Stop being torn in two. Let me get to know him better, don't set a date yet. Let me in, Mac. You used to always give me a swift kick in the ass when I shut you out, now I'm returning the favor."

"You're the worst. You still haven't told me what happened with your ribs." Her words stung.

"I'm keeping you safe, Mac. You have to trust me."

"I do, but you're doing the same thing to me, shutting me out."

"Mac, it's different. Please, don't push it." My tone bordered on whining, but I had to get her to back off. If she knew, she would be pounding on my father's door. Could. Not. Happen.

"I'll make you a deal. I'll stop pushing you away, we can make plans with Jeremiah at the library, and you can continue to get to know him. I do ask you to support me in my decision. If it's the wrong one, I'll figure it out."

"Okay. I do want to get to know Jeremiah more, Mac. It has nothing to do with it. I just don't want you to rush in and find yourself in a situation you don't know how to get out of."

"I appreciate it, but you'll see."

"Are we good? The last few weeks have totally screwed with me. I haven't even left the house."

"What? I'm coming to get you tomorrow, then. We can grab a burger."

"Bring Jeremiah, too."

"You sure?"

"Absolutely."

"Alright. I will."

"Can I ask you something?" I chewed my lip, debating on if I should ask or not.

"Sure."

"Hendrix is back, and he normally comes over to check on Ada Lynn. He hasn't yet, and I—I..."

"Gemma, he's not going to. I've updated him on how you and Ada Lynn are doing. I also told him to stay away from you."

I pushed myself into a sitting position, anger coursing through me.

"What?"

"Hear me out. Honestly, I'm worried about both of you. I know what happened with Alexander and there's no way you can deny you're in love with my brother. I mean like, crazy, mad, intense love. The kind that can set you free or destroy you."

I sucked in a sharp breath.

"And he's the same with you. That hasn't changed, but something has, and I'm honestly worried that if Hendrix finds out what happened...who hurt you...I don't think I could stop him from going after someone. He's finally getting his career off the ground, I can't let him do anything stupid. He deserves to be happy." She stopped long enough to take a breath. "We have both speculated until we're blue in the face, but Hendrix won't act until he has proof. So whatever you're protecting him from? I've decided you're trying to do the right thing, so I supported you. I told him you needed time and to leave you alone."

A sob ripped from my chest. She wasn't trying to be mean; she was backing me up. Mac remained silent while I cried.

"Thank you," I said, wiping my stuffy nose on the sleeve of my shirt.

"You're welcome, but I hope someday you'll tell us. I hope someday, Gemma, you realize you're what's best for Hendrix, and stop thinking you're not giving him what he wants in life. The only thing he really wants is you. The music is keeping him busy for now, but stop wallowing in self-doubt already. You're exactly what he wants and needs. I've never seen him happier than when you two were together in Spokane."

I sat quietly, absorbing what she said. If she knew the truth about my dad and what he'd done...she and Hendrix might think differently.

"Listen, I've got to go, but I'll text you what time I'll pick you up tomorrow. We'll have a few minutes of just girl time before we meet Jeremiah. I've missed it."

"Me too. And Mac?"

"Yeah?"

"Hendrix asked about Alexander." My words cracked with emotion.

"He asked me, too. I told him it was one of Jeremiah's friends, and he was interested in you, but there was nothing to it."

"How did he take it?"

"He was upset. He can always tell when I'm holding something back. Besides, you two aren't together, and it's none of his business if you called out his name when Alexander kissed you. Shit. Sorry."

"Mac!" Horrified, I shut my eyes, trying to remove the visual of Alexander.

"Well, I didn't say any of that to Hendrix at least."

"He'd be furious at me," I said.

"He would get over it. He's not a saint. Hendrix has had a few one-nighters in the past himself."

With his good looks and sexy voice, the girls were all over him. He probably had an offer to get sucked off multiple times a night while on tour.

I cringed, not even wanting to entertain the idea of him with another girl.

"Spare me the details, please."

"Well it was never with Andrea, that's for damned sure."

I grinned. "Thanks, Mac. Love ya."

"You too, bestie. See ya tomorrow."

Mac's words stayed with me throughout the next day. She'd been right, too. Hendrix hadn't stopped by. I peered out the curtain; his car was still parked in the driveway.

"Are you going to go over there or just spend all damned day at the window pining over him?" Ada Lynn asked from her favorite recliner.

"No. I'm not. He's giving me some space, and I need to continue to stay off Dad's radar. So far it's worked, and it's not been a problem."

"I guess I can understand, but I don't like it. However, I'm glad you're getting out with Mac tonight. In fact, we should have her and Jeremiah back over. And if you see anything suspicious about that boy, just know that I'm not beyond snooping around his business."

"What do you mean?"

"I've got friends in this town." She smiled mischievously. "Say the word, and I'll have a full background check on him."

"Are you serious?" I asked, walking toward her, plopping on the couch and seriously considering her offer.

"I'd prefer not to unless we think he's up to some shenanigans. It's an option, though."

"I like the way you think," I said, raising my eyebrow and smiling at her.

My phone buzzed.

"Mac's here. Call me if you need me and I'll be right home."

"I'm fine my blue-eyed girl. You go have some fun. You need it."

I smiled, grabbed my purse, and then stepped out on the porch.

Every time the door closed behind me, I wondered if it might be the last time I saw her. I stopped in my tracks, opened the door, and poked my head back in.

"I love you, Ada Lynn."

She smiled, her eyes glistening, "Love you too, girl."

Pulling the door closed, I glanced over at my house. The curtains remained closed, and there were no signs of life. I suspected he spent the majority of his time drunk or passed out. As long as he left me alone, I didn't give a rat's ass.

Mac opened the passenger car door and waved me forward. It reminded me of the first day I met her in Spokane. She'd honked the car horn right behind me, scaring me shitless. A twinge of longing tugged at me. We'd be playing in the snow right now if things hadn't taken a sharp turn, but life apparently had other plans.

I jumped in and closed the door behind me, a crazy thought hitting me out of nowhere.

"Shit. Are you pregnant?" I asked, my eyes wide. Why hadn't I considered the option before now?

"Well hello to you, too. And *hell* no. I'm on the pill and he uses a condom. After Asher knocked me up, I'm so terrified it might happen again, I actually asked Jeremiah to double wrap."

I barked out a laugh as she pulled out of the driveway. "Did you really?"

"This is a no baby zone." She motioned to her lower abdomen.

"No kidding. I've done that before, too. Not interested."

"Like, never?" she asked, glancing at me quickly as she drove.

"I don't know. After everything with Jordan, I've never wanted kids."

"I get it. I just wonder if you'll change your mind down the road."

I shrugged. Deep down, I doubted it, but I didn't want to say anything to her right now.

"You?"

"Yup, I want three."

My brows shot up. "And Jeremiah?"

"He wants three, a dog, and a cat." She laughed.

"While he's in the military?" I didn't even try to hide the concern in my tone.

Mac arched a brow at me, warning me to tread lightly. We'd just made up, I didn't want to say the wrong thing and blow it again. It was never my intention, I just wanted to lovingly nudge her and help her think things all the way through.

"Three's a good number." I figured if I agreed, we wouldn't go down a bad road. "How's Hendrix?" I asked softly.

"Do you really want to know? Like honestly, or do you want me to blow sunshine up your ass?"

I pondered before I answered. "Honestly."

"He's broken."

My heart sank. It's not what I wanted for him. "Because?" I really couldn't jump to conclusions this time, thinking of the girl on his front porch.

"You, you, you," Mac said, smacking the palm of her hand against the steering wheel. "I can't get more honest than that. And let me tell you what else. I'm stuck on the sidelines, unable to do a damned thing to make either of you happy. You, Gemma, best bestie ever, are the only one who has the power to change this and stop the craziness that's ruining both of you."

My throat tightened, cutting off anything I'd wanted to say in response. I stared out the passenger window, feeling like shit.

"Fix it," Mac demanded.

"If it were only that simple," I replied.

"If you talk to him, it can be that simple. And dammit, I've always wanted a sister-in-law, so get to movin'."

I laughed, then my mood grew serious again. "It was never supposed to have happened like this." I looked at her while she pulled into a parking spot at Red Robin. She slipped the car into park and shut it off, turning to look at me.

"I know. We should all be together in Spokane. Happy. But dammit if Andrea didn't kick off an insane chain of events."

"And Mom." I blinked the tears away, a hollowness seeping deep inside me.

"I know," she said softly. "But tonight, let's just forget all that and enjoy the good company and food. I'm just glad we're out together. I'll drive you home, so try a fun drink or something."

"You do know I'm only nineteen, right?"

"You look twenty-one. Plus I've been here a few times with the guys, and I've never been carded."

I chewed the inside of my cheek, considering it. I wouldn't be around any guys, so I should be able to stay out of trouble and keep my legs closed. Maybe I would have a few, then actually sleep for a change. The pain had lessened in my ribs, but at night it seemed like a dull ache kept me awake more often than I liked.

"I think I will."

We walked inside, and the hostess showed us to the booth where Jeremiah was waiting for us. To my relief, Alexander was nowhere to be seen.

"Hey," I said, giving Jeremiah a quick hug. If he was going to be my brother-in-law, I might as well start embracing it. Not only that, Mac's face lit up the moment I made an effort.

"Are your ribs all better?"

"Much," I said, sliding in the opposite side of the booth from them.

A tall brunette interrupted us as she placed waters on the table. Smiling, she asked for our drink order. Mac stuck with diet soda, and

I ordered a Mai Tai. Jeremiah also stuck with soda. At least they were responsible when driving.

We chatted about school, music, and movies. The more I was around Jeremiah, the more I liked him. I just couldn't stop the growing concern about his military plans and the wedding. Although I'd played the good sport and brought it up, they didn't talk about it much. They had agreed to wait until after finals to really plan the ceremony.

Inside, I was having a full-on freak out, but I couldn't say anything. Mac was twenty, he was twenty-two. Personally, I thought it was too young, but if things had gone differently between Hendrix and me, I might have been wearing an engagement ring soon, too.

Deciding I was acting judgy out of my own fear, I kicked the concerns to the curb and enjoyed my meal and time out of the house.

Three Mai Tai's and several hours later it was time to leave.

"Thank goodness it's after ten. Ada Lynn will be asleep. I don't need a verbal lashing for being irresponsible," I said, giggling on the way to Mac's car.

"I get it, but seriously, I'm amazed you haven't gone on drunken sexcapades. You've had all this shit come at you, and most people would flip out for a while before they came back to their senses. You've done well. A few drinks with friends on occasion is no big deal, don't even worry about it. Ada Lynn would probably think it was funny unless you got into trouble."

"Mm, yeah. Not sure I want to test those waters. I would feel like crap if I gave her a heart attack."

Mac started the car and made sure I was buckled in before she pulled out of the parking lot. "Her heart attack wasn't your fault, ya know."

My head lolled to the side, and I squinted, focusing really hard on her. "I know, but I want her to stay around a lot longer. She's all I've got left other than you. And she knows most of my secrets." I clamped my mouth shut, realizing I'd almost slipped.

"Dammit."

"What's wrong?" I asked, my eyebrows shooting upward.

"Nothing. I just thought you might spill some of those secrets," Mac said.

"You're ornery as hell, Mac. But I wouldn't have it any other way. Ya know what?"

"Hmm?"

"My ribs don't hurt."

"Ya think?" Mac flashed me a toothy grin. "Nothing hurts when you're drunk."

"Not drunk," I said, holding up my first finger for emphasis. "Comfortably tipsy."

"Drink lots of water tonight and eat some bread. It should help stave off a hangover. Ada Lynn would definitely know if you were hungover tomorrow."

I groaned.

"When are you going to tell me the truth, Gemma?" Mac said, quietly.

"Mac, Mac, Mac." I winked and pointed at her. "I can't tell you. I love you too much to involve you. You're going to have to accept that for now. End. Of. Discussion," I said in a sing-song voice.

Mac's expression grew grim, but she didn't push me.

She pulled into the driveway, and I peered through the darkness, scoping the area for any danger. A single light shone from Ada Lynn's living room. I knew for sure she had gone on to bed. The rare times I did leave and stayed out late, she left the light on for me.

"Thanks," I said, hugging Mac. "I'm so glad we're okay. Don't do that again," I said, frowning at her.

"I won't. Are you going to be okay getting up the stairs?"

"Yup, but if you don't mind, just watch me until I'm inside the house?"

"Always."

The fresh night air felt good on my clammy skin. I closed her car door softly, not wanting to gain unwanted attention from the neighbors or from my father. Holding onto the railing, I made it up the steps with no problem. I gave her a small wave and then disappeared inside the house. I leaned against the door, scanning the living room for any signs of Ada Lynn. Creeping down the hall, I checked her bedroom door. It was closed, signaling she was inside sleeping.

I resumed my perch at the living room window and watched Mac's taillights fade into the distance. Recalling her advice, I walked to the kitchen, downed a large glass of water, and stuffed my face with a piece of Wonder Bread. It didn't take long before I no longer felt completely drunk, just halfway.

After the situation with Alexander, not to mention having a drunk for a father, I figured I wouldn't touch alcohol again. My body was relaxed, and my mind slowed down to a dull roar. But the side effect was killing me.

I slipped into the bathroom, checked my makeup, and ran the brush through my hair.

My heart pounded in my chest while I grabbed my phone, checked for my house key, and snuck out the front door.

27

I'd officially gone off the deep end, lost my shit, and given in to insanity.

My words stuck in my throat as the door opened. Then, the reminder of why I was here broke through the alcohol fog.

"Hey," I said, heat climbing up my neck and across my cheeks.

"Gemma?" Hendrix asked. "What are you doing here?"

"Can I come in?"

He opened the door for me, no questions asked.

I stepped inside, inhaling sharply. My attention traveled down his naked chest, his rippled abs, and lingered on his sweatpants.

"Are you busy?" I asked, eyeing his living room behind him. A Dallas Cowboys blanket was wadded up in the corner of his couch. I suspected he'd been watching TV.

"No, I was just working on some music. Are you okay?" he asked, his brows knitting together.

"Yeah. No. I don't know actually," I said, tilting my head and wondering if I'd finally snapped.

"Come on, I'll get us something to drink."

He turned and took a step away from me, and before I realized it, my arm shot out, pulling on his. He whirled around, face to face.

My fingers danced lightly across his chest and trailed slowly down his stomach. His breath hitched, his muscles tightening beneath my touch.

"Gemma?" he asked confusion in his tone.

"I need you." I peered up at him through my eyelashes. My fingers slipped beneath the waistband of his sweats, meeting the tip of his already hard cock.

He gently grabbed my shoulders. "Gemma, look at me. Are you drunk?"

I glanced up, my lower lip forming a pout.

"Shit, don't do that," he growled.

My fingers touched his sensitive head. "I'm not drunk, maybe a little tipsy, but it's beside the point." I stood on my tiptoes, my mouth next to his ear. "I need you inside me. It's been so damned long."

"Jesus," he growled, releasing my arms. "You're not drunk? Like you realize you're in my house with your hand wrapped around my dick?"

I grinned. "Not for long." In one swift motion, I dropped to my knees, pulling his sweats and boxer briefs down with me. His erection throbbed as I wrapped my fingers around it, my tongue licking up his shaft.

"Dammit."

"Do you want me to stop?" I flicked my tongue across his slit.

"No, but if you've been drinking..."

I wrapped my lips around him, slowly taking every inch of him inside my mouth.

"Tell me to stop, and I'll go back home," I said, looking up at him.

His mouth opened, but no words came out.

My mouth slicked him up, and I gripped his cock in my hand and slid it up and down the length of him. I sucked and licked him like he was the best lollipop I'd ever tasted. He was. My panties were soaked. I needed him inside me, but I wanted to suck him off first. I wasn't going anywhere soon, and I knew for a fact he could recover quickly.

My nails dug into his ass cheeks while I stroked him, slowly at first, and then I picked up speed. His hips kept my pace, and his hands threaded through my hair. I'd missed him so damned bad it hurt. My heart and my body ached for him. But tonight, all bets were off. I needed him, I needed to forget all the darkness that was in my life. For one night, I needed him to be my light again.

"I'm going to come." He pulled gently on my hair, but I ignored him, sucking harder. I'd never swallowed before, but if it made him happy, I wanted to try it.

He groaned, his body tensing as he released in my mouth. The warm fluid almost gagged me as it hit the back of my throat, then I swallowed the bitterness. A salty taste lingered in my mouth afterward.

With one last suck, he popped free from my mouth. I stood, wiping the corners of my lips. "Don't get too comfortable," I said. "I'm not finished with you yet."

"Where did all this come from?" he asked, bewildered. I'd never given him a blow job like that before, and I'd certainly never talked to him like this.

"Are you complaining?"

"Hell no, but—"

I held up my hand and stopped him from saying anything else. If he was on board, no other words were necessary, and he obviously hadn't stopped me yet. I pulled off my shirt, tossing it on his living room floor. Next, I slipped out of my jeans.

"Do you want to go to the bedroom?" he asked, his eyes dark with need.

My focus dropped, noticing he was already getting hard again. I stepped toward him, my nails raking down his chest, my gaze holding his.

"No. I want you to fuck me all night long, Hendrix. I want you to bend me over your kitchen counter and take me from behind. I want you on top of your dining room table, and again on your couch. *Then*, you can take me to your bed."

"Holy shit," he mumbled, running both hands over his hair.

"Let's go."

He stepped out of his sweats, leaving them on the living room floor. I sauntered into the kitchen and hopped up on the counter. I was tired of playing by the rules all the time, screw it. I needed some fun, and if the alcohol helped me drop the walls and relax, it was fine with me.

I spread my legs for him, his focus traveling down, slowly. "Do you miss me?" I asked softly, tracing a finger along the thin fabric of my panties.

"You know I do. You're torturing me, Gem." His voice was raspy, his dick nice and hard again.

I slowly pulled the material to the side, exposing my core to him. He growled, his tongue darting across his lips. He moved toward me, kissing the inside of my thigh while my fingers massaged my sensitive flesh. His hand snapped up, grabbed my wrist, and pinned it to the counter. I whimpered as his warm mouth moved up my thigh. My hips tilted upward, needing him.

In one move, Hendrix ripped my G-string off and tossed it to the floor. I gasped while his tongue licked my wet slit, and his thumb massaged my clit. I wasn't going to last long. Thank God for multiple orgasms.

I wrapped my legs around his shoulders, watching him as he looked up at me with those piercing blue eyes that set my world on fire.

His attention never left me while he slid a finger inside me.

I moaned, my head tilting up to the ceiling.

"Oh yeah," he said. "Finally. I've missed you so damned much."

"Stop talking," I gasped. His mouth returned to me, and he slipped another finger inside. He pumped my wet core, licking and teasing me. No one could make me feel so amazing.

My back arched off the counter, as I watched him. My body tingled. I was close. So. Damned. Close.

"Hendrix," I whimpered. Heat spread through my body, pulsing with a desperate need for release.

"Oh God," I said breathlessly, grabbing his long hair. Before I knew it, his mouth left me.

"What?" I squeaked, my core throbbing.

"Get down and turn around. You want me? You got me," he said, his voice gruff.

My feet touched the cool tile floor, and I did as he said. His hand traced gently up my back while he bent me forward, my chest on the counter.

In one swift movement, he slid inside.

I cried out, his fullness deep inside me. It had been a long time, and I needed a minute to adjust to him.

He leaned over, his chest against my back.

"Is this what you want, Gemma?" he asked, moving my hair off my neck, his mouth close to my ear.

Even though I'd said I wanted him to fuck me, he hadn't forgotten I needed to know who I was with. That it was his hands on me, his lips, not my attacker's.

"Yes." I moaned while he moved in and out of me.

"I've missed you so much," he whispered.

I remained quiet, focusing on his deep thrusts. The shock of him inside me had given way to pure, fiery desire. I grabbed ahold of the countertop and pushed back into him, spreading my legs to accommodate him better.

Taking my cue, he picked up the pace, straightened up, and placed his hands on my hips.

He guided me back and forth, and for a minute I let him take control. Biting my lip, I shoved my ass against him, releasing a cry of pain that was quickly replaced by a burning hot need.

"Harder," I said, looking over my shoulder at him. "Fuck me harder, Hendrix."

He slipped his hands between my legs, caressing me as he pumped in and out. The sound of my slickness and his hips hitting my ass turning me on even more. I'd never been so bold before. Although Hendrix suspected it was the alcohol, he had no idea how much it had instigated our night.

A slight pinch to my clit sent me spiraling.

"Oh my God," I gasped. "Hendrix!"

He moaned, twirling my nub between his fingers as he slammed inside me. I screamed, my body shuddering in uncontrollable orgasm. I'd never felt like this before. Hendrix's fingers dug into my hips, and he groaned, his body tensing while he released deep inside me.

He remained still, his hands on the counter next to me, panting. My body ached but in a good way. For the first time in months, I felt alive. He pulled out of me and walked away, leaving me half naked in his kitchen.

I straightened and used the time to catch my breath.

"Bend over," he said, returning.

I did as he said, spreading my legs. A warm washcloth gently cleaned my sensitive area. Tears pricked my eyes at his gentleness. I shut them quickly, refusing to let him in.

I stood and turned toward him. "I'll give you a few minutes to recover before we go again."

His mouth dropped open. "This is you on alcohol?" he asked, rubbing his jawline, analyzing the situation.

"You have a problem with it?" I asked, walking away from him, allowing him a full view of my ass as I made my way to the dining room, then hopped up on the table. Reaching behind me, I flicked open the clasp on my bra and tossed it on the floor. I gave the girls a good shake.

Hendrix's brows shot upward. "I've never seen you like this."

"Things have changed, haven't they?"

He looked away, worry flickering across his beautiful face. I shoved the emotions aside.

"Have you changed, Gemma?" He glanced at me, and then away again. "Have you been with other guys?"

"No. Just you." For a moment, my walls dropped, allowing him to touch my heart again.

He sighed in relief.

"Okay. This time, I pick the position," he said.

My focus traveled down his stomach, and I grinned slowly. He was ready again, and so was I.

"Get on all fours and turn around." I did as he said. His hands grabbed my breasts from behind, twirling my nipples between his thumb and middle fingers. He gave a gentle pinch, then bent down and bit my ass cheek. I gasped. Even though he didn't do it to hurt me, the shock factor worked.

His fingers spread me apart. His tongue licked up my slit, slowly, forcing a long moan out of me. He'd always been so gentle, but I loved this side of him. Maybe we'd moved past it all, and the alcohol had lowered my inhibitions, my fear. My past.

I pushed against his mouth, his tongue flicking across my wet core. I rocked with him; the table creaking beneath my weight. Gasping, he continued to show me how much he'd missed me. And I let him.

He gently flipped me over on my back, his hands cupping my breasts. I grabbed his cock and rubbed it against my throbbing clit. He released a soft moan as I continued. Running it over my core, I gasped. Seeing how turned on he was, I was about to get off again. I moved his dick over my swollen, sensitive folds, moaning. Realizing how close I was, he took my hand and removed it from him.

"Not yet."

My bottom lip stuck out in a pout. He slid inside me, slow and deep. Then, in one swift motion, he tugged on my arms, bringing my upper body flush against his chest, and pulled my hair, tilting my chin up. His lips brushed mine, his tongue darting out against my bottom lip. My mouth parted, welcoming him. His hands cupped the sides of my head, his kiss growing more urgent.

His fingers trailed down my sides, adjusting my hips closer to the edge of the dining table. His mouth dropped to my breast, pulling my nipple gently between his teeth. My back arched into him, and my legs wrapped around his waist even tighter.

"Baby," I said. I cringed at my slip up. This was just sex. There was no way it could be anything more.

His intense gaze traveled up to mine, searching and breaking through my walls again. I closed my eyes, refusing to let him in. His mouth came down on mine in a gentle kiss, his hips moving in a slow circular motion. I dug my nails into his back, raking them down to his ass.

His hand squeezed my breast, and his mouth broke free from mine.

"I love you," he whispered, thrusting deep inside me. A cry escaped me, his words filling me as much as his body.

This couldn't happen. What had I been thinking? Dammit. No. I shut my eyes against the hot tears, slipping down my cheek. I leaned against his shoulder, his pace quickening, leaving me breathless.

"I'm—I'm," I panted, the tears flowing faster. My fingers threaded through a handful of his hair and my core clenched around him. We released together, and at that moment he reached inside my heart, and my entire world split apart. All of the anger, pain, and loneliness I'd shoved down erupted in one messy catastrophic ball of emotions. I whimpered as he forced me to look at him. And then my shoulders shook with my sobs.

"Baby, look at me. It's okay. I'm here." He pulled out of me slowly, picked me off the table, and carried me to his bed.

No matter how hard I tried, I couldn't stop crying. Hendrix tucked me in and settled in the bed next to me. He pulled me against him, kissing the tip of my nose. "I've got you. I'm here." His hand ran up and down my back, soothing the pain away while my tears landed on his chest.

Eventually they slowed, and I stayed curled up next to him and fell asleep.

28

My skull pounded like a son of a bitch the next morning. Forcing my eyes open, I groaned and rubbed my forehead.

"I suspect you have a hangover?" Hendrix said, placing a glass of water and some Advil on the nightstand.

"Thanks," I said, my hair hanging down and hiding my shame. I'd come over here and literally attacked him last night.

"Do you feel sick or anything?"

I shook my head no and grimaced.

"Good. I hoped you wouldn't, but I wasn't sure. I'd never seen you like that before."

I glanced up at him; he stood fully dressed with his hands shoved deep inside his pockets.

"I know you're dealing with a lot. When you lose a parent—you don't really ever get over it. Plus whatever happened with your ribs and shit." He paused and rubbed his chin. "I've tried to give you some space to process Andrea's confession. And even though it really scared you, I think somewhere inside, you knew she was lying. I totally got it, Gem." He paused, looking away for a moment. "You're such a beautiful, insanely talented, strong woman. You know I love you, but I need to know what last night was." He rocked back and forth on his heels, his anxiety apparent.

I got out of bed and walked out of the bedroom. Silently gathering my clothes all over the house, I began to dress. He followed me, but still gave me some space. I kept my back to him while I tugged my jeans over my hips. I was about to do the walk of shame right out of his front door. I'd royally messed things up last night, torturing us both after I'd told him to leave. I couldn't take him to hell with me. He wasn't safe here with my dad. I wasn't safe here, but I couldn't stand to leave Ada Lynn. There was only one way to fix it.

I turned toward him slowly, tucking a stray hair behind my ear. My gaze traveled up to his while a million emotions swirled inside me at once. I squared my shoulders. I hoped the next words out of my mouth would save him.

"It was a one-night stand, Hendrix. Nothing more."

His jaw tensed, his pulse throbbing in his neck. I'd pushed him too far. He was about to break.

He stared at the floor, and then looked at me, his expression full of anger and pain.

"This is it. Today, Gemma. When you go back to Ada Lynn's, I need you to think about it. Do you want to be with me or not? If not, then at four o'clock today I'm on my way to the airport. I've been offered a tour in Europe. If you show up here by then and tell me you love me, and that we can be together, I'll tour in the United States instead. If not, I'm going. There won't be any more chances. This, whatever is going on," he motioned between us, "is fucking gutting me. You need to give me an answer one way or another for good."

I averted my gaze and chewed on my thumbnail. Europe? Oh, my God. How could he say no to touring Europe? At the same time, how could he leave me? I nodded, and without another word, I slipped out the front door and walked back to Ada Lynn's.

"You could have left me a note if you weren't going to be home last night," Ada Lynn said, meeting me at the front door.

"I'm so sorry. It won't happen again." My cheeks warmed.

"I was about to go beat on your father's door to see if you were there. You scared the shit out of me. What got into you? Your hair is a mess—" She stopped mid-sentence, realization dawning on her. She knew there were only a few places I could have been. "Oh. You were with Hendrix last night?"

I raised my hand, halting any further conversation about him.

"I'm so so sorry. I will never do that to you again. For now, I need some coffee and a shower."

She frowned, but nodded, letting me go.

The hot water did little to soothe the ache inside me. My body was sore from all the sex, but he'd given me an ultimatum. I had only hours to figure out my life. Honestly, my decision had little to do with his career. It was either Europe or the United States. He had a tour either way.

My hands rested against the shower wall. I was numb. After the last round of sex, everything had erupted inside me. Mom, Dad, Hendrix, Ada Lynn, Mac. It all intertwined into one huge ass ball of fucked up mess. I wasn't sure what string to pull on to unravel it to give my heart a break. To heal.

Finally, I stepped out of the shower, my head hating me a little less. My stomach growled, but I wasn't interested in food. I dressed and walked to my bedroom. It was strange living here, but I would probably be dead by now if it hadn't been for Ada Lynn.

I collapsed onto my bed, sleep claiming me quickly.

M y eyes shot open, and I sat up, gasping. Sweat beaded across my forehead as my pulse double-timed. Finally, I realized I was at Ada Lynn's. Dammit, what time was it? I grabbed my phone. It was three fifty-four. I got out of bed, slipped on my tennis shoes, and ran into the living room.

"I'll be right back," I said to Ada Lynn, as I flew past her and out the front door. I willed my feet to move faster, flying across the street and up Hendrix's porch steps. I knocked, a little breathless from my sprint.

The door flung open. He looked like hell, and for the first time since I'd met him, his shirt was wrinkled. Half-moon shadows had settled beneath his eyes, too.

"Hey," he said, rolling out his suitcase on the porch. He locked the door behind him and turned to look at me. His guard was up. I'd toyed with his emotions, constantly pushing him away. But it had been to protect him, to keep him safe.

"I—Thank you for taking care of me last night," I said, chewing my lip.

He nodded, searching for any indication of what might come out of my mouth next.

"I, um...I came to tell you goodbye, Hendrix." My words caught in my throat. He glanced up, his jaw tightening, then his eyes locked on mine.

"I'd hoped it was going to be a different answer. I'd give up everything for you, Gemma. I love you that much."

An ache spread through me. He had no idea how hard this was, how I wanted the opposite of what I'd just said. "I would never ask you to do that for me, though. Never." Tears clouded my vision. "Go live your life. Let me go," I whispered, my heart jumping into my throat.

His eyes glistened as I leaned in and kissed him softly on the cheek.

"Take care," he said, his fingers tracing down my face.

A flurry of relief, distress, and numerous other emotions I didn't know how to process stirred inside me. At least we'd had one last night together. Even if I was drunk, I knew I'd wanted to be with him. I'd just lied to myself about it.

I stood on his porch as he lifted his suitcase and descended the stairs. He never looked back as he reached the car and got in. As the Lexus purred to life, I couldn't breathe. This was it. There would be no more back and forth.

He backed out of the driveway and drove down the street. I released the breath I'd been holding. I'd done it. I'd set him free. I'd saved him from my father, and all of the secrets I carried with me.

My feet descended the steps as I watched his car grow farther and farther away. With every second that passed, he took my heart with him, shattering it into a million pieces.

"Shit," I muttered, then my feet propelled me out of his yard and onto the street. I took a sharp left down the road after him.

"Hendrix!" I screamed, my arms pumping at my side. I was choking on my tears and screams simultaneously. "Hendrix!" I picked up speed, but he was too far down the road. He couldn't hear me. His left turn signal came on. "Hendrix!" I screamed one more time, then his car turned, his tail lights winking at me while they disappeared forever around the corner.

Gasping for air, my feet slowed, then I came to an abrupt stop. My sobs doubled me over. He was gone. I'd lost him. There was nothing I could do to change it. Ever. I'd tried to protect him, and it had cost me everything. I stood, my vision struggling against the tears and bright sun. I turned around and began to walk back to Ada Lynn's, defeated. My entire body felt heavy, each step was almost impossible to take. I wanted to lie down in the middle of the road and die. In my mind, I'd done the right thing and protected Hendrix, but my heart had other ideas. Now it was shattered into pieces, and Hendrix was the only one that could have put it back together.

"Gemma!"

I whirled around.

Hendrix had backed up around the corner and was out of his car, taking cautious steps toward me.

"Hendrix," I choked out. My legs finding new life. I bolted toward him. "Hendrix!"

He ran toward me. "Gem?" he asked, unsure of what was going on.

I slammed into him, nearly knocking him over. Grabbing him by his neck, I jumped up, my legs wrapping around his waist. His hands grabbed my ass, and I squeezed him tighter.

"Don't leave me," I said, breathlessly, planting little kisses all over his face. "I love you, don't leave," I hiccupped.

"Gem? Is this it? Are you coming back to me?" I pulled back slightly, hope filling his features.

I nodded while my tears flowed freely. "I love you, Hendrix. Don't ever leave me again, please." I kissed him. All of my love for him was in that one kiss.

"I won't. Not ever again. Just promise me. Look at me for a minute," he said.

I stopped kissing him and looked at him, his blue eyes piercing my soul.

"Are you sure? I can't do the back and forth anymore. I need to know this is it."

I nodded. "Yes. This is it. I'm not ever letting you go again."

His mouth crashed down on mine, and my fingers grabbed handfuls of his hair.

"Get in the car," he ordered. He set me down, and I hurried to get into the passenger side. I guess Hendrix was shaken up because he backed all the way up the street instead of turning around. I giggled as we reached his house. He grabbed his suitcase, and we hustled up the stairs.

He unlocked the door and we hurried inside. I closed the door with my hip and flipped the bolt.

"I love you," he said, tilting my chin up toward him. "We have a lot to discuss, but dammit, I feel like you just put my heart back together again."

"I'm so sorry. I'm so sorry, Hendrix. I lost myself. I love you, that never changed." I stood on my tiptoes and kissed him again. His arms wrapped around me, pulling me into him.

"As much fun as last night was, I want to take you to my bed and make love to you."

I nodded. "Please." And with that, he scooped me into his arms and carried me to his bedroom.

29

$\mathcal{H}$endrix gently laid me on his bed. He flipped open the button on my jeans and slid them along with my G-string, over my hips and discarded them to the side. His eyes roamed hungrily up and down my body, devouring me and leaving me breathless.

"Sit up," he coaxed.

I did as he asked, and he pulled my soft pink sweater over my head. His fingers lightly traced down my back and released the clasp on my black bra. My nipples hardened against the cool air while he slipped the straps off my shoulders and tossed it on the floor. His hand gently cupped the back of my neck.

"I love you," he whispered. Goosebumps dotted my skin. His sweet breath tickled my ear. His mouth took mine, and we sank back into his bed. He kissed the side of my neck, and I tilted my head, allowing him access. His fingers traced down my sensitive skin, over my collarbone, and gently cupped my breast. I arched into his touch, losing myself in our kiss, and in his arms. My heart pounded in anticipation of being with him again, but this time I didn't have to leave.

I fumbled with the button on his jeans and freed his erection, my hand wrapping around him. He moaned in my mouth while I stroked him, slowly but firmly.

Even though I was sore from the night before, my body ached for him as he traced small circles down my stomach and to the inside of my thighs.

"I need you," I said.

He stood and discarded his Levi's and shirt. I stared at him, soaking in every beautiful detail about his hard body. I licked my lips, thinking about him coming in my mouth the night before. His eyes darkened as his gaze fell between my legs. He pulled me to the edge of the bed and parted my legs. Not wasting any time, he dipped his head and licked across my sensitive flesh. I moaned, my eyes closing as I grasped his soft hair and arched off the bed, needy with desire. For him. With a small nip of his teeth, my eyes popped open, and his finger slipped inside me.

"Baby look at me," I whispered, pinning him with my gaze. "No one else, ever. It's always been you."

He stopped and stared at me, his eyes overflowing with love and need. In one swift motion, he slid inside me.

"You're mine," he growled.

"Yes," I panted while he moved his hips in slow, deliberate circles. "Only yours."

He thrust inside me, reclaiming every part of me for himself. And I willingly gave it to him.

Lifting my hips off the bed, I moaned while his tongue played with my nipple. His hot mouth teased me relentlessly.

Suddenly, I flipped him over and straddled him. Grinning, I took control and planted my palms on his chest. He smiled and grabbed my hips, lifting me up and down his shaft.

"You feel so good," I whimpered, rocking my hips forward.

"Tell me you love me," he said, staring at me with an intense gaze.

"I love you, Hendrix Harrington. I always have."

His pace quickened with my words, and I leaned forward, kissing him long and deep. Our bodies rocked together, searing heat building up inside me.

"Baby," I whimpered. "You're going...harder," I moaned.

He groaned in response, his grip on my hips tightening while I remained leaning forward.

"Come for me, Gem. I need to see your face when you tighten around me. You're so wet," he said, moving deep inside me.

With a sudden surge of power, he lifted me off him, positioning me over his face. I slowly lowered down, his mouth latching on to my clit.

"Hendrix!" I cried as he made love to me with his tongue. "Oh, my God." I moved gently, unsure what to expect while he pushed me to the brink. I leaned my hand against the wall, rocked against him, and allowed the pleasure to build.

An intense sensation swirled inside me, and my body tensed, my climax rippling through me. His hands moved up, pulling my nipples as I came. I didn't want him to stop. Ever.

Panting, I glanced down at him. I lifted up and then slid him inside me.

"You taste so good," he said, wiping his mouth.

My cheeks flushed. "I might have liked that," I whispered, smiling shyly.

He arched his hips in response and moved inside me. A moan of sheer pleasure escaped me.

"Come inside me," I said, nipping at his bottom lip with my teeth.

He groaned as my core clenched around him, pleading for another release while his hand teased my clit.

"You feel so damned good," he said, his voice deep and husky.

"Like this?" I asked, grinding against him. The familiar, sweet feeling began to build again.

"Oh my God. I—"

"That's it, babe. Oh yeah," he slammed up inside me, his body tensing. His fingers dug into my flesh as he released.

"Aggh!" he yelled.

I picked up my pace, unable to hold on any longer, coming with him. Seconds later, I collapsed on top of his chest, sweaty and happily exhausted.

"I love you," I said, glancing up at him through my eyelashes.

"You're so damned sexy when you look at me like that." He smoothed my hair away from my face and kissed me. I smiled at him, content.

"Thank you for running after me," he said softly.

"I should have never let you go in the first place. I'm so sorry. I've been a total disaster."

"You've had a lot on your plate, babe. And now you're *my* disaster, and we'll put us back together again. Stronger than ever before."

I nodded, mentally chiding myself for thinking I could ever tell him goodbye. But there was something still looming over us. My father.

"I'll be right back," I said, kissing him on the nose. I lifted myself off Hendrix and stepped into the bathroom. Glancing at my side, I no longer saw the bruises, but it still ached. With all the activity over the last two days, the pain had increased, but I didn't want to say anything to Hendrix. He wouldn't make love to me until I felt better, and I needed him more than ever right now.

When I returned, Hendrix was sprawled out on the bed, a big, silly grin eased his face. He pushed up on an elbow, his attention traveling up and down my body.

"I can't believe you're here," he said, patting the bed. I crawled in beside him and tossed a leg over his, facing him.

"Believe it," I said. "You're stuck with me now."

He tilted my chin up and kissed me softly.

"Last night," he started, "was insane."

I propped up on my elbow, giving him my undivided attention, "You didn't like it?" I asked, worry lines creasing my forehead.

His fingers trailed down my cheek. "I loved it, but you were drunk. My question is why?"

I dropped my eyes, embarrassed. "Mac thought a few drinks would help me relax, but apparently not only am I a lightweight, but I become Jungle Gemma." I peeked at him for his reaction. I'd never been comfortable or confident enough with sex, much less barging into his house and ordering him around.

Hendrix barked out a laugh. "Jungle Gemma?"

"Well, yeah. I mean, your kitchen counter and your table. I'm going to turn ten shades of red when we have friends over, and we're serving them dinner. Someone will end up sitting in the exact spot we had sex. Remind me to Lysol the hell out of those surfaces."

"I love it," Hendrix chuckled. He quieted, his expression growing more serious. "That's all it was?"

"Yeah, I've only drank a few times since I've been home. I don't think Mac knows what to do to help me manage all this shit other than being a designated driver for me on occasion."

Hendrix nodded. "How is she? I mean, I've talked to her on the phone, but I haven't seen her lately."

I sat up, looking at him. "I thought you were going to do something about Jeremiah?" My brows knitted in concern.

"I am, but I haven't met him yet."

"Oh," I said, disappointment obvious in my tone. "Well, we have six months. You're her brother and she loves you, so if she's going to listen to anyone, it will be you. I can't do anything except support her, or I'll lose our friendship." My shoulders slumped with the mere idea of not having Mac in my life.

"I understand," he said, taking my hand and kissing the inside of my palm. He cleared his throat and then changed the subject. "You never came over to the studio," he said gently.

I rolled over on my back and stared at the ceiling.

"It was—so fucking hard not to, Hendrix." I turned to look at him. "There wasn't a day that didn't go by I didn't think about you. But I also thought about what Andrea said. It was enough to keep me away most days. Other days, I caved when you snuck in a kiss or a visit. Every time I considered begging you to take me back, I would see Andrea in my mind or hear her words. Until there was proof...the fear always nagged at me."

Hendrix blew out a breath. "I've never felt more powerless in my adult life. With Kendra, yeah, but this destroyed me just as much, Gem. I would never hurt you or any other woman. Forcing someone to have sex—. Not okay. Ever. I don't know why pricks like Brandon even exist."

I flinched at the mention of Brandon's name. Hendrix frowned and pulled me to him, kissing the top of my head.

"He's nowhere close," he ensured me.

"But, what if we go back? *Will* we go back?"

He tilted my chin up, our gaze locking. "We need to talk about Spokane if you're okay with making plans for our future."

"All I know is my future can't be without you," I said, tracing my fingers along his cheek.

"Same here," he whispered and leaned his forehead against mine. "Do you think we can write together again?" Hendrix asked, his eyes hopeful.

"I would love to," I said, beaming at him. "But wait, how do you know I didn't come over to the studio? What if I had and just sat there?" Suspicion tickled me. There was more to it.

A mischievous smile spread across his face. "Because I had something waiting for you. It sat right on the console, so I would know if you'd been here."

"What?" My brows shot up with the details.

Hendrix's phone buzzed on his nightstand. He gave me a quick peck and rolled over to grab it. My focus traveled over his well-sculpted body. A boxer's body. His muscles rippled as he stretched his arm to get the phone. I chewed my bottom lip, contemplating all the ways I wanted to get my hands and mouth on him again.

Setting it down, he turned back toward me, his expression not revealing who it was. For the second time in my life, jealousy reared its ugly head.

"Who was it?" I asked, not wanting to reveal my feelings.

"Just business, it can wait."

"Producers daughter again?" He'd never hidden anything from me before. In Spokane, he'd been an open book. The second we were officially together, he told me his schedule, who he was with, and anything else he thought I might want to know. Not because I'd asked, but because he didn't want me to feel disconnected or unsafe.

My bottom lip jutted out.

"Are you jealous?" he asked, a grin pulling at the corner of his mouth.

My eyes narrowed. "No...maybe...she just..." I sat up, folding my arms across my naked chest. "I don't know what to even do with this. She was all over you, Hendrix. I am sure you have girls offering up the goods at your shows on a regular basis. I'm not stupid."

He sat up, his hand cupping my chin.

"Gem, I've not been with anyone. It's you and only you. This life is nothing new to me. I've been telling girls no for a long time. It's not who I am. I don't have to sleep with multiple women to feel like a man. I have you and my music. There's nothing else in this world I need."

"Really?" I asked, dropping my arms. "I'm scared, Hendrix. What if I lose you again?"

"The best thing I can do to help you through it is to show you, again and again, I'm a man of my word, and you're the only one for me."

I leaned on his shoulder while he stroked my hair, then sat up and kissed him gently. "Wait, your phone interrupted our conversation." I tapped my chin, smiling at him. "What did you have for me in the studio. Is it still there?" I asked, giddy with the idea of possibilities.

He sighed and lay back down. I straddled him, realizing more sex was inevitable if I stayed in this position for long. We'd still not bothered getting dressed, but I was loving every moment of spending time with him naked. I'd never done it before.

His hands gripped my waist.

"Do you want to finish this conversation, or do you want to play again, because you're making it incredibly difficult for me right now."

"What?" I asked, feigning innocence. "Spit it out, mister." I leaned forward and shifted my hips, his dick popping to life.

"Ugh," he groaned, closing his eyes for a moment.

I ground against him, flashing him a mischievous smile. Then sat up and allowed enough space between us so that I could grab him and rub the tip of his erection against my clit.

"Shit," he said.

"Spill or I'll leave you hanging."

"Gem! Come on, you're torturing me for information. You realize, that right?"

I giggled my response.

"Fine," he gasped while I firmly wrapped my hands around him. "I had backstage passes for you to meet the X Ambassadors and Billy Raffoul."

I let him go and flew off him, my mouth gaping with the information.

"What?" I screeched, bouncing up and down on the bed. "Are you fucking kidding me? Oh my God!"

"Babe," he said, rolling over to face me. "The concert was last month."

My entire body collapsed with disappointment. "Oh." I bit my lip in order to not cry. It didn't work.

"Gem, babe, don't cry," he said, wiping away my tear.

"What...what did you do with them?"

"I gave them to Mac."

"What? She never said a word to me about it." I gawked at him, stunned. She'd actually kept her mouth closed.

"I told her if she did, she would never get backstage passes again." His chuckle rumbled through the room.

"I hope she had fun." My gaze fell, and I pulled a small thread on his plush silver comforter. "Dammit, I wish I would have known, but honestly, with everything going on...and Mom...I don't think I would have gone, anyway. But thank you. Thank you for trying to help me."

"But the text I got a few minutes ago..." he reminded me, grinning.

Staring at him, I waited for more news that would continue to induce my funk.

"It was Billy."

"*The* Billy? Like *the* Billy Raffoul? He just texted you?" I asked, incredulously.

Hendrix laughed. "Yeah, it's why I didn't mind telling you about the tickets."

My head tilted, waiting for the rest of the explanation.

"I'm going to perform on the same stage with him."

"Holy shit! Are you serious?" I asked, straddling him and pinning him to the mattress with my hands. A beautiful smile lit up his face.

"Yeah. It's pretty fucking awesome, huh?"

"Oh my God! I'm so proud of you!" I leaned forward, covering his face with little kisses, his laughter filling the room.

"There's more."

"Spill." I leaned back, waiting impatiently.

"Don't be mad. This is not set in stone in any way, it was a general conversation, okay?"

I folded my hands over my chest, bracing myself for the worst.

"The first night we hung out," he started.

"Wait, you and Billy *just* hung out?" I asked, stunned. Shit, Hendrix had been busy over the last few months while I'd rotted at home and attempted to keep him at a distance. A moment of sadness washed over me. We should have been together.

"It was after a gig, and some people introduced us. After multiple drinks, we ended up in the studio, just messing around. We were talking about how we got where we are, where we wanted to go, and shared some music ideas. It got late, and...I was drunk, honestly." His admittance pulled me out of my haze.

"What? Hendrix, you never get drunk," I whispered, worry tugging at me.

"I know. It was after the goodbye kiss on your porch, and I folded."

I remained silent, unsure of what to say since that was behind us now.

"Anyway, I had a habit of carrying our song with me on a thumb drive. I kept it in my pocket everywhere I went. That way I could listen to your voice whenever I needed to. You were always with me, Gem." His eyes softened, his thumb lightly stroking my cheek.

I blinked my tears away and took his hands in mine. "Never again."

He smiled. "Never again." He inhaled deeply. "I played our song for him, and he loved it."

Stunned, my eyes widened.

"He just sent me a text. He's going to be in Shreveport soon and wants to meet you. He also suggested some studio time with us."

"Oh. My. God!" I screamed, jumping off him. I was like a five-year-old little girl, jumping up and down on Hendrix's bed.

He laughed and pulled me down to him. "You're fucking hot when you do that," he said, grinning.

"Holy shit, Hendrix. I'm so sorry. I'm totally fangirling over another guy in front of you!" My hands covered my face, embarrassed after my initial reaction. I peered through my fingers at him. "Are you mad?"

"After seeing you jump up and down naked on my bed? Hell no." His grin was infectious as he kissed me. "So, is that a yes? You want to meet him and chat about singing?"

"Yeah," I replied. "But let me make something very clear. I don't want anything else to come between us, so if I pass up the opportunity, it's because you're what's important to me."

"I love you so damned much," he said, his mouth brushing against mine.

I leaned back on his bed, allowing him to claim every part of me again. This was the happiest I'd been in years.

30

ear tugged at me while I lay quietly, my head resting on Hendrix's chest. His career was taking off, and although I was ecstatic, I was afraid I would get left behind at some point. My heart had been battered enough.

"Hey, what are you thinking?" he asked, softly smoothing my hair with his palm.

"How fast life can change." I shifted and looked up at him. "When are you and Billy performing? And where is the concert? I can't leave Ada Lynn, Hendrix. Not after her heart attack."

"I know, babe. It's close, actually. It's in a month, late March, in Shreveport. You'll only be gone for a night. As I said, if you don't want to go…"

"It's not that," I said, sitting up. "You know I want to go. I just need to make arrangements for Ada Lynn. And can Mac come? You'll be on the stage, performing. It would be nice to have her with me."

"Yeah, I think it would be best if you had someone with you, too. Why don't you talk to Ada Lynn and see how she feels about it? I'm pretty sure she'll want you to go."

"I don't doubt that, but what if she has another heart attack? She was unconscious and unable to call 911. I would never forgive myself."

Hendrix nodded, compassion filling his eyes. "We have time to make arrangements. If I need to hire a nurse to be with her that night, then consider it done."

"Really? You'd do that for her?"

"I'd do it for both of you." He squeezed my hand.

There were so many times I forgot Hendrix had money. The expense of a nurse for Ada Lynn was nothing for him. If Ada Lynn agreed, I was going to meet Billy Raffoul. Hope nudged me.

I slid to my side of the bed and allowed my feet to dangle off the edge. My toes grazed over the soft tan carpet. "I'm sore," I said as I stood, flashing him a smile. "It's your fault I've spent the entire day in bed."

He chuckled. "*Our* bed."

I cocked my eyebrow at him, stretching. "Technically, it's yours."

He stood and pulled his jeans on while I hunted for my shirt and G-string. Hendrix sauntered over to me and tucked my hair behind my shoulder.

"You were about to move in with me in Spokane when you got the call about your mom."

"Yeah, I remember," I replied, wistfully.

His hands rubbed my arms, his gaze intent. "Move in with me now, Gem. Go get your stuff and come back. Talk to Ada Lynn about the concert, but come home to me tonight."

My eyes widened with his suggestion. "Hendrix, are you sure?" I asked, my nerves springing to life. What if things didn't work out? What if he changed his mind? What would Ada Lynn think?

"I've never been more sure about anything in my life, Gem. You'll be across the street and can visit Ada Lynn every day. I'll even go with you sometimes."

"Really?"

"Yeah. Come home. Please." His expression grew intense while he waited for me to respond.

I wrapped my arms around him and nuzzled his chest. The rhythm of his heartbeat lulled me into safety. This is what I wanted, to be next to him every day and wake up with him every morning.

I stood on my tiptoes, kissing him. "I have no idea how Ada Lynn is going to take this."

"Gem, do you not want to?" He dropped his arms, fear flickering across his expression.

"No, I absolutely do. Please, it's not that. Ada Lynn is eighty-three, and I'm not sure how she feels about me living with a guy. It's never come up before is all. I want nothing more than to be here with you," I assured him.

His shoulders sagged in relief. "I get it. I do. Let's see what she says, okay?"

I nodded. "I'm going to get dressed and go on over."

"I'll go with you," he said, protectively.

I smiled. "I've been crossing this road by myself since I was four, I'll be fine. Plus I need to have this conversation woman-to-woman. I don't want to put her on the spot if you're with me. She'll think I'm bulldozing her, and I don't want to do that. I need to show her some respect."

Hendrix frowned. "Yeah, alright. I don't like it, though. Let me walk you over at least."

"Babe, you do realize I've lived here my entire life, right? Don't hover. I'm going to Ada Lynn's, and I'll be back," I said, hoping I sounded convincing. "I love you."

If Hendrix suspected my dad was the one who hurt me, he was doing everything he could to make sure it didn't happen again. Honestly, it wasn't my father I was concerned about anymore. Hendrix couldn't get involved. And I was the only one who could make sure he stayed out of it. He needed to remain focused on his career now that it was taking off.

"Fine." Irritation filled his tone. "Text me if you need me to come over, though."

"I will. I'll be back in an hour with some of my stuff."

"I'm going to shower and make us something to eat. Hurry back." He kissed me goodbye, and I smiled like an idiot while I walked through his living room and out the front door.

Although it had only been a few hours, it felt like it had been days since I had emerged from his house. Dusk was setting in as I walked down his porch steps and sidewalk. My house was directly across from his. I rolled my eyes when I noticed the mail bulging out of our box. Dad hadn't bothered checking it again. He apparently was holed up in the house in a drunken stupor. At least he was leaving everyone alone. Hell, I didn't care if his power and water were turned off, but I needed to see if there was any mail for me.

Approaching the box, I tugged on the mail, and several letters fluttered to the ground. I groaned and collected them, the Washington college logo catching my eye. I stuck it in my back pocket and then shuffled through the rest of the mail. No other letters were addressed to me, only bills and junk mail. Curiosity tugged at me, and I shoved the remainder back in the box and flipped the lid closed. Reaching for my letter from Spokane, I tore it open and scanned it.

Dear Ms. Thompson,

I am reaching out to you today to offer our condolences for the loss of your mother. At this time, we have marked your classes as incomplete which will allow you to finish them when you are ready to return. We will also continue to extend a full scholarship.

Best Wishes,

Dean Montgomery

A mixture of gratitude, grief, and dread ran through me. The letter was from Brandon's father. Did he have any idea that his son was a monster?

Lost in thought, I shoved the letter back into the envelope and turned toward Hendrix's house. We would have to talk about Washington and what our future looked like together. From what I had experienced of Spokane, I loved it. But I couldn't leave Ada Lynn alone again. Hendrix's form moved inside his living room, and I smiled. My heart sang. Honestly, it didn't matter. I had everything I needed right here, and Hendrix and I were finally back together.

Butterflies fluttered in my stomach. I was ready to go home. To him. But first, I needed to check in on Ada Lynn.

"It sure as hell took you long enough." I froze at the sound of my father's voice.

A meaty hand covered my mouth, and the other wrapped around my waist, pulling me toward my childhood home. I screamed against his palm, clawing and kicking, mentally pleading for my release. I landed with a thud in my living room, my father closing the front door behind him. Scurrying to stand, I tripped over the corner of the area rug. Disbelief washed over me as I took in his dirty, crumpled clothes. This person no longer resembled the man I knew as my father.

"What are you doing?" My voice shook as I finally managed to stand.

"Did you think you could just scurry away like a little rat and hide from me?" He growled. His bloodshot eyes were sharp with anger.

"What are you talking about?" I asked calmly, backing into the kitchen. If I could grab a knife from the butcher block, I might have a chance to get out in one piece.

"Are you screwing that boy?" He walked toward me, stalking me as though I were his prey instead of his daughter.

"What? Daddy, what are you talking about?" Even though calling him daddy hadn't worked last time, I prayed it would this time. Anything to break through to the man I used to know.

"Are you fucking him?" He roared.

I scrambled to the kitchen table, scanning the area for anything to use as a weapon. But for the first time since I'd been home, the clutter was gone. The room had been cleaned. Had he planned this?

"Dad, let's talk about this. Sit down, I'll make some coffee." I pulled out a chair for him and patted the seat. My legs trembled while I moved slowly toward the cabinet. His hawk-like attention remained on me, his hands clenching and unclenching at his sides.

"Do you want me to cook? You're absolutely right, we haven't spent a lot of time together. I'm sorry. It's all my fault."

Confusion clouded his unshaven face. Was it working? Was I

getting through to him? I quickly removed the coffee from the cupboard and angled my body where I could see him. Oddly enough, he sat down at the table.

"There are a lot of secrets in this little town," he started, rubbing his chin. His gaze intensified, and fear ripped through me. I couldn't let him know, though. He couldn't think he had an advantage over me.

I remained silent.

"There are these clubs so to speak...secret societies," he said, pausing.

I wondered how drunk he was at the moment and why in the world he would want to talk about a club. I quickly started brewing the coffee, the gurgle of the machine breaking the silence. I folded my arms over my chest and leaned against the counter. No matter what, I had to keep a safe distance from him. My phone was in my back pocket, but I wasn't sure how I could get to it yet without setting him off.

"After you left, your mother found out."

Ada Lynn's words rang in my ears with her suspicions about how Mom had died. Fear and nausea nearly doubled me over.

"Found out what?" I asked gently.

He glanced around the kitchen and rubbed his hands along his pajama pants. By the look and smell of him, he no longer wasted time taking a shower or changing clothes.

"One of the guys I was friends with, Carl Roberts, he had a niece about your age. She was beautiful, too. Long brown hair, petite, but just the right curves." His eyes filled with lust.

My stomach churned. "Dad, don't," I said, holding up my hands to indicate it was time to stop. This was worse than I imagined. I needed to get the hell out of here.

"Don't you dare tell me what to do!" he said, shooting out of the chair. I cringed and attempted to move backward, but bumped against the counter. I'd been so focused on not turning my back to him, I'd not paid enough attention to my surroundings. I had no escape route.

"We traded girls. I knew who raped you because I handed you to him on a silver platter," he sneered.

Sheer terror speared through me and little black dots floated in and out of my vision. There was no way I'd heard him right.

"You arranged for a man to brutally rape me?" I asked, gasping for air. "You hurt another girl?" My voice no longer sounded like my own.

"Don't be so surprised. It's been going on for years around here," he chided.

"Did you cover up my rape?" My knees buckled, and I clutched at the counter, forcing myself to stay upright. He ignored my question and continued talking.

"Your mother found out. Apparently she did a lot of digging while I was sick, and eventually she uncovered the truth. We got into a big fight, and I threw her against the living room bookshelf. She hit her head really hard."

"You killed my mom?" Tears spilled down my face, everything I'd ever known to be true had just shattered into a million pieces.

White hot rage flickered to life inside me. With a new clarity, the pieces clicked together, and an eerie calm washed over me. My legs straightened, my eyes narrowed, and I willed him to put his hand on me. He'd just confessed to murder and raping little girls. It was up to me to bring the sick bastard down and make sure he never hurt anyone again.

"You mean to tell me you hid behind your religion, you sick shit?" I spat. "You call yourself a man? You're a fucking pussy."

In two steps he stood in front of me, his fingers wrapped tightly around my neck. Panic filled me, and I gasped for air. His facial features twisted, revealing the monster he really was. While his eyes were locked on my face, I reached my arm out, fumbling for the coffee pot on the counter.

In one motion, I grabbed the half-full pot of steaming coffee and threw it in his face. He stumbled backward, his scream ripping through the air. I gasped for a breath, still holding the pot in my hand. I quickly stepped around the spilled coffee on the floor and swung the glass pot. A sickening crack sounded as it made contact with the side of his head. Shards of glass shattered and flew in every direction. I ducked, attempting to avoid the pieces myself.

Peeking up, a cry escaped me. The son of a bitch hadn't gone down, he was still standing. All I'd managed to do was piss him off. I shuffled backward, my feet slipping in the coffee.

"You little bitch!" he thundered, his shoulders hunched over as he ran toward me. "You're letting some little shit fuck you every night, and you have the audacity to judge *me*?"

If I was going down, I was going to tell him exactly what I thought of him.

"You're no longer my father!" I screamed at him. "Fuck you! I fucking hate you. I hope you rot in hell!"

A loud thud broke my screaming, and I dropped to the floor, my surroundings fading into darkness.

31

A whimper escaped me as I tried to focus through the cloudy haze. Dad's blue slippered feet stood inches away, guarding me. He wasn't taking any chances of me walking out the door this time. I lay still and wondered how much time had passed since I'd left Hendrix's. Shit. I'd told him to give me an hour. Had I just dug my own grave? If Dad caused Mom's death, was mine next?

Before I realized it, Dad grabbed a hold of my shirt, gave a hard tug, and pulled me up. The room began to spin while I attempted to find my footing.

"I've had enough of you," he growled. His other hand flew up, making contact with my jaw. A scream ripped through me, and a small trickle of blood dripped from my lip.

"If you're going to kill me then do it. At least I'll die knowing what a disgusting son of a bitch you really are," I said, steel in my voice.

He let go of my shirt with a shove, sending me flying. My skull smacked the side of the kitchen counter, and another scream ripped from my lungs.

"One more move, Kyle and I'll put a bullet right through you. I won't even blink twice." A click echoed through the room, and my attention darted toward the voice, my vision blurry. "Let her go," Ada Lynn demanded.

Dad raised his hands, and sobs wracked my body as I crumpled to the linoleum floor.

"Ada Lynn?" I whispered.

"You hang on, baby. Ada Lynn's here," she said and aimed at my father's head.

"Step away, Kyle. If you touch her again, you're done." She waved her pistol at him, and he slowly backed away, his hands raised in the air. I suspected he was beginning to sober up with a gun trained on him. Ada Lynn was a kind woman, but you didn't want to cross her. And he'd officially stepped over the line.

"Gemma!" A figure flashed past Ada Lynn and knelt down next to me. "Babe. I'm here. Goddammit, why did I let you go alone?" Hendrix asked, his voice shaking with anger.

I whimpered when his hand suddenly left me. My gaze followed him the best I could.

"You're a sick bastard and a horrible excuse for a father and a human being," Hendrix said, landing a quick and strong punch to my father's stomach. If I could have cheered, I would have. Dad's body bowed forward, and Hendrix brought his fist up again with a sharp uppercut, sending Dad backward. He landed on the floor with a thud. Hendrix straddled him, pinning him beneath his weight. The last thing I remembered was the sound of Hendrix's fist pounding into my father's face over and over again.

A sharp ache pulled me from the darkness.

"Babe, the paramedics are here. I'm next to you. Ada Lynn is waiting for you, too." Hendrix squeezed my hand. The inside of the ambulance came into slow focus as someone poked and prodded me. A bright light blinded me momentarily, and fingers kneaded along my jaw.

"Shit," I said, inhaling sharply. "You don't have to be so rough."

"Sorry miss. I know it's tender, I just need to make sure nothing is broken." The woman gave me a gentle smile. "Your vitals are good, and there's nothing that seems to be broken. You'll be sore for a few days, though. You're lucky." She gave my hand a little pat. She glanced at Hendrix. "Keep an eye on her and wake her every two hours. Don't take any chances. If you're concerned, get her to the hospital."

"I will," Hendrix replied. Somehow, I doubted he would leave my side for a while.

"Thank you," I said, attempting to sit up. My skull pounded furiously with every move. Hendrix wrapped his arm around my waist, escorted me out of the ambulance, and to the porch swing where Ada Lynn anxiously waited for us.

"Are you alright?" she asked, clutching my hand, crying.

"I'm okay. Thank you." I leaned down slowly and hugged her.

Hendrix sat next to Ada Lynn on the swing and pulled me into his lap. Ada Lynn never even blinked.

"Is he dead?" I asked, mumbling through the pain.

Hendrix's jaw tensed, his pulse throbbing in his neck. "He's alive. For now."

The police bustled in and out of the house and within minutes they escorted my father out onto the front porch in handcuffs. One of his eyes was swollen shut and blood trickled from a now disfigured and most likely broken nose. His lip was puffy and bloody, too. Tiny cuts ran across his cheek. I suspected it was from the glass in the coffee pot. A moment of pride took hold inside me. I'd fought back. I'd not cowered down. And thanks to Hendrix and Ada Lynn, a monster hadn't won.

Disbelief hovered over me as everything began to sink in. The man had raised me, forced me to have a child, and swore he was a bible following, God-fearing man. But in reality, he set up my rape in trade for sex with another young girl. Was this really my life?

I shot off Hendrix's lap, doubled over the porch railing and tossed the contents of my stomach in Mom's now dead rose bushes. Hendrix stood beside me, holding my hair back as I heaved. Finally, I straightened slowly and crumpled against him.

"Ma'am, I'm Officer Forbes. We'll need a statement from you." A tall, balding, burly cop stood in front of me.

"Now?" Hendrix asked, wrapping his arms around me protectively. He knew the rules, though.

"It's okay," I mumbled.

Hendrix glanced at Ada Lynn, and she nodded.

"Can we at least take her home? You all can talk to her there, but I need to at least take her where she'll feel safe."

"Depends on where that is," the officer responded, his hand on his hip.

"Across the street."

The officer looked over his shoulder and then nodded. "Yeah, it's fine."

Hendrix scooped me into his arms, and Ada Lynn stood, following us as Hendrix carried me across the road and into his house.

He gently laid me on the couch, and Ada Lynn sat next to me in the recliner.

"How did you know?" I asked, glancing up at her while Hendrix left the room, returning with some water and aspirin.

"I heard some commotion from your dad's house and called you, but there was no answer."

I frowned. I never heard my phone go off. I leaned on my side, pulling it from my pocket. "Shit, it's dead." Even if I'd been able to reach it when Dad was attacking me, it wouldn't have done me any good.

"Next, I called your boyfriend," Ada Lynn nodded to Hendrix as he settled in next to me, gripping my hand in between his. "When he said you were supposed to be at my place, I knew where you were. Then a muffled scream came from your father's house. I grabbed my pistol, loaded it, and told Hendrix to meet me there."

"She doesn't mess around," he said, smiling at her and tucking my hair behind my ear.

A knock on the front door interrupted our conversation. Hendrix answered, and two police officers entered his house.

"How are you feeling?" Officer Forbes asked, pulling up a dining room chair. The female cop followed his lead.

"Honestly? Pretty lousy. I can't say I've had a very good day."

"Your father is in deep water, Gemma."

"Good." My body shuddered. Logically, I realized I was in shock and wondered when I would fall apart. I hoped it was after the police were gone.

The female cop leaned back in her chair, eyeing me.

"I'm Officer Smith." She paused. "We found some things in your house," she said.

Shit. "Wait!" I held my hand up, indicating for them to stop. "I want a paramedic here, please."

"Are you okay?" Hendrix said, attentive to my every move.

"It's not for me. This conversation is going to get nasty. Ada Lynn is eighty-three and on heart medication. She had a heart attack a few months ago, and I need someone here to monitor her."

"I don't think that's possible. They have already left and have other emergencies to tend to."

I leaned forward, growing a major pair of balls for the second time that day. "I know things that will allow you to bring down some dirty people. If you want me to talk, you get someone in here to take care of one of the few people who has never betrayed me." Steel laced every word I spoke.

Silence filled the room, and I caught Hendrix attempting to hide a smile. Apparently he liked this side of me.

"We can do that," Officer Forbes said. He stood and walked toward the door, radioing in for a paramedic. Within minutes one showed at the door and stood next to Ada Lynn. I reached for her hand.

"I love you," I said.

"Love you, too, my blue-eyed girl," she responded softly.

I peeked at Hendrix. "Forgive me," I whispered. Confusion clouded his features.

"Let's get started," I said, sipping my water. For the first time in my life, even under the circumstances, I felt strong and safe. Even though Hendrix would beat himself up for not walking me across the street, I'd been the one that had refused his help. Now I no longer had to protect him, everything had exploded, and I was free. I could finally tell the truth.

My back straightened, and I cleared my throat.

"When we arrested your father, we searched the house. We found child porn on his computer. Did you know about it?" Officer Smith asked.

Ada Lynn gasped, and Hendrix shot out of his seat, pacing across the floor. His hands clenched and unclenched at his sides. I glanced at Ada Lynn, tears pooling in my eyes.

"I didn't know about the computer, but in recent events, I suspected my father was a pedophile. Unfortunately, I didn't know the extent of it until this evening."

"You knew?" Hendrix asked pain etched deep into his face. "Why in the hell wouldn't you have told me? I could have protected you. My father could have helped."

"I had to protect you," I explained, fear lacing itself in my words. "He's a monster and if he knew I loved you—" My words choked off. Hendrix sank to his knees next to me, finally understanding why I'd pushed him away. I ran my hand over his head, comforting him, the softness of his hair soothing me. I knew him well enough to understand he was trying not to lose his shit in front of the cops.

"You had knowledge he liked little girls?" Officer Forbes asked while he leaned forward in his chair, his beady eyes narrowing at me.

"Stop talking," Hendrix said and stood quickly. "She's not saying anything else without an attorney present." He said, firmly.

I peered at Ada Lynn, and she nodded in agreement. Shit. What was happening?

"We'll meet you at the police station tomorrow. I need to make some phone calls first." Hendrix said, dismissing them with his statement.

The officers stood, there was nothing else they could do legally.

"Fine. We'll see you tomorrow, Gemma." Officer Smith nodded as the police stood and then let themselves out the front door.

It had never occurred to me I would be in trouble. The only thing I'd taken into consideration was protecting the people I loved. Hendrix, Ada Lynn, and Mac.

32

*A*fter the paramedic made a quick exit, Hendrix pulled his phone out of his pocket.

"Don't move, either one of you," Hendrix ordered. I'd never seen him take command like this before. If the circumstances had been better, I would have pulled him into the bedroom and ripped his clothes off. He was sexy as hell.

"I'm sorry," I said, turning toward Ada Lynn. The aspirin was beginning to help, but my head still throbbed. "Are you okay?"

Her hand trembled while she covered her mouth, muffling a sob. I slid out of my chair and kneeled down next to her. Unable to hold my own tears back any longer, I took her hand.

"Did he?" she hiccupped.

I shook my head furiously and stopped her from even saying it. "Never. He never touched me."

Her shoulders shook, and a wail escaped her as she folded over in her seat, crying. I kissed her hand and waited for her to settle down. Hendrix's muffled voice came from the other room and then fell silent. I assumed he was on the phone with his Dad.

"I'll go to the house and pack some things for you ... your medicine, some clothes. You're staying here with us tonight. I highly doubt Hendrix is letting either of us out of his sight."

I turned at the sound of his footsteps. "We need some things from Ada Lynn's. I'll go since I know where her medication is."

"No. Hell no. We can all go together. Ada Lynn, are you okay to walk over with us?" He approached her with a box of tissues. Then he bent over and planted a tender kiss on her head. She reached up and grabbed his shoulder, pulling him down for a hug. I chewed my lip and watched them. Somehow, while I'd pushed Hendrix away, they'd developed a special relationship.

"Thank you for taking care of her and making sure that bastard won't ever hurt her again," Ada Lynn said, her voice trembling.

"I should have been there sooner." His shoulders sagged with guilt. "I let you both down. I'm so sorry, Ada Lynn," he said softly.

She dabbed at her eyes with the Kleenex. "Young man, if you let her down, I let her down worse than that. You just got here. I lived next door to her for years. I knew he had a temper, but I had no idea about the rest."

A cry escaped me. My father's actions had rippled through an entire community.

"Stop, both of you. No one let me down. I'm grown. I made a choice to protect you both. *I* made a choice to keep you away from him tonight, Hendrix. *I* flat out refused you walking me across the street. And no, I had no idea he would attack me, but he's the reason I pushed you away. By the time Andrea had confessed, I already knew enough about my father to know he would kill you. He killed my mother!" I cried. "He killed my mom." My knees collapsed with the confession, and I sank to the floor, the heaviness more than I could handle.

The next thing I knew, Hendrix had scooped me up and settled into the couch with me on his lap. He rocked me as I leaned against his shoulder and cried.

All of the secrets were coming out, and there was no longer anyone else I needed to protect.

I scanned Ada Lynn's tidy living room for items to bring over to Hendrix's house, then it dawned on me.

"Where's the gun? Ada Lynn, didn't you have a gun?" I asked, the fog and shock wearing off for a minute.

"I have it," Hendrix said. "It's not registered, and I didn't want Ada Lynn to get in trouble."

It was great news for Ada Lynn, but now my worry was targeted toward my boyfriend.

"What if Dad says something?"

"We'll take care of it. Don't worry about it," he said, kissing the tip of my nose.

What other choice did I have than to let him manage the situation? It wouldn't stop me from worrying, though.

Once again, I piled my belongings in my duffel bag while Hendrix helped Ada Lynn gather her medicine, some clothes, and her favorite pillow. He carried our bags across the street. When his door closed and locked behind us, I finally began to feel a little bit safe.

He disappeared and then returned empty-handed. I assumed he'd dropped the bags off in the bedrooms.

"You ladies can either sit at the dining room table or join me in the kitchen on the bar stools. I'm going to make us some food." He disappeared into the kitchen.

"I'll be right back," I said to Ada Lynn and followed him.

"Hey," I said. He slowly turned to me, his eyes filled with so many emotions I struggled to get a good read of where he was at.

"Are you mad at me?" I asked, softly. I stood a few feet away from him and allowed him some space. I wasn't sure what he needed. "Do you still want me to live here?"

"What?" he asked, shock registering in his face. In two steps he wrapped me in his arms and rested his chin on the top of my head. "I want you here. Always. Nothing will change that. Nothing," he whispered in my hair. "I almost lost you tonight, Gem. Sometimes I wonder if I'm really the right guy for you."

I pulled away, my mouth gaping open. "Don't you ever say that again." Anger flashed through me. "You're the best thing that has ever happened to me. You're the best choice I've ever made. I finally got something right. Let it go, Hendrix. Let it go. I wanted to be next to you the moment Andrea confessed. But I couldn't. Shit had already hit the fan, and I had to do the right thing. If you'd have known...I'm afraid you would have killed him, or he would have killed you."

He inhaled sharply. "I would have, Gem. You'd be visiting me in prison right now."

"I don't want that life for us, Hendrix. I need you next to me. Please don't beat yourself up about tonight anymore. I need you now. And all I wanted was to keep you safe, but now I might be in trouble with the cops."

He held me tightly against him, the steady beat of his heart reminding me of his quiet strength.

I pulled away and gave him a quick kiss. "I'm going to help Ada Lynn and then get settled myself. Where did you put my bag?"

His eyebrow arched. "In our bedroom."

For the first time all evening, I smiled. "*Our* bedroom?"

"You're no longer a guest or my girlfriend spending the night. This is your house, too. And if we really want to get technical about it, it's yours and Ada Lynn's, it's not even mine."

My pulse raced. I'd forgotten he'd done that for us.

"Thank you," I said softly and kissed him on the cheek. I left Hendrix in the kitchen and met Ada Lynn in the guest bedroom.

"Do you need anything other than some dinner?" I asked, helping her put a few clothes in the dresser.

She sank down on the edge of the bed, her brown eyes traveling up to mine. Weariness was etched in her face. We had been through so much in such a short time. I was so worried about her. I sat down on the end of the bed and took her hand.

"It's not your fault he was sick. You didn't know. Neither did Mom."

"She didn't?" Ada Lynn's attention snapped to me.

"No. He told me tonight. But I think I should tell you and Hendrix all at once. Apparently, I might end up in some hot water legally. Hendrix's Dad can help...I think."

When we sat down at the dining table, my cheeks flushed crimson red.

"Are you feeling okay?" Ada Lynn asked, concern in her tone.

"Yeah, it's just been a long day." If Hendrix had been here with us, he would have laughed. She'd have another spell if she knew Hendrix and I had had sex on this table.

The aroma of burgers and fries filled the air while Hendrix prepared our plates. He popped open a bottle of wine and poured three glasses.

"I figured we have a pretty good reason to have a few drinks," he said, sitting down with us.

I giggled and gave Ada Lynn a knowing glance. "If that's the case, we should be in the moonshine tonight."

"Oh lord," Ada Lynn said, chuckling. "The night before you left for Spokane...I remember. Your expression was hilarious." It was nice to hear her laugh.

Hendrix's focus bounced between us, grinning. It was a nice break from the insanity we'd dealt with all evening.

We ate, keeping the conversation light. I cut my hamburger into small pieces in order to chew better. Even though my father hadn't used his fist, my cheek and jaw still hurt from his hit.

Hendrix's gaze traveled to me often. Whether it was to make sure I wasn't going to shatter into a million pieces or disbelief that I was here to stay with him for good, I wasn't sure.

After dinner, Hendrix cleared our plates and refilled our wine glasses. Ada Lynn yawned, and I looked at my phone. It was almost ten.

"I need to call Mac soon," I told Hendrix. "I'm really dreading the conversation."

"I understand, and we will. She needs to know we're back together, too. But first, I need all of the details so we can make sure you're legally protected." He reached across the table, squeezing my hand in his.

"I'm going to get Ada Lynn's nitroglycerin, first. I can't take any chances." I scooted my chair back.

Ada Lynn raised her hand to stop me. "Got it right here," she said, pulling a few tablets from her pocket and placing them on the dining room table.

I glanced at Hendrix, wondering if he realized he'd bent me over in that exact spot. The mischievous look in his eye told me he did.

I sighed and took another sip of my wine.

"Ask me a question. It's all bouncing around in my brain like a boomerang, and I can't grab ahold of it to slow it down."

"When did you find out your dad killed your mom?"

I reached up to scratch my cheek, internally shrinking away from the question. Franklin had most likely taught him to go straight for the meat in his questioning.

"I—It was Ada Lynn who told me the police suspected foul play. Her cop friend shared the information with her. But—it was tonight when he admitted it...said he'd shoved her, and she hit her head on the bookshelf in the living room. Shit," I said, rubbing my temples.

"Take your time, Gem," Hendrix coaxed.

"The first time...when he broke my ribs. It's when he hinted that he liked young girls." My body shuddered, recalling the lust and the insanity in his crazed facial expression. Then the scorching memories of my rape bombarded me. I leaned forward and covered my face with my hands while I rocked in my chair. A muffled cry escaped me.

Warm, strong hands pulled my palms away from my face, forcing me to peer up.

"Look at me, Gem. You're safe. Take a deep breath. You're right here with Ada Lynn and me. It's okay." Tears slipped down my cheeks. I leaned forward, kissing him. The softness of his mouth on mine centered me again.

I nodded, and he returned to his seat.

"Do you know what they do to pedophiles in prison?" Ada Lynn asked, her skin sickly pale.

"No," Hendrix squeezed my hand. Something inside me told me he already knew what she was about to say.

"They kill them. Even murderers can't stand men who hurt children. Gemma, it would serve you best if you prepared to say goodbye to your father."

"I can only hope," I choked out. An odd combination of grief and relief stirred inside me with the thought of him dead.

I took a few minutes to collect myself before continuing.

"He told me...There's an organization, a society for men to trade and have sex with young girls." I felt the color drain from my face as the words left my lips. "My father traded me to one of them. He not only knew who raped me, but he set it up."

The sound of Hendrix's chair shooting backward, snapped me out of my daze. Trembling with the truth, I curled up inside myself. I was done. Admitting it out loud was somehow more horrifying than I'd been able to comprehend.

"Goddammit," Hendrix yelled, his hands fisting together while he walked through the dining room and straight out his front door. I could hear his footsteps pacing across the front porch.

Ada Lynn stared at me. Her mouth gaped open for a moment, then she hurried over to me.

"Gemma," she said, pulling me tightly to her. "I'm so sorry. You did nothing wrong." She rocked me back and forth and patted my back. "Hendrix will be back. He's upset and didn't want you to see it. You've dealt with enough."

"I know. He's trying not to lose his shit in front of us," I mumbled into her shoulder. "This is a nightmare, Ada Lynn. I don't know how we're all supposed to handle it, but you're the one I'm most worried about. Are you okay?" I asked, leaning back in my chair.

Her expression grew stern.

"Hell is too good for him. If I had a chance, I'd set the bastard on fire and laugh as he burned alive."

Although I'd never heard her say anything so harsh, I completely understood. I was right there with her. I lay my head against the table and took her hand in mine. Only time would dictate how quickly we healed or didn't heal. Right now, all I could do was wait for Hendrix to blow off some steam and calm down. He would be back in when he was ready.

"Can you sleep?" I asked her.

"I'm going to take my prescription to help me tonight. I only take it if I have to, but I need to get some rest."

"Let us help take care of you. It's the least I can do. But," I sat up, "where in the world did you buy a gun?"

The memory of her pointing a gun at my dad sent a chill up and down my spine. If she'd not gotten to me in time and stopped him, I wouldn't be here with her right now. She was my hero.

"I've had that gun for a long time now. When you're as old as I am, you take precautions. I'd hoped I would never have to use it, but thank God it was there when I needed it."

"You saved my life," I whispered. "Thank you."

"I'd do it again, too. But don't you for one minute dismiss what Hendrix did. If I'd not had the key and gun, he would have broken the front door down. He's a powerhouse. I have to admit, I was in a bit of awe when he beat the hell out of your father. I don't know what all he's been through, but those waters run deep. It's a good thing he's on your side." She reached up, her hand shaking slightly while she patted my cheek.

"I love him. I was just trying to keep him safe."

"Girl, you had it all backward. you should have allowed him to keep you safe. But I get it. Your heart was in the right place. You tried to protect us all, but it cost you dearly. Your father wasn't worth protecting. In this case, there is strength in numbers."

I nodded.

Kissing her on the cheek, I helped her to the guest bedroom and tucked her into bed.

"Love you, Ada Lynn."

"Love you too, my blue-eyed girl."

I turned off the light and shut her door. For the first time all evening, no one else was with me, and I no longer had to pretend to be strong. I hurried to the master bathroom and closed the door behind me. Turning on the shower, I stripped down and stepped in. The hot water trailed down my body, washing all the dirt and filth from the day away. My legs wobbled beneath me, and I slid down into the tub. I curled into a fetal position while powerful sobs wracked my body.

33

The water turned cool as I stared at the spray, numbly. The sound of the shower door opening broke through my hazy thoughts, and I glanced up. Hendrix stood above me, his blue eyes rimmed with red.

"Babe," he said quietly. His hand flicked beneath the spray, and then he leaned over, turning the water off. He grabbed a thick plush towel from the rack and held it up. "Can you stand?" he asked guilt and worry heavy in his tone.

I nodded. On autopilot, I stood up and allowed him to wrap me in the towel. He guided me out of the shower and into his bedroom.

"The house—it's similar to Spokane with the décor," I mumbled while he dried me off. I lifted my arms like I did when I was a child and Mom would pat me dry after a bath. But then, I was a carefree little girl. Untouched. Whole. Innocent.

"I did my best. If you came back to me, I wanted it to remind you of the good times we had. Our connection. Plus I needed you with me in every way possible."

"The first time I saw your house, it was with Ada Lynn...I knew. And the picture of me in your living room. I knew you still loved me. I just couldn't reach out to you."

He wrapped me in the towel and brought me to him. "Nothing is standing in our way anymore, Gem. It's you and me. All the shit is over. Your father is in jail, and you're finally safe."

He held me against him, allowing me the ability to block everyone and everything else out. It was just Hendrix and me against the world.

"I assume you're in shock." He placed a kiss on my forehead. "Let's dry your hair. Just go sit down, and I'll take care of it."

Numbly, I walked back into the bathroom and sat on the toilet. A shiver shot through me.

Hendrix plugged in the hairdryer and over the next twenty minutes, he dried and brushed my hair. No one had ever done something so simple yet so intimate for me. How did I get so lucky? He was a combination of quiet strength and gentleness intertwined with a ferocious lion who had the ability to kill a man in a single blow.

My thoughts drifted back to earlier today, my dad attacking me. I wondered why Hendrix hadn't killed him right then. Wouldn't it have been self-defense? I don't know what finally stopped him from beating my father to death, but I suspected Ada Lynn had something to do with it.

"Let's get you in some clothes and to bed," he said, breaking me away from my thoughts.

I followed him into his bedroom. He'd already unpacked my duffel bag, placing my clothes in the dresser next to his.

"This okay?" he asked, holding up a tank top and matching pajama shorts. I nodded and he dressed me. Minutes later, I snuggled up against him in bed. He leaned over toward his nightstand and turned the lamp off. The warmth of his body quickly lulled me into a deep sleep.

A scream ripped through the darkness. My body trembled as I jumped from the bed and landed with a thud on all fours. Nausea twisted my stomach.

"Shit," I said, bolting toward the bathroom. I flipped the toilet lid up in time to empty the contents of my dinner.

"Jesus," Hendrix said, hurrying in beside me. He sat on the tub, holding my hair back while I continued to hurl. Sweat beaded my forehead, my skin clammy with fear. Finally, I sank onto the floor, shaking violently.

He slid down next to me, his back against the bathtub. He pulled me into him, and I nestled between his legs as he wrapped me in his strong, protective arms. l leaned back against his bare chest and listened to the steady rhythm of his heartbeat in my ear.

"It was just a bad dream, you're safe," he said and nuzzled my hair with his nose.

His arms tightened around me, providing the love and stability I needed to consider the possibility of a real future with him.

My neck screamed profanities at me while I lifted my head off Hendrix's chest. We'd slept the rest of the night on the bathroom floor. He had never left me.

"Babe?" I asked, my voice cracking.

"Yeah?" he replied, his eyes fluttering open and glancing around.

"I'm a bit stiff, how are you?" I asked, sitting up and stretching. I squinted against the bright sunlight that filtered through the bathroom window. "There was no way you were comfortable."

He scrubbed his face with his hands and smiled gently. "I've felt worse. Don't forget I was the state boxing champion. I've taken a few hits. Way more than the side of a tub could do to me."

I stood and gave him a soft smile. Although my experience was extremely limited, I doubted a lot of guys would have slept in the bathroom with their girlfriends. I was so damned lucky to have him. I extended my hand and helped him off the floor, his neck and knees cracking as he stood.

"I need to check on Ada Lynn. Can we get some coffee started?"

"First," he said, pulling me against him. My hands landed on his broad chest, the beat of his heart against my hand. His head dipped down, his lips gently brushing mine. "I know the circumstances are shitty, but this is our first morning together in Louisiana. I love you, and I'm so happy you're here with me." He rested his forehead against mine.

"I love you so much, Hendrix," I said a bit breathlessly. His erection pressed against me through his sweatpants. "I would love to have you inside me right now," I said, threading my fingers through his hair, "but I need to check on Ada Lynn."

He responded with a passionate kiss, then grabbed a shirt from the dresser in the bedroom and slipped it on. We walked into the living room hand in hand.

"It's about time you two got up," Ada Lynn said from the dining room table. A cup of coffee sat in front of her as she read the paper. I grinned at her. There was no way my world would ever be complete without her.

"What time is it?" I asked while Hendrix sauntered into the kitchen and I sat down next to her.

"It's after nine."

"What? I'm usually up a little after seven and at your place around nine."

"It was a big day yesterday. It will take some time for you to get your energy back. How are you feeling by the way?"

"Sore," I said, staring at my hands, the images bombarding me. "I'm shocked my head doesn't hurt worse. He slammed it against the kitchen counter." I averted my focus quickly, attempting to block the sound of the impact from my mind, but it was too late. My body tensed, and I relived the horror.

"It's going to take some time," she said softly, taking my hand.

My gaze flicked up to hers, and Ada Lynn's lips pursed. "I've told you the biggest stuff, but I think moving forward I should talk to Hendrix and whatever attorney he finds for me. I can't put you through anymore," I said.

"You're right," Hendrix said, placing a large mug of hot coffee in front of me and pulling up a chair to join us. "We don't want to pull

Ada Lynn into this anymore. Right now, it's all hearsay from you, but she needs to stay out of it as much as possible. What is said in this house, stays in this house." His attention bounced between Ada Lynn and me. "Everyone good with that?"

I nodded. I would do anything to keep her safe.

"I just talked to Dad, Gem. He has contacts all around the country. We'll meet with a local attorney in a few hours."

"Seriously? Your dad got me an attorney?"

"Yeah. When I told him everything, he was happy to do it. He likes you, babe. He also hates anyone who targets children." He paused, his eyes flashing with anger. "There's no charge, either. These guys trade favors all the time. Not like your dad did, though. Legal help." His words were laced with disgust. I didn't blame him. I was beyond disgusted myself.

"Please tell him thank you." I sipped my coffee, grateful for Franklin's help and embarrassed at the same time. Who wanted to admit they had a sick and twisted, perverted parent?

"Well, you'll have the opportunity to thank him yourself. He's coming as well."

"What?" I asked nearly spitting my drink out. "Is he mad at me for involving you?" I asked softly. "I know this affected you and it wasn't what I meant to do."

"No, Gem, he's not mad at you. The exact opposite. He has a lot of respect for what you've gone through. He recognized you're not a quitter, plus you tried to keep the people you love safe. How could he not like you?"

I relaxed in my chair.

"He also recommended we not discuss anything else with Ada Lynn. He and Marcus will be here by four this afternoon."

My focus darted between him and Ada Lynn. "So fast?" I asked, my hands wringing together.

"Honey, you need to get this over with as soon as possible. They'll investigate, but the more you provide, the longer they can put him away for," Ada Lynn assured me.

"I know. But never in a billion years did I think I'd offer information that would put my father behind bars."

Both of them reached for my hands at the same time.

Four o'clock rolled around fast. A part of me wanted to get it all over with. The other part was terrified Franklin might not be able to help, and I was in massive trouble. If that were the case, and I was faced with jail time, Hendrix and I would be separated once again.

We all agreed Ada Lynn would be okay at home for a while, and I strongly urged her to get some rest. Whether she could or not was another story. Everyone was on edge, our minds running a million miles an hour with different scenarios.

The doorbell rang, and my nerves sped into overdrive.

Franklin and a shorter man with tight, curly, dark brown hair walked into the house. Franklin gave Hendrix a hug, patting him on the back.

"You look good, son. I'm real proud of you for pursuing your music."

"Thanks," Hendrix replied, grinning.

"Gemma," Franklin said, giving me a warm hug. "Glad you and Hendrix were able to work things out." He smiled. "In my opinion, you're the best decision he's made."

My cheeks warmed with the support.

"Thank you, Franklin. I'm sorry I got into some hot water and needed your help, but I'm relieved you're here."

"Gemma, I'm Marcus. I'm a long-time friend of Franklin's. Sounds like we need to keep you out of jail."

I blanched.

Franklin chuckled, "You're not going to jail, Gemma. It's okay."

"How can you be sure? I withheld information. I didn't mean to, I was just trying to protect everyone."

"I've dealt with this type of situation before," Marcus assured me. "Everything will be fine."

I nodded, and Hendrix led us to the living room where we all sat down. I sank into the corner of the couch, and Hendrix sat next to me. He pulled me into him while he wrapped his arm around my shoulder.

"You're in good hands," he whispered.

"When we're done here, we'll call the police and meet with them at the station. You're an adult, so they'll question you one on one, but Franklin and I will be with you. If I tell you not to answer, you need to do what I tell you. Agreed?"

I nodded. This couldn't be happening. This shit only happened to criminals or on TV. I was in neither situation.

For the next two hours, I shared what my father had told me about my rape, the society, my mom, and that the police had found child porn on his computer. The lawyers discussed deals that would possibly keep me out of trouble if I willingly provided the information and the name of the man my father had coordinated my attack with. Honestly, I was happy to. And someday, I wanted to track Carl's niece down if I could. I just needed to know she was okay. The rape had nearly destroyed me. I wondered if she'd done better than I had.

The police station had been overwhelming, to say the least. After I provided all of the details, they had enough to not only investigate my father but to look into the group of men who preyed on girls. Deep inside me, I knew it extended beyond the borders of my small town. I just hoped I'd been able to provide enough for them to take every sick fucker down.

Marcus had already prepared paperwork that released me from any charges for withholding information in a criminal case. He must have been good at what he did because there wasn't any arguing or bartering on the cop's side. Honestly, I don't think they cared anything about me, I think they were more interested in taking down the group of pedophiles.

Relief flowed over me when Franklin, Marcus, and I were free to go.

"Are you doing okay? That was a lot to deal with," Franklin asked me, concern in his eyes.

"No, not really. I'm exhausted, too." I rubbed my arms, attempting to not fall apart in public.

"Do you want to see him?" Marcus asked. "Your dad?"

Emotions cluttered my head. I'd not thought about it yet, but Ada Lynn's voice interrupted my thoughts. This might be the only opportunity I had to say what I needed to. I squared my shoulders, my chin jutting up.

"I should say goodbye." Regardless of what anyone thought, I wanted to say goodbye for me, not for him.

Within minutes, I sat at a table across from the man who I shared a bloodline with. Guards were scattered throughout the room, hands on their waist, pacing and eyeing everyone. Franklin insisted he be at a nearby table. I wondered if Hendrix had asked him to stay close, or if he felt sorry for me and chose to. Regardless, I wasn't going to turn down his support.

"Are you finally sobered up now?" I asked, searching him for any sign of remorse. The alcohol and Mom's death had aged him significantly. Nothing about him even closely resembled the man I'd left behind when I had moved to Washington.

"Yeah," he muttered and ran a hand over his hair. It had grown out over the last few months, and the gray streaks were now more pronounced.

He looked different, broken. I didn't know how someone like him could break, though. He had no conscience. Maybe he'd heard the same rumors Ada Lynn had and was scared he'd be killed in prison. But he wasn't there yet, the trial and sentencing still had to happen.

"For some reason, I felt it necessary to say goodbye. I guess I need some closure. I lost Mom thanks to you, and now you're going away, hopefully for the rest of your life. Also, let me be clear. Make no mistake, I will not visit you. Ever. I'll see you at the trial, but as soon as I testify, I'm done. I won't be back."

"So, you're just going to bail on me?" he asked, self-pity written all over his face.

"Fuck you," I whispered harshly. "You turned your back on me when you offered me to a sick man at the age of fourteen. And how many others? Huh? How many did you hurt, scarring them for the rest of their lives?" My hands fisted, and I could feel the burn of anger in my cheeks with every question. In truth, I didn't want to hear his answer. It would most likely come out in the trial.

He remained silent. It was probably for the best. If the guards hadn't been nearby, I would have flown over the table and clawed his eyes out for what he'd done to me. I hated him. I hated him more than I knew I was even capable of. If the other inmates stepped in, death would be too good for him, but at least the world would be rid of one more sicko. And so would I.

"Goodbye, Kyle." I stood, turned, and walked away on shaky limbs.

34

Although I wanted to call Mac, I wasn't ready to answer all of her questions. Hendrix had offered to let her know he was in town and explain everything. Relieved and exhausted, I took him up on it.

Since Dad was no longer at his house, there was no reason for me not to walk over to Ada Lynn's by myself. I needed to let her know I was back from the police station, so she wouldn't worry. For the first time in years, I had a small taste of freedom, and fear no longer dangled itself in front of me everywhere I turned.

I knocked on the door and waited for her to answer. It cracked open, her eye peering through the small space the chain allowed. The door closed, the sound of the chain slipping out of its slot.

"Wasn't sure you'd make it over tonight," Ada Lynn said.

"I know it's late, but I just got home from a long discussion with the cops." I crumpled into her couch and stared at my hands. "How are you holding up?" I asked, tilting my head.

"Under the circumstances, not too bad. I took a long nap. Some sleep seemed to have helped. Also, knowing the son of a bitch won't be home—well, I know you're safe."

I nodded. "Yeah, I was thinking the same thing. I saw the yellow tape across the front of the door, too. Guess his computer made it a crime scene..." My voice trailed off.

"What's next?" she asked.

"The trial, then I'm done as far as I know. I can try to put it behind me." I chewed on my thumbnail, mentally reviewing what had happened at the station. How had I gotten through it all? How was I still here? Anxiety hummed beneath my skin, and I took a deep breath. "I did visit him while I was there."

Ada Lynn's eyebrow arched.

"I told him goodbye, and it was the last time I would see him." I stared at her, "I didn't do it for him. I did it for me. Other than the trial, I'm finished. No parent does what he did to me. I don't think I'll ever forgive him, Ada Lynn." Hurt and anger hinged on every word.

"No judgment here. All I want for you is to move on. You and Hendrix have time to enjoy each other now."

She was right. I needed to focus on the good that was in front of me and learn how to deal with the past. I wasn't sure how I would do it, but now would be a good time to start. A shy smile pulled at my mouth. "Are you okay if I stay at his place with him? I'll be over every day to see you, plus you have both of our cell phone numbers. I just wasn't sure how you would feel about it."

"Child, back in my day you didn't live with someone without being married, but it's not a big deal now. I look at it this way: you two love each other, you've lost your youth, and both your parents. If Hendrix makes you happy, grab hold of him, and don't you ever let go. You deserve a good life. You hear me?" Her tone was firm.

"Thank you," I said quietly, tears burning the back of my eyes. "Thank you again for saving me from Dad...Kyle."

"I'm just sorry I didn't get there sooner. I'm still kicking myself for it."

"If I have to move on, so do you," I said, gently.

She nodded. "Fair enough. After some thought, I think it might be a good idea if Hendrix showed you a few boxing moves to keep you safe. He sure is a whirlwind of power."

"I've been thinking about it, too. I know he will if I ask. He boxed competitively for years."

"It shows," she said, rocking in her chair. She didn't bother hiding her yawn.

"It's late, so you should get some rest. Hendrix was calling Mac for me. I didn't have the energy to tell her."

"Good. I'm glad he did. She'll need her brother to help her digest all of this mess. You get some rest too, and I'll see you tomorrow."

"Okay." I stood, kissed her forehead, and let myself out.

The walk back to Hendrix's seemed like it took all of the energy I had left. Mental and physical exhaustion seeped deep inside me, weighing me down.

"Hey," I said, walking through his front door. "How'd it go with Mac?" I locked the door behind me and approached him in the living room.

He sat forward on his couch, his hands steepled, deep in thought. He stood when I entered the room, his expression filled with relief while he wrapped me in his arms. "She's okay. Pissed and upset, but she's okay. Like the rest of us, she's angry with herself for not keeping you safe." His hand threaded through my hair, gently playing with a few strands.

"I'm safe now," I said, peering up at him, my arms around his waist. "I'll talk to Mac tomorrow. I just needed some time to wrap my noggin around everything that happened today."

I sank into his couch and tucked my legs beneath me and patted the spot next to me. "I saw my father."

Hendrix sat down, searching for any telltale signs of how the conversation went.

"I told him goodbye. And other than seeing him at the trial, I'm done. I have no plans of ever visiting him again."

Hendrix took my hand. His warmth and strength calmed my raw nerves. "I'm sure you needed the closure, babe. I would have done the same thing."

I nodded. "I also had a good talk with Ada Lynn," I said, leaning over and planting a kiss on his mouth.

"Yeah?" he asked.

"You're stuck with me for real. I'm here to stay. Ada Lynn was fine with me moving in. She didn't even bat an eye."

A soft smile eased across his face. "So you're here with me for good?" he asked, running his hand through his hair.

"If you're sure," I whispered.

"I've never been more sure about anything in my life." He kissed me tenderly, still being mindful of my sore face.

"Me too," I said, sighing against his lips.

He pulled away and tucked my hair behind my shoulder.

"I've grown very fond of Ada Lynn. She's pretty amazing," he said.

"Yeah, she is. And a total badass with a gun. I had no idea, and I've spent a lot of time with her over the years."

Hendrix's low chuckle filled the room. "I suspect there are more surprises inside her."

I covered my mouth with my arm and yawned.

"It's late, and I know you didn't get a lot of sleep last night. Why don't we get into bed?"

His fingers skimmed down my cheek, and I leaned into his touch.

"Hopefully I can sleep tonight. I need to spend some time with Mac tomorrow."

"I need to meet Jeremiah, too," he said, taking my hand and leading me into our bedroom.

"Oh boy," I mumbled behind him. "That should be interesting."

Hendrix figured the best way to deal with Mac, and help me manage my energy and emotions, was to invite her and Jeremiah over to our place for lunch.

The doorbell rang around noon, and I hurried to peek through the peephole. I smiled and swung it open.

"Bestie," Mac said, entering Hendrix's house and nearly knocking me over with her hug.

It seemed like it had been weeks since I'd seen her.

"I'm so glad you're okay," she sniffled quietly in my ear. She pulled away from me and squeezed my hand.

"It's all good," I assured her. My gaze traveled to Jeremiah. "Hey, come on in." I offered him a warm smile. Today was the day Hendrix would check him out and find out what his intentions were with his sister. For a moment, I almost felt sorry for him, then it faded. It was a big brother's job to be protective of his sister. And maybe, maybe he would be able to talk to Mac in a way I couldn't. I wasn't opposed to Jeremiah, just the wedding occurring so soon.

"You guys want a beer or some tea?" I asked, showing them into the living room.

"So, you live here now?" Mac asked, bouncing up and down on her toes.

I laughed. "Yeah. As you know, I don't have a lot to move, so we brought it over the other night after—" My words were cut off while she bounded over to me, nearly knocking the wind out of me with her hug.

"I'm so happy!" She exclaimed. "Now I can think about the real possibility of you becoming my sister-in-law. You'll never get rid of me then." She giggled and let me go. A rush of air filled my lungs.

"One thing at a time," I said a bit breathless. "Jeremiah, I'm sorry, you've not been here yet. Let me show you around."

Mac nodded and fell into place next to him as I gave him a quick tour. Afterward, we stopped in the kitchen and grabbed a few beers. If everyone drank today, they could stay in the guest room, so it was as good a time as any to just relax.

I opened the door off the kitchen and stepped onto the back deck with Hendrix. The early spring air was crisp, and the sun was bright. I'd not spent any time out back yet, so I was excited the day had turned out nice enough to enjoy the outdoors. The BBQ chicken and hamburgers sizzled on the grill. Suddenly, my stomach growled in anticipation.

Mac took Jeremiah's hand in hers and smiled at her brother.

"Jeremiah, this is my brother, Hendrix. Hendrix, my fia—my boyfriend, Jeremiah."

The two shook hands, Hendrix eyeing him up and down. Jeremiah was a few inches taller, but I had no question in my mind that Hendrix could take him down if he had too.

"Hey, man, good to meet you. Mac talks about you all the time," Jeremiah said, all smiles.

"Nice," Hendrix said, glancing at Mac. "She hasn't said a single thing about you, so I'm glad you're here."

Poor Jeremiah's mouth dropped, and so did his hand. Mac turned whiter than a sheet, and she shot her brother a pleading look. I wondered how things had gone down with Asher, but I did recall Hendrix liking him. At least until recently.

"Have a seat," Hendrix said to Jeremiah, nodding toward a patio chair. He smiled and turned to flip the burgers.

"Well, I think Mac and I will go inside and get the salad and other food ready," I said, kissing Hendrix on the cheek. "She can't know you know about the engagement. Behave," I whispered.

"Never," he said softly against my ear. His eyes twinkled as he glanced at me and then focused on the food again.

I had a feeling he was going to enjoy every second of making Jeremiah squirm. Although he and Mac hadn't told Hendrix their wedding plans, I had, and there was no way Hendrix wasn't going to grill Jeremiah about his entire life. I just had to trust he'd do it in a way that didn't send Mac rushing the wedding even more.

The second the door closed behind us, Mac took a big swallow of her beer.

"Holy hell, what have I just done?" she asked, fanning herself with her hand.

I smiled. "Come help me with the food and let's catch up."

"Hendrix. I forgot what he's like when he meets someone I'm dating." The color drained from her face again.

"You did almost slip up on that one," I said, pulling the ingredients for the salad from the stainless-steel fridge and meticulously placing everything on the counter.

"I know," she groaned, sliding into the barstool across from me.

"I think one thing you and I can both agree on about Hendrix is that he's fair. He's protective of us, but he's fair and a good judge of people. Let him do what he needs to. Let the guys be guys." I raised an eyebrow at her, wondering if she understood what I was trying to say.

Her body relaxed. "You're right. And how are you giving me advice on dealing with my brother?" she asked, giving me a toothy grin.

I rolled my eyes at her. "Life took a few turns, huh?"

"Yeah, which..." Her words trailed off, and she took another drink of her beer. "Hendrix told me about your dad. He also said not to bring it up in front of Jeremiah. And I totally respect that. I've not said a word about any of it. I figured this is between family for now."

I chopped the tomatoes and tossed them with the salad in a large wooden bowl. Was she not considering Jeremiah family yet? That was interesting.

"Why didn't you tell me, Gemma? I could have gotten you out of there."

"No, you couldn't have. Plus I wouldn't have left Ada Lynn. With her health and recent heart attack, I need to stay close, Mac. On the bright side, even though it was under shitty circumstances, I was able to give the cops some leads on some really bad men. If it saves even one little girl...it was worth it," I said, my voice hovering above a whisper and putting the knife down. My emotions had spiked too high to continue chopping the vegetables safely.

"He arranged your rape," she blurted out. "What kind of sick fuck does that to his own daughter?"

A dull throb started in my head. I was so tired of answering questions, but I needed to help Mac process it because when it was all said and done, she'd be there for me on the bad days. We were there for each other.

Realizing I needed to give her my undivided attention, I grabbed my beer and took a long drink. I sank into the bar stool next to her.

"Yeah. I was beyond stunned when he told me. It's like it's still not real, ya know? I guess my brain disengaged when reality became too much for me. Between him attacking me and the horrible things he said, I'm surprised I remember much, honestly."

"But you're safe now, and you and Hendrix are back together, too." She flashed me a smile. "He told me everything, and there's no way it can be easy for you to talk about. Hell, I'm not sure I can talk much about it. I mean, I stayed with you guys for three weeks. It never crossed my mind he was a monster."

"Me either. Apparently he was very skilled at hiding who he really was. Mom didn't even know for a long time. And when she found out...she lost her life." A tear streamed down my cheek, and Mac reached for my hand.

"I miss her so much," I said, the tears flowing. "She tried to turn him in, and it destroyed her."

"I'm so sorry, Gemma." Mac leaned forward, hugging me while I cried. "It's going to take some time for you to put it all together. Maybe you should consider talking to someone who's professionally trained to help in this area, too. You're going to have some rough days, but Hendrix and I are here for you, and so is Ada Lynn. You're with family again, where you belong." She patted my arm reassuringly.

Finally, I sat up and sniffled, my nose stuffy from crying.

The back door opened, and Hendrix waltzed in.

"Hey," he said smiling, but it faltered quickly. "Gem?" He hurried toward me, his fingers tilting my chin up and kissing my cheek. "You okay?"

I nodded. "Yeah, we're just talking about stuff. About Mom."

He wrapped me up in a protective hug, and my hands immediately went around his waist.

"I'm so fucking happy you two finally got your shit together!" Mac said, a huge grin splitting her face.

Hendrix chuckled, and I smiled at her.

"Did you need some help with anything?" I asked Hendrix. "More importantly, are you being nice to Jeremiah?"

An ornery smile graced his face. "Marriage, Mac?"

Mac slinked right out of her chair and darted for the back door.

What the hell? I'd never seen her do that before. She'd always met her brother head on. I barked out a laugh.

The rest of the day went by peacefully. Mac and Hendrix laughed and teased each other about old times while Jeremiah and I sat back and listened. If Hendrix had given him a bad time, Jeremiah hadn't let on about it. The more time I spent with him and Mac, the more I liked him, but I still felt incredibly uneasy about the upcoming nuptials. But for now, at this moment, I had everything I wanted, and I didn't want to waste time worrying about the future.

Quiet filled the house as Hendrix slipped into bed next to me. It was after midnight when we said goodbye to Mac and Jeremiah, and I was eager to find out what had happened between the guys.

"Well?" I asked, peering up at him through my eyelashes.

"Well what?" he asked, teasing.

I propped up on my elbow and smiled. "You know exactly what I'm after. What did you say to Jeremiah? Do you like him? How did you find out about the engagement? I mean other than me. Did he tell you? You're holding out on me, and I need deets."

Hendrix's low and throaty chuckle filled the room. "You're so cute when you're feisty," he said, kissing the tip of my nose.

"Hendrix! You're killing me over here," I said, smacking my palm on the blankets.

Apparently he thought that was funny, too.

"He seems to be an all right guy, Gemma."

"And?" I asked, my brows shooting upward.

"He told me about the engagement first. I never brought it up. I mean, I would have, but he was completely upfront and manned up about not talking to me before he asked Mac."

"What? And so that just makes up for everything?" I sat up, my eyes wide with concern. How could Hendrix just let it go?

"Of course not. All I'm saying was he didn't skirt the issue. I honestly don't think he's hiding anything. He explained to me about enlisting in the military, and he wanted Mac by his side. He loves her. Seriously, it was that simple."

I flung myself back against the mattress and groaned. "You're her older brother, aren't you supposed to at least torture him or act like you're not okay with all of this?"

"Babe, I'm not okay with it at all, but I know Mac. The second anyone starts to push her, she's going to push back, and in this case she'll end up married even faster. Neither of us wants that, right?"

I nodded, hating to admit he was right.

"Now that you and I are back together, we'll spend more time with them. I'll invite him to a show, and we can hang out afterward, just him and me. I want to see him in some social situations without Mac. It will tell me a lot. This is going to take some time. Plus Mac knows me. She knows how I analyze and evaluate situations. I have to handle this one with kid gloves."

I massaged my pounding temples. For some dumb reason, I thought the marriage situation would have been settled tonight.

"Ya know," I said, looking up at him. "I do like Jeremiah, it's not that. It's how fast the relationship is moving."

"Me too, but Mac is an adult. We all are. The worst that can happen is she has to undo the marriage at some point in time."

"That's not the worst," I groaned, sitting upright. "Hendrix, I realize we've had a total shit show going on lately, but what if Jeremiah gets stationed in Iraq? Or somewhere else overseas and we aren't with her?"

Silence filled the space between us. "I know. I've thought about it, too. I can't guarantee an outcome, Gem. But I'll do my best to slow the wedding down, alright?"

My overworked nerves stood on end. I couldn't stand it if anything happened to Mac, and I wasn't there for her.

Dread washed over me, and I quietly slid into the bed and laid my head against Hendrix's chest, focusing on the steady rhythm of his heartbeat. It was amazing how one heart could keep two people alive.

"Just make it better, please," I said, my voice barely above a whisper. But somewhere inside myself, I knew I wasn't just referring to Mac anymore.

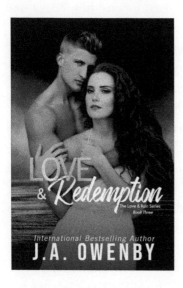

Join Hendrix and Gemma in the final chapter of The Love & Ruin Series in *Love & Redemption*. Just one click here.

You can also join my Facebook group, J.A. Owenby's One Page At A Time, for exclusive giveaways and sneak peeks of future books.

ALSO BY J.A. OWENBY

Bestselling Romance

The Love & Ruin Series

Love & Ruin

Love & Deception

Love & Redemption

Love & Consequences, a standalone novel

Love & Corruption, a standalone novel

Love & Seduction, Coming Soon!

Romantic Thriller

Let Me Love You Series

The Essence of You

Let Me Love You, Coming Soon!

Standalone Novels

Where I'll Find You

Coming of Age

The Torn Series, Inspired by True Events

Fading into Her, a prequel novella

Torn

Captured

Freed

Love & Deception

J.A. OWENBY

Edited by: Deb Markanton

Cover Art by: iheartcoverdesigns

Photographer: CJC Photography

First Edition

ISBN-13: 978-1-949414-17-2

Gain access to previews of J.A. Owenby's novels before they're released and to take part in exclusive giveaways. www.jaowenby.com

A NOTE FROM THE AUTHOR:

Dear Readers,
If you have experienced sexual assault or physical abuse, there is free confidential help. Please visit:
Website: https://www.rainn.org/
Phone: 800-656-4673

This book may contain sensitive material for some readers. Gemma and Hendrix's story is considered a dark romance with language, sex, and violence.

ABOUT THE AUTHOR

J.A. Owenby lives in the beautiful Pacific Northwest with her husband and cat.

She also runs her own business as a professional resume writer and interview coach—she helps people find jobs they love.

J.A. is an avid reader of thrillers, romance, new adult, and young adult novels. She loves music, movies, and good wine. And call her crazy, but she loves the rainy Pacific Northwest; she gets her best story ideas while listening to the rain pattering against the windows in front of the fireplace.

You can follow the progress of her upcoming novel on Facebook at Author J.A. Owenby and on Twitter @jaowenby.

Sign up for J.A. Owenby's Newsletter:
BookHip.com/CTZMWZ

Like J.A. Owenby's Facebook:
https://www.facebook.com/JAOwenby

J.A Owenby's One Page At A Time reader group:
https://www.facebook.com/groups/JAOwenby

Lightning Source UK Ltd.
Milton Keynes UK
UKHW010720111022
410294UK00001B/26